Serbocroat

HIPPOCRENE HANDY DICTIONARIES

For the traveler of independent spirit and curious mind, this practical series will help you to communicate, not just get by. Easier to use than a dictionary, the comprehensive listing of words and phrases is arranged alphabetically by key word. More versatile than a phrasebook, words frequently met in stores, on signs, or needed for standard replies, are conveniently presented by subject.

ARABIC
ISBN 0-87052-960-9

PORTUGUESE
ISBN 0-87052-053-9

CHINESE
ISBN 0-87052-050-4

THAI
ISBN 0-87052-963-3

DUTCH
ISBN 0-87052-049-0

TURKISH
ISBN 0-87052-982-X

GREEK
ISBN 0-87052-961-7

SERBO-CROATIAN
ISBN 0-87052-051-2

JAPANESE
ISBN 0-87052-962-5

SWEDISH
ISBN 0-87052-054-7

Books may be ordered directly from the publisher. Each book costs $6.95. Send the total amount plus $3.50 for shipping and handling to: Hippocrene Books, Inc.
171 Madison Avenue
New York, NY 10016.

HIPPOCRENE HANDY DICTIONARIES

Serbocroat

at your Fingertips

compiled by

LEXUS

with

Andrijana Hewitt

HIPPOCRENE BOOKS
New York

Published in the United States of America in 1991 by
HIPPOCRENE BOOKS, INC., New York,
by arrangement with Routledge, London

For information, address:
HIPPOCRENE BOOKS, INC.
171 Madison Ave.
New York, NY 10016

ISBN 0-87052-051-2

Contents

Pronunciation Guide

Because you are likely to want to speak most of the Serbocroat given in this book, rather than just to understand its meaning, an indication of the pronunciation has been given in square brackets. If you pronounce this as though it were English, the result will be clearly comprehensible to a Yugoslav.

In some cases, however, we have decided it was not necessary to give the entire pronunciation for a word or phrase. This may be because it would more or less duplicate the ordinary Serbocroat spelling, or because the pronunciation of a particular word or words has already been given within the same entry. In these cases we have simply shown how to pronounce the problematic parts of the word or phrase. Some comments on the pronunciation system used:

VOWELS

a	as in 'and'	o	as in 'hot' never as in 'do'
ay	as in 'say'	oo	as in 'book'
e	as in 'fed'	oy	as in 'boy'
I	as in 'I' or the 'i' in 'kite'		

CONSONANTS

ch	as in 'church'
g	always hard as in 'get'
н	sounded at the back of the throat like the 'ch' in Scottish 'loch'
j	as in 'jam'
ȷ	like the 's' sound in 'pleasure'
y	is always like the 'y' in 'you', never like the 'y' in 'sty'

When the print for a letter or for two letters is in bold type this means that this part of the word should be stressed. Note that a final 'e' in Serbocroat is always pronounced. For example, 'ime' is pronounced 'ee-me'.

For references of the type (+A) see the Reference Grammar, pages 104–105.

SOME KEY CHARACTERS IN SERBOCROAT

c	= ts	dž, đ	= j	ž	= the 's' sound
č, ć	= ch	j	= y		in 'pleasure'

VARIANTS OF SERBOCROAT

Yugoslavia has a mixture of languages but Serbocroat is spoken by about three-quarters of the population. If you are intending to travel to Slovenia or Macedonia, you will find that Serbocroat will be understood, although it is not the spoken language. There are some differences in the Serbocroat spoken by Yugoslavs in Serbia (which is the eastern part of the country) and Croatia (the western part, including most of the Adriatic coast down to Montenegro). In this book we have indicated some of these differences, although the main effort has always been to provide translations that will be usable throughout the country. Capital S (italic) stands for Serbian, C for Croatian.

English-Serbocroat

A

a: 90 dinars a bottle devedeset dinara boca *[deenara botsa]*; *see page 102*

about: about 25 oko 25 *[oko]*; **about 6 o'clock** oko 6 sati; **is the manager about?** da li je tu direktor? *[lee ye too deerektor]*; **I was just about to leave** upravo sam se spremao otići *[oopravo sam se spremao oteechee]*; **how about a drink?** jeste li za piće? *[yeste lee za peeche]*

above iznad *[eeznad]*; **above the village** iznad sela

abroad (S) u inostranstvu *[oo eenostranstvoo]*; (C) u inozemstvu *[eenozemstvoo]*

abscess apsces *[apstses]*

absolutely: it's absolutely perfect više nego savršeno *[veeshe nego savursheno]*; **you're absolutely right** potpuno ste u pravu *[potpoono ste oo pravoo]*; **absolutely!** apsolutno! *[apsolootno]*

absorbent cotton vata

accelerator pedala gasa

accept prihvatiti *[preeнvateetee]*

accident nesreća *[nesrecha]*; **there's been an accident** dogodila se nesreća *[dogodeela se nesrecha]*; **sorry, it was an accident** izvinite, bilo je slučajno *[eezveeneete beelo ye sloochɪno]*

accommodation(s) smještaj *[smyeshtɪ]*; **we need accommodation(s) for four** treba nam smještaj za četvoro *[treba nam smyeshtɪ za chetvoro]*

accurate (S) tačan *[tachan]*; (C) točan *[tochan]*

ache: I have an ache here ovdje me boli *[ovdye me bolee]*; **it aches** boli

across: across the street preko puta *[preko poota]*

actor glumac *[gloomats]*

actress glumica *[gloomeetsa]*

adapter (*elec*) ispravljač *[eespravlyach]*

address adresa *[adresa]*; **what's your address?** koja je vaša adresa? *[koya ye vasha]*

address book adresar

admission: how much is admission? pošto je ulaz? *[poshto ye oolaz]*

adore: I adore ... (*this country, this food etc*) obožavam ... *[oboɔavam]*

Adriatic Jadransko more *[yadransko]*

adult odrastao

advance: I'll pay in advance platit ću unaprijed *[plateet choo oonapreeyed]*

advertisement oglas *[oglas]*

advise: what would you advise? šta biste savjetovali? *[shta beeste savyetovalee]*

aeroplane avion *[aveeon]*

affluent imućan *[eemoochan]*

afraid: I'm afraid of heights bojim se visine *[boyeem se veeseene]*; **don't be afraid** ne bojte se *[boyte]*; **I'm not afraid** ne bojim se *[boyeem]*; **I'm afraid I can't help you** bojim se da vam ne mogu pomoći *[boyeem se da vam ne mogu pomochee]*; **I'm afraid so** bojim se da je tako; **I'm afraid not** bojim se da nije *[neeye]*

after: after you poslije vas *[poslye]*; **after 9 o'clock** poslije 9 sati

afternoon poslije podne *[poslye podne]*; **in the afternoon** poslije podne; **good afternoon** dobar dan; **this afternoon** danas poslije podne

aftershave losion za brijanje *[loseeon za breeyanye]*

afterwards kasnije *[kasneeye]*

again opet

against protiv *[proteev]*; **against the wall** do zida *[zeeda]*

age starost (*f*); **under age** maloljetan *[malolyetan]*; **not at my age!** ne u mojim godinama *[oo moyeem godeenama]*; **it takes ages** to traje beskrajno dugo *[trɪye beskrɪno doogo]*; **I haven't been here for ages** ovdje nisam bio ko zna otkad *[ovdye neesam beeo ko zna otkad]*

agency agencija *[agentseeya]*
aggressive agresivan *[agreseevan]*
ago: a year/week ago prije godinu/
nedjelju dana *[preeye godeenoo/
nedyelyoo dana]*; **it wasn't long ago**
nije bilo davno *[neeye beelo davno]*
agony: it's agony muka je to *[mooka
ye to]*
agree: do you agree? slažete li se?
[slaJete lee]; **I agree** slažem se
[slaJem]; **it doesn't agree with me** ne
prija mi *[preeya mee]*; **I don't agree**
ne slažem se
AIDS SIDA *[seeda]*
air (S) vazduh *[vazdooн]*; (C) zrak; **by
air** avionom *[aveeonom]*
air-bed (S) vazdušni dušek
[vazdooshnee dooshek]; (C) zračni
madrac *[zrachnee madrats]*
air-conditioning klimatizacija
[kleemateezatseeya]
air hostess stjuardesa *[styooardesa]*
airmail: by airmail avionskom po-
štom *[aveeonskom poshtom]*
airmail envelope (S) avionska koverta *[aveeonska koverta]*; (C)
avionska kuverta *[kooverta]*
airplane avion *[aveeon]*
airport aerodrom *[a-erodrom]*
airport bus autobus za aerodrom
[aootobus za a-erodrom]
airport tax aerodromska taksa
airsick: I get airsick u avionu mi je
mučno *[oo aveeonoo mee ye
moochno]*
à la carte po narudžbi *[naroodJbee]*
alarm uzbuna *[oozboona]*
alarm clock (S) budilnik
[boodeelneek]; (C) budilica
[boodeeleetsa]
Albania Albanija *[albaneeya]*
Albanian (*adjective, language*) albanski
[albanskee]; (*man*) Albanac *[albanats]*;
(*woman*) Albanka *[albanka]*; **the
Albanians** Albanci *[albantsee]*
alcohol alkohol *[alkohol]*
alcoholic: is it alcoholic? je li alkoholno? *[ye lee alkoholno]*
alive živ *[Jeev]*; **is he still alive?** je li
još živ? *[ye lee yosh]*
all: all the hotels svi hoteli *[svee
hotelee]*; **all of them** svi oni *[onee]*;
all my money sav moj novac *[moy
novats]*; **all of it** sve to; **all right** u

redu *[oo redoo]*; **I'm all right**
(*nothing wrong*) dobro mi je *[dobro
mee ye]*; **that's all** to je sve; **it's all
changed** sve se promijenilo
[promyeneelo]; **thank you — not at
all** hvala — nema na čemu
[chemoo]
allergic: I'm allergic to ... alergičan
sam na ... *[alergeechan]*
allergy alergija *[alergeeya]*
all-inclusive sve je uključeno
[ooklyoocheno]
allowed dozvoljen *[dozvolyen]*; **is it
allowed?** je li dozvoljeno? *[ye lee
dozvolyeno]*; **I'm not allowed to eat
fish** ne smijem jesti ribu *[smyem
yestee reeboo]*
all-risks svi rizici *[svee reezeetsee]*
almost gotovo
alone sam; **are you alone?** jeste li
sami? *[yeste lee samee]*; **leave me
alone** ostavite me na miru *[ostaveete
me na meeroo]*
already već *[vech]*
also takođe *[takodje]*
alteration promjena *[promyena]*
alternative: is there an alternative?
postoji li alternativa? *[postoyee lee
alternateeva]*; **we had no alternative**
nije bilo alternative *[neeye beelo
alternateeve]*
alternator alternator
although mada, iako
altogether sasvim *[sasveem]*; **what
does that come to altogether?** koliko
to dođe sve skupa? *[koleeko to dodje
sve skoopa]*
always uvijek *[ooveeyek]*
a.m.: at 8 a.m. u 8 ujutro *[oo osam
ooyootro]*
amazing nevjerojatno *[nevyeroyatno]*
ambassador ambasador
ambulance kola hitne pomoći *[kola
нeetne pomochee]*; **get an ambulance**
pozovite kola hitne pomoći
[pozoveete]
America Amerika *[amereeka]*
American (*adjective*) američki
[amereechkee]; (*man*) Amerikanac
[amereekanats]; (*woman*) Amerikanka
[amereekanka]; **the Americans**
Amerikanci *[amereekantsee]*
American plan puni pansion *[poonee
panseeon]*

among među *[medjoo]*

amp: a 13 amp fuse osigurač od 13 ampera *[oseegoorach od treenaest ampera]*

an(a)esthetic anestetik *[anesteteek]*

ancestor predak

anchor sidro *[seedro]*

anchovies ringlice *[reengleetse]*

ancient drevan; (*suitcase etc*) prastar

and i *[ee]*

angina angina pektoris *[angeena pektorees]*

angry ljut *[lyoot]*; **I'm very angry about it** vrlo sam ljut zbog toga *[vurlo sam lyoot zbog toga]*

animal životinja *[Jeevoteenya]*

ankle gležanj *[gleJan-yuh]*

anniversary: it's our (wedding) anniversary today danas je naša godišnjica (vjenčanja) *[danas ye nasha godeeshnyeetsa (vyenchanya)]*

annoy: he's annoying me dosađuje mi *[dosadjooye mee]*; **it's so annoying** tako je dosadno *[ye]*

anorak vjetrovka *[vyetrovka]*

another (*extra*) još jedan *[yosh yedan]*; (*different*) drugi *[droogee]*; **another bottle, please** još jednu bocu, molim *[yosh yednoo botsoo, moleem]*; **can we have another room?** možemo li promijeniti sobu? *[moJemo lee promeeyeneetee soboo]*

answer: there was no answer nije bilo odgovora *[neeye beelo odgovora]*; **what was his answer?** šta je odgovorio? *[shta ye odgovoreeo]*

ant: ants mravi *[mravee]*

antibiotics antibiotici *[anteebeeoteetsee]*

anticlimax antiklimaks *[anteekleemaks]*

antifreeze antifriz *[anteefreez]*

antihistamine antihistaminik *[anteeheestameeneek]*

antique: is it an antique? je li antikvitet? *[ye lee anteekveetet]*

antique shop antikvarnica *[anteekvarneetsa]*

antisocial: don't be antisocial nemojte biti nedruštveni *[nemoyte beetee nedrooshtvenee]*

any: have you got any rolls/milk? imate li peciva/mlijeka? *[eemate lee petseeva/mlyeka]*; **I haven't got any**
nemam

anybody iko *[eeko]*; **can anybody help?** može li iko pomoći? *[moJe lee eeko pomochee]*; **there wasn't anybody there** tamo nije bilo nikog *[tamo neeye beelo neekog]*

anything išta *[eeshta]*; **I don't want anything** ništa ne želim *[neeshta ne Jeleem]*; **don't you have anything else?** zar nemate ništa drugo? *[nemate neeshta droogo]*

apart from osim *[oseem]*

apartment stan

aperitif aperitiv *[apereeteev]*

apology izvinjenje *[eezveenyenye]*; **please accept my apologies** molim vas primite moje izvinjenje *[moleem vas preemeete moye eezveenyenye]*

appalling užasan *[ooJasan]*

appear: it would appear that ... čini se da ... *[cheenee]*

appendicitis upala slijepog crijeva *[oopala slyepog tsryeva]*

appetite apetit *[apeteet]*; **I've lost my appetite** izgubio sam apetit *[eezgoobeeo]*

apple jabuka *[yabooka]*

apple pie pita od jabuka *[peeta od yabooka]*

application form prijava *[preeyava]*

appointment sastanak; **I'd like to make an appointment** želio bih da zakažem vrijeme *[Jeleeo beeн da zakaJem vryeme]*

appreciate: thank you, I appreciate it puno vam hvala *[poono vam нvala]*

approve: she doesn't approve ona ne odobrava

apricot (S) kajsija *[kıseeya]*; (C) marelica *[mareleetsa]*

April (S) april *[apreel]*; (C) travanj *[travan-yuh]*

aqualung oprema za podvodno disanje *[oprema za podvodno deesanye]*

arch(a)eology arheologija *[arнeologeeya]*

are *see page 114*

area: I don't know the area ne poznajem kraj *[poznıyem krı]*

area code pozivni broj *[pozeevnee broy]*

arm ruka *[rooka]*

around *see* **about**

arrangement: will you make the

arrangements? hoćete li vi to srediti?
[hochete lee vee to sredeetee]
arrest uhapsiti *[oohapseetee]*; **he's been arrested** uhapšen je *[oohapshen ye]*
arrival dolazak
arrive: when do we arrive? kad stižemo? *[steeɹemo]*; **has my parcel arrived yet?** je li moj paket već stigao? *[ye lee moy paket vech steegao]*; **let me know as soon as they arrive** obavijestite me čim stignu *[obavyesteete me cheem steegnoo]*; **we only arrived yesterday** stigli smo tek juče *[steeglee smo tek yooche]*
art umjetnost (*f*) *[oomyetnost]*
art gallery umjetnička galerija *[oomyetneechka galereeya]*
arthritis artritis *[artreetees]*
artificial umjetan *[oomyetan]*
artist umjetnik *[oomyetneek]*
as: as fast as you can šta brže možete *[shta burɹe moɹete]*; **as much as you can** šta više možete *[shta veeshe]*; **as you like** kako hoćete *[kako hochete]*; **as it's getting late** pošto je vrijeme odmaklo *[poshto ye vryeme odmaklo]*
ashore: to go ashore iskrcati se *[eeskurtsatee]*
ashtray pepeljara *[pepelyara]*
aside from osim *[oseem]*
ask zamoliti *[zamoleetee]*; **could you ask him to phone me back?** možete li ga zamoliti da mi telefonira? *[moɹete lee ga zamoleetee da mee telefoneera]*; **that's not what I asked for** nisam to tražio *[neesam to traɹeeo]*
asleep: he's still asleep još spava *[yosh spava]*
asparagus (*S*) špargla *[shpargla]*; (*C*) šparoga *[shparoga]*
aspirin aspirin *[aspeereen]*
assault: she's been assaulted napadnuta je *[napadnoota ye]*; **indecent assault** napastvovanje *[napastvovanye]*
assistant (*helper*) pomagač *[pomagach]*; (*in shop*) pomoćnik *[pomochneek]*
assume: I assume that ... pretpostavljam da ... *[pretpostavlyam]*
asthma astma
astonishing zapanjujući *[zapanyoo*

yoochee]
at: at the restaurant u restoranu *[oo restoranoo]*; **at the hotel** u hotelu *[hoteloo]*; **at 8 o'clock** u 8 sati; **see you at dinner** vidimo se za večerom *[veedeemo se za vecherom]*; **at work** na poslu *[posloo]*; **at the bookshop** kod knjižara *[knyeeɹara]*; **at night** noću *[nochoo]*
Atlantic Atlantski okean *[atlantskee]*
atmosphere atmosfera
attractive privlačan *[preevlachan]*; **you're very attractive** vrlo ste privlačni *[vurlo ste preevlachnee]*
aubergine plavi patlidžan *[plavee patleedjan]*
auction aukcija *[aooktseeya]*
audience publika *[poobleeka]*
August (*S*) avgust *[avgoost]*; (*C*) kolovoz
aunt: my aunt moja tetka *[moya]*
Australia *[aoostraleeya]*
Australian (*adjective*) australski *[aoostralskee]*; (*man*) Australijanac *[aoostraleeyanats]*; (*woman*) Australijanka *[aoostraleeyanka]*; **the Australians** Australijanci *[aoostraleeyantsee]*
Austria Austrija *[aoostreeya]*
Austrian (*adjective*) austrijski *[aoostreeskee]*; (*man*) Austrijanac *[aoostreeyanats]*; (*woman*) Austrijanka *[aoostreeyanka]*; **the Austrians** Austrijanci *[aoostreeyantsee]*
authorities vlasti *[vlastee]*
automatic automatski *[aootomatskee]*
automobile automobil *[aootomobeel]*
autumn jesen (*f*) *[yesen]*; **in the autumn** na jesen
available: when will it be available? kada će se moći dobiti? *[kada che se mochee dobeetee]*; **when will he be available?** kada će se do njega moći doći? *[nyega mochee dochee]*
avenue avenija *[aveneeya]*
average: the average Yugoslav prosječan Jugoslaven *[prosyechan yoogoslaven]*; **an above average hotel** hotel iznad prosjeka *[eeznad prosyeka]*; **a below average hotel** hotel ispod prosjeka *[eespod]*; **the food was only average** hrana je bila sasvim prosječna *[нrana ye beela sasveem prosyechna]*; **on average**

prosječno *[prosyechno]*
awake: is she awake? je li budna? *[ye lee boodna]*
away: is it far away? je li daleko? *[ye lee]*; **go away!** odlazi! *[odlazee]*
awful grozan
axle osovina *[osoveena]*

B

baby beba
baby-carrier nosiljka za bebu *[noseelyka za beboo]*
baby-sitter osoba koja čuva djecu *[osoba koya choova dyetsoo]*; **can you get us a baby-sitter?** možete li nam naći nekoga da nam pričuva djecu? *[moJete lee nam nachee nekoga da nam preechoova dyetsoo]*
bachelor neženja *[neJenya]*
back: I've got a bad back imam problema s leđima *[eemam problema s ledjeema]*; **at the back** straga; **in the back of the car** od ostraga u kolima *[ostraga oo koleema]*; **I'll be right back** odmah se vraćam *[odmaH se vracham]*; **when do you want it back?** kad treba da vam vratim? *[vrateem]*; **can I have my money back?** možete li mi vratiti novac? *[moJete lee mee vrateetee novats]*; **come back!** vratite se! *[vrateete]*; **I go back home tomorrow** sutra se vraćam kući *[sootra se vracham koochee]*; **we'll be back next year** doći ćemo i iduće godine *[dochee chemo ee eedooche godeene]*; **when is the last bus back?** kad se vraća zadnji autobus? *[vracha zadnyee aootoboos]*
backache: I have a backache bole me leđa *[bole me ledja]*
back door stražnja vrata *[straJnya]*
backgammon triktrak *[treektrak]*
backpack ruksak *[rooksak]*
back seat stražnje sjedište *[straJnye syedeeshte]*
back street sporedna ulica *[sporedna ooleetsa]*
bacon slanina *[slaneena]*; **bacon and eggs** jaja sa slaninom *[yIya sa slaneenom]*
bad loš *[losh]*; **this meat's bad** ovo meso je pokvareno *[ye]*; **a bad headache** gadna glavobolja *[glavobolya]*; **it's not bad** nije loše *[neeye loshe]*; **too bad!** šteta! *[shteta]*
badly: he's been badly injured teško je ozlijeđen *[teshko ye ozleeyedjen]*
bag torba; *(suitcase)* kovčeg *[kovcheg]*; *(carrier bag)* vrećica *[vrecheetsa]*
baggage *(S)* prtljag *[purtlyag]*; *(C)* prtljaga *[purtlyaga]*
baggage allowance dozvoljena težina prtljaga *[dozvolyena teJeena purtlyaga]*
baggage checkroom garderoba
bakery pekara
balcony balkon; **a room with a balcony** soba sa balkonom; **on the balcony** na balkonu *[balkonoo]*
bald ćelav *[chelav]*
ball lopta
ballet balet
ball-point pen *(S)* hemijska olovka *[hemeeska]*; *(C)* kemijska olovka
banana banana
band *(music)* orkestar
bandage zavoj *[zavoy]*; **could you change the bandage?** možete li promijeniti zavoj? *[moJete lee promyeneetee]*
bandaid flaster
bank banka; **when are the banks open?** kad su otvorene banke? *[soo]*
bank account bankovni račun *[bankovnee rachoon]*
bar kafić *[kafeech]*; **let's meet in the bar** nađimo se u kafiću *[nadjeemo se oo kafeechoo]*; **a bar of chocolate** tabla čokolade *[tabla chokolade]*
barbecue roštilj *[roshteel-yuh]*
barber *(shop)* *(S)* berbernica *[berberneetsa]*; *(C)* brijačnica *[breeyachneetsa]*
bargain: it's a real bargain baš je

jeftino *[bash ye yefteeno]*
barmaid konobarica *[konobareetsa]*
barman barmen
barrette (S) šnala za kosu *[shnala za kosoo]*; (C) kopča za kosu *[kopcha]*
bartender barmen
basic: the hotel is rather basic hotel je prilično skroman *[ye preeleechno]*; **will you teach me some basic phrases?** da li biste me naučili nekoliko osnovih izraza? *[lee beeste me naoocheelee nekoleeko osnovneeн eezraza]*
basket (S) korpa; (C) koš *[kosh]*
bath kupanje *[koopanye]*; **can I take a bath?** mogu li se okupati? *[mogoo lee se okoopatee]*
bathing kupanje *[koopanye]*
bathing costume kupaći kostim *[koopachee kosteem]*
bathrobe bademantil *[bademanteel]*
bathroom (S) kupatilo *[koopateelo]*; (C) kupaonica *[koopaoneetsa]*; **can I use your bathroom?** mogu li se poslužiti vašim kupatilom/vašom kupaonicom? *[mogoo lee se posloojeetee vasheem]*
bath towel (S) peškir za kupanje *[peshkeer za koopanye]*; (C) ručnik za kupanje *[roochneek]*
battery akumulator *[akoomoolator]*; **the battery's flat** akumulator je prazan *[ye prazan]*
bay (S) zaliv *[zaleev]*; (C) zaljev *[zalyev]*
be biti *[beetee]*; **be reasonable** budite razumni *[boodeete razoomnee]*; **don't be lazy** ne budite lijeni *[boodeete lyenee]*; **where have you been?** gdje ste bili? *[gdye ste beelee]*; **I've never been to Korčula** nikad nisam bio na Korčuli *[neekad neesam beeo na korchoolee]*; *see pages 114-116*
beach plaža *[plaлa]*; **on the beach** na plaži *[plaлee]*; **I'm going to the beach** idem na plažu *[eedem na plaлoo]*
beach mat asura za plažu *[asoora za plaлoo]*
beach towel (S) peškir za plažu *[peshkeer za plaлoo]*; (C) ručnik za plažu *[roochneek]*
beach umbrella suncobran *[soontsobran]*

beads perle
beans (S) pasulj *[pasool-yuh]*; (C) гран
beard brada
beautiful lijep *[lyep]*; **thank you, that's beautiful** lijepo je, hvala *[lyepo ye, нvala]*
beauty salon kozmetički salon *[kozmeteechkee salon]*
because zato što *[zato shto]*; **because of the weather** zbog vremena
bed krevet; **single bed** krevet za jednu osobu *[yednoo osoboo]*; **double bed** bračni krevet *[brachnee]*; **you haven't made my bed** niste spremili moj krevet *[neeste spremeelee moy]*; **he's still in bed** još je u krevetu *[yosh ye oo krevetoo]*; **I'm going to bed** idem spavati *[eedem spavatee]*
bed and breakfast noćenje s doručkom *[nochenye s doroochkom]*
bed linen posteljina *[postelyeena]*
bedroom spavaća soba *[spavacha soba]*
bee pčela *[pchela]*
beef govedina *[govedeena]*
beer pivo *[peevo]*; **two beers, please** dva piva, molim *[dva peeva moleem]*
before: before breakfast prije doručka *[preeye doroochka]*; **before I leave** prije mog odlaska; **I haven't been here before** ovdje nisam bio ranije *[ovdye neesam beeo raneeye]*
begin: when does it begin? kad počinje? *[pocheenye]*
beginner početnik *[pochetneek]*; **I'm just a beginner** ja sam tek početnik *[ya]*
beginning: at the beginning u početku *[oo pochetkoo]*
behavio(u)r ponašanje *[ponashanye]*
behind iza *[eeza]*; **the driver behind me** vozač iza mene *[vozach eeza]*
beige bež *[beл]*
Belgium Belgija *[belgeeya]*
Belgrade Beograd
believe: I don't believe you ne vjerujem vam *[vyerooyem]*; **I believe you** vjerujem vam
bell zvono; (small) zvonac *[zvonats]*
belong: that belongs to me to je moje *[to ye moye]*; **who does this belong to?** čije je ovo? *[cheeye ye ovo]*
belonging: all my belongings sve moje lične stvari *[sve moye leechne*

stv*aree]*
below: below the knee ispod koljena *[eespod kolyena]*
belt (*clothing*) pojas *[poyas]*
bend (*in road*) okuka *[okooka]*
berth ležaj *[leʃi]*
beside: beside the church pokraj crkve *[pokrɪ tsurkve]*; **sit beside me** sjedite pokraj mene *[syedeete]*
besides: besides that pored toga
best najbolji *[nɪbolyee]*; **the best hotel in town** najbolji hotel u gradu *[hotel oo gradoo]*; **that's the best meal I've ever had** nikad nisam bolje jeo *[neekad neesam bolye yeo]*
bet: I bet you 500 dinars kladim se s vama u 500 dinara *[kladeem se s vama oo petsto deenara]*
better bolji *[bolyee]*; **that's better!** to je bolje! *[ye bolye]*; **are you feeling better?** osjećate li se bolje? *[osyechate lee]*; **I'm feeling a lot better** osjećam se mnogo bolje *[osyecham se mnogo]*; **I'd better be going now** sad treba da idem *[treba da eedem]*
between između *[eezmedjoo]*
beyond iza *[eeza]*; **beyond the mountains** iza planina *[planeena]*
bicycle bicikl *[beetseekl]*; **can we rent bicycles here?** možemo li ovdje iznajmiti bicikle? *[moʒemo lee ovdye eeznɪmeetee beetseekle]*
big velik *[veleek]*; **a big one** veliki *[veleekee]*; **that's too big** to je preveliko *[ye preveleeko]*; **it's not big enough** nije dovljno velik *[neeye dovolyno]*
bigger veći *[vechee]*
bike bicikl *[beetseekl]*
bikini bikini (*m*) *[beekeenee]*
bill račun *[rachoon]*; **could I have the bill, please?** račun, molim! *[moleem]*
billfold novčanik *[novchaneek]*
billiards bilijar *[beeleeyar]*
bird ptica *[pteetsa]*
biro (*tm*) (*S*) hemijska olovka *[hemeeska]*; (*C*) kemijska olovka
birthday rođendan *[rodjendan]*; **it's my birthday** rođendam mi je *[mee ye]*; **when is your birthday?** kad je vaš rođendan? *[ye vash]*; **happy birthday!** sretan rođendan
biscuit keks
bit: just a little bit for me samo malo

za mene *[samo malo za mene]*; **a big bit** veliki komad *[veleekee]*; **a bit of that cake** malo tog kolača *[kolacha]*; **it's a bit too big for me** malo je prevelik za mene *[ye preveleek]*; **it's a bit cold today** danas je prohladno *[ye proHladno]*
bite ujesti *[ooyestee]*; **I've been bitten** nešto me ujelo *[neshto me ooyelo]*; **do you have something for bites?** imati li nešto protiv ujeda? *[eemate lee neshto proteev ooyeda]*
bitter (*taste*) gorak
bitter lemon 'bitter lemon'
black crn *[tsurn]*; **black and white film** crno-bijeli film *[tsurno-byelee feelm]*
blackout: he's had a blackout onesvijestio se *[onesvyesteeo]*
bladder mjehur *[myehoor]*
blanket (*S*) ćebe *[chebe]*; (*C*) deka; **I'd like another blanket** molim vas još jedno ćebe/jednu deku *[moleem vas yosh yedno]*
blazer blejzer *[blayzer]*
bleach (*for toilet etc*) bjelilo *[byeleelo]*
bleed krvariti *[kurvareetee]*; **he's bleeding** krvari *[kurvaree]*
bless you! (*after sneeze*) nazdravlje! *[nazdravlye]*
blind slijep *[slyep]*
blinds roletne
blind spot (*driving*) slijepa tačka *[slyepa tachka]*
blister plik *[pleek]*
blocked blokiran *[blokeeran]*
block of flats stambena zgrada
blond (*adjective*) plav
blonde (*woman*) plavuša *[plavoosha]*
blood krv *[kurv]*; **his blood group is ...** njegova krvna grupa je ... *[nyegova kurvna groopa ye]*; **I have high blood pressure** imam visok krvni pritisak *[eemam veesok kurvnee preeteesak]*
bloody mary 'bloody mary'
blouse bluza *[blooza]*
blue plav
blusher (*cosmetic*) rumenilo za obraze *[roomeneelo za obraze]*
board: full board puni pansion *[poonee panseeon]*; **half-board** polupansion *[poloopanseeon]*
boarding house pansion *[panseeon]*

boarding pass bording karta
boat čamac *[chamats]*; (*large*) brod *[burod]*
body tijelo *[tyelo]*
boil (*on body*) čir *[cheer]*; **boil the water** (*S*) prokuvati vodu *[prokoovatee vodoo]*; (*C*) skuhati vodu *[skoohatee]*
boiled egg (*S*) bareno jaje *[bareno yiye]*; (*C*) kuhano jaje *[koohano]*
boiling hot (*weather, food*) vreo
bomb (*noun*) bomba
bone kost (*f*)
bonnet (*of car*) hauba *[haooba]*
book knjiga *[knyeega]*; **I'd like to book a table for two** želio bih rezervirati stol za dvije osobe *[jeleeo beeн rezerveeratee stol za dvye osobe]*
bookshop, bookstore knjižara *[knyeejara]*
boot (*on foot*) čizma *[cheezma]*; (*of car*) prtljažnik *[purtlyajneek]*
booze piće *[peeche]*; **I had too much booze** previše sam pio *[preveeshe sam peeo]*
border (*of country*) granica *[graneetsa]*
bored: I'm bored dosadno mi je *[dosadno mee ye]*
boring (*person, trip, film*) dosadan
born: I was born in ... (*date*) rođen sam ... *[rodjen]*; (*place*) rođen sam u ... *[oo]*
borrow: may I borrow ...? mogu li posuditi? *[mogoo lee posoodeetee]*
boss šef *[shef]*
both obojica (*m*), obadvije (*f*), oboje (*n*) *[oboyeetsa, obadveeye, oboye]*; **I'll take both of them** uzet ću oba (*m,n*)/obe (*f*) *[oozet choo oba/obe]*; **we'll both come** doći ćemo obojica *[dochee chemo]*
bother: sorry to bother you izvinite što vas uznemiravam *[eezveeneete shto vas ooznemeeravam]*; **it's no bother** ne uznemirava me *[ooznemeerava]*; **it's such a bother** to je velika gnjavaža *[ye veleeka gnyavaja]*
bottle boca *[botsa]*; **a bottle of wine** boca vina *[veena]*; **another bottle, please** još jednu bocu, molim *[yosh yednoo botsoo moleem]*
bottle-opener otvarač za boce

[otvarach za botse]
bottom dno; (*of person*) (*S*) zadnjica *[zadnyeetsa]*; (*C*) stražnica *[strajneetsa]*; **at the bottom of the hill** u podnožju brda *[oo podnojyoo burda]*
bottom gear prva brzina *[purva burzeena]*
bouncer izbacivač *[eezbatseevach]*
bowels crijeva *[tsuryeva]*
bowling kuglanje *[kooglanye]*
box kutija *[kooteeya]*
box lunch lanč-paket *[lanch-paket]*
box office blagajna *[blagina]*
boy dječak *[dyechak]*
boyfriend: my boyfriend moj dečko (*m*) *[moy dechko]*
bra (*S*) prsluče *[purslooche]*; (*C*) grudnjak *[groodnyak]*
bracelet narukvica *[narookveetsa]*
brake fluid (*S*) tečnost (*f*) za kočnice *[technost za kochneetse]*; (*C*) tekučina za kočnice *[tekoocheena]*
brake lining obloga kočnice *[obloga kochneetse]*
brakes kočnice *[kochneetse]*; **there's something wrong with the brakes** kočnice nisu ispravne *[neesoo eespravne]*; **I had to brake suddenly** morao sam naglo kočiti *[morao sam naglo kocheetee]*
brandy konjak *[konyak]*; (*local variety*) rakija *[rakeeya]*
brave нrabar
bread (*S*) hljeb *[нlyeb]*; (*C*) kruh *[krooн]*; **could we have some bread?** molim vas malo hljeba/kruha *[moleem vas malo нlyeba/krooha]*; **some more bread, please** još malo hljeba/kruha, molim *[yosh]*; **white bread** bijeli hljeb/kruh *[byelee]*; **brown bread** crni hljeb/kruh *[tsurnee]*; **wholemeal bread** hljeb/kruh s mekinjama *[mekeenyama]*; **rye bread** raženi hljeb/kruh *[rajenee]*
break slomiti *[slomeetee]*; **I think I've broken my ankle** mislim da sam slomio gležanj *[meesleem da sam slomeeo glejan-yuh]*; **it keeps breaking** stalno se lomi *[lomee]*
breakdown: I've had a breakdown kola su mi u kvaru *[kola soo mee oo kvaroo]*; **nervous breakdown** (*S*) nervni slom *[nervnee]*; (*C*) slom

živaca *[Jeevatsa]*
breakfast doručak *[doroochak]*;
English/full breakfast engleski
doručak *[engleskee]*; **continental
breakfast** kontinentalni doručak
[konteenentalnee]
break in: somebody's broken in neko
je provalio *[neko ye provaleeo]*
breast-feed dojiti *[doyeetee]*
breasts grudi *[groodee]*
breath daн; **out of breath** bez daha
breathe disati *[deesatee]*; **I can't
breathe** ne mogu disati *[mogoo]*
breeze povjetarac *[povyetarats]*
breezy svjež *[svyeɹ]*
bridal suite apartman za mladence
[apartman za mladentse]
bride (*S*) mlada; (*C*) nevjesta
[nevyesta]
bridegroom mladoženja *[mladoɹenya]*
bridge (*over river etc*) most
brief (*stay, visit*) kratak
briefcase tašna *[tashna]*
bright (*colour*) svijetao *[svyetao]*
brilliant (*idea, colour*) sjajan *[syɪyan]*
bring donijeti *[donyetee]*; **could you
bring it to my hotel?** možete li
donijeti u moj hotel? *[moɹete lee
donyetee oo moy hotel]*; **I'll bring it
back** vratit ću to *[vrateet choo]*; **can
I bring him too?** mogu li dovesti i
njega? *[mogoo lee dovestee ee nyega]*
Britain Britanija *[breetaneeya]*
British britanski *[breetanskee]*; **the
British** Britanci *[breetantsee]*
brochure brošura *[broshoora]*; **do you
have any brochures on ...?** imate li
brošura o ...? *[eemate lee]*
broke: I'm broke nemam ni prebijene
pare *[nemam nee prebeeyene pare]*
broken slomljen *[slomlyen]*; **you've
broken it** vi ste to slomili *[vee ste to
slomeelee]*; **it's broken** slomljen je
[ye]; **broken nose** razbijen nos
[razbeeyen]
brooch broš *[brosh]*
brother: my brother moj brat *[moy]*
brother-in-law: my brother-in-law (*S*)
moj djever *[moy dyever]*; (*C*) moj
šurjak *[shooryak]*
brown smeđ *[smedj]*; **I don't go
brown** ja ne crnim *[ya ne tsurneem]*
browse: may I just browse around?
mogu li samo malo pogledati?

[mogoo lee samo malo pogledatee]
bruise (*noun*) modrica *[modreetsa]*
brunette crnka *[tsurnka]*
brush (*noun*) četka *[chetka]*; (*artist's*)
kist *[keest]*
bucket vedro
buffet bife (*m*) *[beefe]*
bug (*insect*) stjenica *[styeneetsa]*; **she's
caught a bug** dobila je virus *[dobeela
ye veeroos]*
building zgrada
bulb (*elec*) (*S*) sijalica *[seeyaleetsa]*; (*C*)
žarulja *[ɹaroolya]*; **a new bulb** nova
sijalica/žarulja
Bulgaria Bugarska *[boogarska]*
Bulgarian (*adjective, language*) bu-
garski *[boogarskee]*; (*man*) Bugarin
[boogareen]; (*woman*) Bugarka *[boo-
garka]*; **the Bulgarians** Bugari
[boogaree]
bull bik *[beek]*
bump: I bumped my head udario
sam glavu *[oodareeo sam glavoo]*
bumper odbojnik *[odboyneek]*
bumpy (*road*) neravan; (*flight*) nemi-
ran *[nemeeran]*
bunch of flowers svežanj cvijeća
[sveɹan-yuh tsvyecha]
bungalow prizemna kuća *[preezemna
koocha]*
bunion upaljena oteklina na velikom
prstu na nozi *[oopalyena otekleena
na veleekom purstoo na noze]*
bunk ležaj *[leɹɪ]*; **bunk beds** (*S*) kreveti
na sprat *[krevetee]*; (*C*) kreveti na
kat
buoy plovak
burglar provalnik *[provalneek]*
**burn: do you have an ointment for
burns?** imate li mast za opekotine?
[eemate lee mast za opekoteene]
burnt: this meat is burnt ovo meso je
izgorjelo *[ye eezgoryelo]*; **my arms
are so burnt** ruke su mi toliko
izgorjele *[rooke soo mee toleeko
eezgoryele]*
burst: a burst pipe pukla cijev *[pookla
tsyev]*
bus autobus *[aootoboos]*; **is this the
bus for ...?** je li ovo autobus za ...?
[ye lee ovo]; **when's the next bus?**
kad ima slijedeći autobus? *[eema
slyedechee]*
bus driver vozač autobusa *[vozach*

aootoboosa]

business posao (*m*); **I'm here on business** ovdje sam poslom *[ovdye]*; **it's a pleasure to do business with you** zadovoljstvo je s vama sarađivati *[zadovolystvo ye s vama saradjeevatee]*

bus station (S) autobuska stanica *[aootobooska staneetsa]*; (C) autobusni kolodvor *[aootoboosnee]*

bus stop (S) stanica za autobus *[staneetsa za aootoboos]*; (C) autobusno stajalište *[aootoboosno stiyaleeshte]*; **will you tell me which bus stop I get off at?** hoćete li mi reći na kojoj stanici silazim? *[hochete lee mee rechee na koyoy staneetsee seelazeem]*

bust (*of body*) grudi *[groodee]*

bus tour ekskurzija autobusom *[ekskoorzeeya aootoboosom]*

busy (*street, restaurant*) prometan; **I'm busy this evening** večeras sam zauzet *[vecheras sam zaoozet]*; **the line was busy** (*tel*) linija je bila zauzeta *[leeneeya ye beela zaoozeta]*

but ali *[alee]*; **not ... but ...** ne ... ali ...

butcher mesar

butter (S) buter *[booter]*; (C) maslac *[maslats]*

butterfly leptir *[lepteer]*

button dugme *[doogme]*

buy: I'll buy it kupit ću *[koopeet choo]*; **where can I buy ...?** gdje mogu kupiti ...? *[gdye mogoo koopeetee]*

by: by car/boat kolima/brodom *[koleema/brodom]*; **who's it written by?** ko je to napisao? *[ye to napeesao]*; **it's by Meštrović** od Meštrovića je *[meshtroveecha]*; **I came by myself** došao sam sam *[doshao]*; **a seat by the window** mjesto pored prozora *[myesto]*; **by the sea** uz more *[ooz]*; **can you do it by Wednesday?** možete li uraditi do srijede? *[moJete lee ooradeetee do sryede]*

bye-bye doviđenja *[doveedjenya]*

bypass (*road*) zaobilazni put *[zaobeelaznee poot]*

C

cab (*taxi*) taksi *[taksee]*

cabaret kabare (*m*) *[kabare]*

cabbage kupus *[koopoos]*

cabin kabina *[kabeena]*

cable (*elec*) kabl *[kabul]*

cablecar žičara *[Jeechara]*

café (S) kafana; (C) kavana

caffeine kafein *[kafe-een]*

cake kolač *[kolach]*; **a piece of cake** komad kolača *[komad kolacha]*

calculator računar *[rachoonar]*

calendar kalendar

call: what is this called? kako se ovo zove?; **call the manager!** zovnite direktora *[zovneete deerektora]*; **I'd like to make a call to England** želio bih telefonirati u Englesku *[Jeleeo beeн telefoneeratee oo engleskoo]*; **I'll call back later** (*come back*) navratit ću kasnije *[navrateet choo kasneeye]*; (*phone back*) telefonirat ću

opet *[telefoneerat choo]*; **I'm expecting a call from London** očekujem poziv iz Londona *[ochekooyem pozeev eez]*; **would you give me a call at 7.30?** da li biste mi nazvali u 7.30? *[lee beeste mee nazvalee oo sedam ee treedeset]*; **it's been called off** otkazano je *[ye]*

call box telefonska govornica *[telefonska govorneetsa]*

calm (*person, sea*) miran *[meeran]*; **calm down!** smirite se! *[smeereete]*

Calor gas butan-gas *[bootan-gas]*

calories kalorije *[kaloreeye]*

camera foto-aparat

camp (S) kampovati *[kampovatee]*; (C) kampirati *[kampeeratee]*; **is there somewhere we can camp?** gdje možemo kampovati/kampirati? *[gdye moJemo]*; **can we camp here?** možemo li ovdje kampovati/

kampirati? *[lee ovdye]*
campbed poljski krevet *[polyskee]*
camping (S) kampovanje *[kampovanye]*; (C) kampiranje *[kampeeranye]*
campsite kamping *[kampeeng]*
can (*tin*) konzerva; **a can of beer** konzerva piva *[peeva]*
can: can I ...? mogu li ...? *[mogoo lee]*; **can you ...?** možete li ...? *[moJete]*; **can he ...?** može li ...? *[moJe]*; **can we ...?** možemo li ...? *[moJemo]*; **can they ...?** mogu li ...? *[mogoo]*; **I can't ...** ne mogu ...; **he can't ...** ne može ...; **can I keep it?** mogu li zadržati? *[zadurJatee]*; **if I can** ako mogu; **that can't be right** to ne može biti tačno *[beetee tachno]*
Canada Kanada
Canadian (*adjective*) kanadski *[kanadskee]*; (*man*) Kanađanin *[kanadjaneen]*; (*woman*) Kanađanka *[kanakjanka]*
cancel otkazati *[otkazatee]*; **can I cancel my reservation?** mogu li otkazati svoju rezervaciju? *[mogoo lee otkazatee svoyoo rezervatseeyoo]*; **can we cancel dinner for tonight?** možemo li večeras otkazati večeru? *[moJemo lee vecheras otkazatee vecheroo]*; **I cancelled it** otkazao sam
cancellation otkazivanje *[otkazeevanye]*
candies bombone; **a piece of candy** bombona
candle svijeća *[svyecha]*
canoe kanu *[kanoo]*
can-opener otvarač za konzerve *[otvarach za konzerve]*
cap (*headwear*) kapa; **bathing cap** kapa za kupanje *[koopanye]*
capital city glavni grad *[glavnee]*
capital letters velika slova *[veleeka]*
capsize: it capsized prevrnuo se *[prevurnoo-o]*
captain kapetan
car kola (*with plural verb*)
carafe boca *[botsa]*
carat: is it 9/14 carat gold? je li to deveto/četrnaestokaratno zlato? *[ye lee to deveto/cheturna-estokaratno]*
caravan kamp prikolica *[preekoleetsa]*
carbonated pjenušav *[pyenooshav]*

carburet(t)or karburator *[karboorator]*
card: do you have a (business) card? imate li visitkartu? *[eemate lee veezeetkartoo]*
cardboard box kartonska kutija *[kartonska kooteeya]*
cardigan džemper na raskopčavanje *[djemper na raskopchavanye]*
cards karte; **do you play cards?** igrate li karte? *[eegrate lee]*
care: goodbye, take care zbogom, pazite se *[zbogom pazeete]*; **will you take care of this bag for me?** hoćete li mi pričuvati ovu torbu? *[hochete lee mee preechoovatee ovoo torboo]*; **care of ...** KOD ...
careful: be careful pazite *[pazeete]*
careless: that was careless of you vrlo ste nespretni *[vurlo ste nespretnee]*
careless driving neoprezna vožnja *[neoprezna voJnya]*
car ferry trajekt *[trayekt]*
car hire iznajmljivanje kola *[eeznImlyeevanye kola]*
car keys ključevi od kola *[klyoochevee od kola]*
carnation karanfil *[karanfeel]*
carnival karneval
car park parking *[parkeeng]*
carpet tepih *[тереен]*
car rental iznajmljivanje kola *[eeznImlyeevanye kola]*
carrot (S) šargarepa *[shargarepa]*; (C) mrkva *[murkva]*
carry nositi *[noseetee]*; **could you carry this for me?** možete li mi ovo ponijeti? *[moJete lee mee ovo ponyetee]*
carry-cot nosiljka za bebu *[noseelyka za beboo]*
car-sick: I get car-sick mučno mi je u kolima *[moochno mee ye oo koleema]*
carton kutija *[kooteeya]*; **a carton of milk** mlijeko u tetrapaku *[mlyeko oo tetrapakoo]*
carving rezbarija *[rezbareeya]*
carwash pranje kola *[pranye kola]*
case (*suitcase*) (S) kofer; (C) kovčeg *[kovcheg]*; **in any case** u svakom slučaju *[oo svakom sloochIyoo]*; **in that case** u tom slučaju; **it's a special case** to je specijalan slučaj

[ye spetseeyalan sloochɪ]; **in case he comes back** u slučaju da se vrati *[vratee]*; **I'll take two just in case** uzet ću dva za svaki slučaj *[oozet choo dva za svakee]*

cash gotovina *[gotoveena]*; **I don't have any cash** nemam gotovine *[nemam gotoveene]*; **I'll pay cash** (S) platiću gotovinom *[plateechoo gotoveenom]*; (C) platit ću u gotovini; **will you cash a cheque/check for me?** da li biste mi unovčili ček? *[lee beeste mee oonovcheelee chek]*

cashdesk kasa

cash register registar-kasa *[regeestar-kasa]*

casino kasino (m) *[kaseeno]*

cassette kaseta

cassette player, cassette recorder kasetofon

castle zamak

casual: casual clothes sportska odjeća *[sportska odyecha]*

cat mačka *[machka]*

catamaran splav

catastrophe katastrofa

catch: where do we catch the bus? gdje možemo uhvatiti autobus? *[gdye moɪemo ooʜvateetee aootoboos]*; **he's caught some strange illness** dobio je neku čudnu bolest *[dobeeo ye nekoo choodnoo bolest]*

catching: is it catching? je li (bolest) zarazna? *[ye lee (bolest) zarazna]*

cathedral katedrala

Catholic katolički *[katoleechkee]*

cauliflower karfiol *[karfeeol]*

cause uzrok *[oozrok]*

cave pećina *[pecheena]*

caviar kavijar *[kaveeyar]*

ceiling (S) tavanica *[tavaneetsa]*; (C) strop

celebrations proslave

celery celer *[tseler]*

cellophane celofan *[tselofan]*

cemetery groblje *[groblye]*

center centar *[tsentar]*; *see also* **centre**

centigrade Celzijus *[tselzeeyoos]*; *see page 121*

centimetre, centimeter centimetar *[tsenteemetar]*; *see page 120*

central centralan *[tsentralan]*; **we'd prefer something more central** više bismo voljeli nešto bliže centru

[veeshe beesmo volyelee neshto bleeɪe tsentroo]

central heating centralno grijanje *[tsentralno greeyanye]*

central station (S) glavna stanica *[glavna staneetsa]*; (C) glavni kolodvor *[glavnee kolodvor]*

centre centar *[tsentar]*; **how do we get to the centre?** kako da dođemo do centra? *[kako da dodjemo do tsentra]*; **in the centre** (of town) u centru *[oo tsentroo]*

century (S) vijek *[vyek]*; (C) stoljeće *[stolyeche]*; **in the 19th/20th century** u 19./20. vijeku *[oo devetna-estom/dvadesetom vyekoo]*

ceramics keramika *[kerameeka]*

certain siguran *[seegooran]*; **are you certain?** jeste li sigurni? *[yeste lee seegoornee]*; **I'm absolutely certain** potpuno sam siguran *[potpoono]*

certainly svakako; **certainly not** svakako ne

certificate potvrda *[potvurda]*; **birth certificate** rodni list *[rodnee]*

chain lanac *[lanats]*

chair stolica *[stoleetsa]*

chalet (in mountains) planinska koliba *[planeenska koleeba]*

chambermaid sobarica *[sobareetsa]*

champagne šampanjac *[shampanyats]*

chance: quite by chance sasvim slučajno *[sasveem sloochɪno]*; **no chance!** ni govora! *[nee]*

change: could you change this into dinars? možete li ovo promijeniti u dinare *[moɪete lee ovo promyeneetee oo deenare]*; **I haven't got any change** nemam ništa sitno *[nemam neeshta seetno]*; **can you give me change for a 20,000 dinar note?** možete li mi usitniti novčanicu od 20,000 dinara? *[moɪete lee mee ooseetneetee novchaneetsoo ... deenara]*; **do we have to change (trains)?** moramo li presjedati? *[lee presyedatee]*; **for a change** za promjenu *[promyenoo]*; **you haven't changed the sheets** niste promijenili plahte *[neeste promyeneelee plahte]*; **the place has changed so much** mjesto se toliko izmijenilo *[myesto se toleeko eezmyeneelo]*; **do you want to change places with me?** želite li

da se zamjenimo za mjesta? *[Jeleete
lee da se zamyeneemo za myesta]*;
can I change this for ...? mogu li
ovo zamijeniti za ...? *[mogoo lee ovo
zamyeneetee]*
changeable promjenljiv *[prom-
yenlyeev]*
channel: the English Channel La-
manš *[lamansh]*
chaos Haos
chap čovjek *[chovyek]*; **the chap at
reception** čovjek na recepciji
chapel kapela
charge: is there an extra charge? ima
li dodatnih troškova? *[eema lee
dodatneeн troshkova]*; **what do you
charge?** koliko naplaćujete? *[koleeko
naplachooyete]*; **who's in charge
here?** ko je ovdje odgovorno lice?
[ye ovdye odgovorno leetse]
charming *(place, thing)* čaroban
[charoban]; *(person)* šarmantan
[sharmantan]
chart *(for navigation)* pomorska karta
charter flight čarter let *[charter]*
chassis šasija *[shaseeya]*
cheap jevtin *[yevteen]*; **do you have
something cheaper?** imate li nešto
jevtinije? *[eemate lee neshto
yevteeneeye]*
cheat: I've been cheated prevarili su
me *[prevareelee soo]*
check: will you check? da li biste
provjerili? *[lee beeste provyereelee]*;
will you check the steering? da li
biste provjerili volan?; **will you
check the bill?** da li biste provjerili
račun? *[rachoon]*; **I've checked it**
provjerio sam *[provyereeo]*
check *(financial)* ček *[chek]*; **will you
take a check?** da li ćete primiti ček?
[lee chete preemeetee]
check *(bill)* račun *[rachoon]*; **may I
have the check please?** račun,
molim! *[moleem]*
checkbook čekovna knjižica *[chekovna
knyeeJeetsa]*
checked *(shirt etc)* kariran *[kareeran]*
checkers dame
check-in otprema putnika *[pootneeka]*
checkroom *(for coats)* garderoba
cheek *(on face)* obraz; **what a cheek!**
kakva drskost! *[kakva durskost]*
cheeky *(person)* drzak *[durzak]*

cheerio *(bye-bye)* do viđenja
[doveedjenya]
cheers *(toast)* živjeli! *[Jeevyelee]*; *(thank
you)* нvala
cheer up! samo veselo!
cheese sir *[seer]*
cheesecake kolač od sira *[kolach od
seera]*
chef *(S)* kuvar *[koovar]*; *(C)* kuhar
[koohar]
chemist *(shop)* *(S)* apoteka; *(C)* ljekarna *[lyekarna]*
cheque ček *[chek]*; **will you take a
cheque?** da li ćete primiti ček? *[lee
chete preemeetee]*
cheque book čekovna knjižica
[chekovna knyeeJeetsa]
cheque card čekovna kartica
[chekovna karteetsa]
cherry trešnja *[treshnya]*
chess šah *[shaн]*
chest *(of body)* grudi *[groodee]* *(with
plural verb)*
chewing gum žvakaća guma
[Jvakacha gooma]
chicken piletina *[peeleteena]*
chickenpox male boginje *[bogeenye]*
child dijete *[dyete]*
child minder osoba koja čuva djecu
[osoba koya choova dyetsoo]
child minding service služba za ču-
vanje djece *[slooJba za choovanye
dyetse]*
children djeca *[dyetsa]*
children's playground igralište za
djecu *[eegraleeshte za dyetsoo]*
children's pool bazen za djecu
[dyetsoo]
children's portion dječja porcija
[dyechya portseeya]
children's room soba za djecu
[dyetsoo]
chilled *(wine)* ohlađen *[oнladjen]*; **it's
not properly chilled** nije dobro
ohlađeno *[neeye dobro oнladjeno]*
chilly нladno
chimney dimnjak *[deemnyak]*
chin brada
china *(S)* porcelan *[portselan]*; *(C)*
porculan
chips *(S)* pržen krompir *[purJen
krompeer]*; *(C)* krumpir *[kroompeer]*;
potato chips čips *[cheeps]*; *(gambling)*
žetoni *[Jetonee]*

chiropodist pediker *[pedeeker]*
chocolate čokolada *[chokolada]*; **a chocolate bar** tabla čokolade; **a box of chocolates** bombonjera *[bombonyera]*; **a hot chocolate** topli napitak od čokolade *[toplee napeetak]*
choke (*on car*) čok *[chok]*
choose: it's hard to choose teško je izabrati *[teshko ye eezabratee]*; **you choose for us** izaberite za nas *[eezabereete]*
chop: a pork chop svinjski kotlet *[sveenyskee]*
Christian name ime *[eeme]*
Christmas Božić *[boⱼeech]*; **merry Christmas** sretan Božić
church crkva *[tsurkva]*; **where is the Orthodox/Catholic church?** gdje je pravoslavna/katolička crkva? *[gdye ye katoleechka]*
cider jabukovača *[yabookovacha]*
cigar cigara *[tseegara]*
cigarette cigareta *[tseegareta]*; **tipped/plain cigarettes** cigareta s filterom/bez filtera *[feelterom/bez feeltera]*
cigarette lighter upaljač *[oopalyach]*
cine-camera filmska kamera *[feelmska]*
cinema (*S*) bioskop *[beeoskop]*; (*C*) kino *[keeno]*
circle krug *[kroog]*; (*in theatre*) (*S*) serkl; (*C*) **dress circle** mezanin *[mezaneen]*; **upper circle** *[balkon]*
citizen: I'm a British/American citizen ja sam britanski/američki državljanin *[ya sam breetanskee/amereechkee durⱼavlyaneen]*
city grad
city centre, city center centar grada *[tsentar grada]*
claim (*noun: insurance*) zahtjev (za naknadu štete) *[zaнtyev (za naknadoo shtete)]*
claim form odštetni formular *[odshtetnee formoolar]*
clarify razjasniti *[razyasneetee]*
classical klasičan *[klaseechan]*
clean (*adjective*) čist *[cheest]*; **it's not clean** nije čist *[neeye]*; **may I have some clean sheets?** mogu li dobiti čiste plahte? *[mogoo lee dobeetee cheeste plaнte]*; **our apartment hasn't been cleaned today** naš apartman

danas nije očišćen *[nash apartman danas neeye ocheeshchen]*; **can you clean this for me?** možete li mi ovo očistiti? *[moⱼete lee mee ovo ocheesteetee]*
cleaning solution (*for contact lenses*) rastvor za ispiranje *[rastvor za eespeeranye]*
cleansing cream mlijeko za čišćenje lica *[mlyeko za cheeshchenye leetsa]*
clear: it's not very clear nije sasvim jasno *[neeye sasveem yasno]*; **ok, that's clear** u redu, jasno je *[oo redoo, yasno ye]*
clever bistar *[beestar]*
cliff litica *[leeteetsa]*
climate klima *[kleema]*
climb: it's a long climb to the top dugo se treba penjati do vrha *[doogo se treba penyatee do vurнa]*; **we're going to climb Triglav** (*S*) penjaćemo se na Triglav *[penyachemo se na treeglav]*; (*C*) penjat ćemo se na Triglav
climber planinar *[planeenar]*
climbing boots planinarske cipele *[planeenarske tseepele]*
climbing holiday planinarski odmor *[planeenarskee odmor]*
clinic klinika *[kleeneeka]*
clip (*ski*) kopča *[kopcha]*
cloakroom (*for coats*) garderoba *[garderoba]*; (*WC*) klozet
clock sat
close: is it close? je li blizu? *[ye lee bleezoo]*; **close to the hotel** blizu hotela; **close by** blizu
close: when do you close? kad zatvarate?
closed zatvoreno; **they were closed** bili su zatvoreni *[beelee su zatvorenee]*
closet (*cupboard*) (*S*) plakar; (*C*) ormar
cloth (*material*) tkanina *[tkaneena]*; (*rag*) krpa *[kurpa]*
clothes odjeća *[odyecha]*
clothes line (*S*) konopac za sušenje rublja *[konopats za sooshenye rooblya]*; (*C*) konop za sušenje rublja
clothes peg, clothespin štipaljka *[shteepalyka]*
cloud oblak; **it's clouding over** vrijeme se muti *[vreeyeme se mootee]*
cloudy oblačno *[oblachno]*

club klub *[kloob]*

clubhouse klupska kuća *[kloopska koocha]*

clumsy nespretan

clutch (*car*) kvačilo *[kvacheelo]*; **the clutch is slipping** kvačilo klizi *[kleezee]*

coach (*bus*) autobus *[aootoboos]*

coach trip izlet autobusom *[eezlet aootoboosom]*

coast obala; **at the coast** na obali *[obalee]*

coastguard (*S*) obalska straža *[straJa]*; (*C*) obalna straža

coat (*overcoat etc*) kaput *[kapoot]*; (*jacket*) sako (*m*)

coathanger vješalica za odijela *[vyeshaleetsa za odyela]*

cobbled street kaldrmisana ulica *[kaldurmeesana ooleetsa]*

cobbler (*S*) obućar *[oboochar]*; (*C*) postolar

cockroach žohar *[Johar]*

cocktail koktel

cocktail bar aperitiv-bar *[apereeteev—]*

cocoa kakao (*m*)

coconut kokosov orah

code: what's the (dialling) code for ...? koji je pozivni broj za ...? *[koyee ye pozeevnee broy]*

coffee kafa; **a white coffee, a coffee with milk** bijela kafa *[byela]*; **a black coffee** crna kafa *[tsurna]*; **a Turkish coffee** turska kafa *[toorska]*; **two coffees, please** dvije kafe, molim *[dvye kafe moleem]*

coin kovani novac *[kovanee novats]*

Coke (*tm*) koka-kola

cold (*adjective*) Hladan; **I'm cold** hladno mi je *[Hladno mee ye]*; **I have a cold** prehlađen sam *[preHladjen]*

coldbox (*for carrying food*) putni frižider *[pootnee freeJeeder]*

cold cream (*S*) pomada; (*C*) krema za lice *[za leetse]*

collapse: he's collapsed on se srušio *[sroosheeo]*

collar okovratnik *[okovratneek]*

collar bone ključna kost *[klyoochna]*

colleague: my colleague moj kolega *[moy kolega]*; **your colleague** vaš kolega *[vash]*

collect: I've come to collect ... došao sam po ... *[doshao]*; **I collect ...** (*stamps etc*) skupljam ... *[skooplyam]*; **I want to call New York collect** želim da telefoniram u Njujork na račun broja u Njujorku *[Jeleem da telefoneeram oo nyooyork na rachoon broya oo nyooyorkoo]*

collect call telefonski razgovor na račun broja koji se zove *[telefonskee razgovor na rachoon broya koyee se zove]*

college koledž *[koledj]*

collision sudar *[soodar]*

cologne kolonjska voda *[kolonyska]*

colo(u)r boja *[boya]*; **do you have any other colo(u)rs?** imate li u drugim bojama? *[eemate lee oo droogeem boyama]*

colo(u)r film film u boji *[feelm oo boyee]*

comb (*noun*) češalj *[cheshal-yuh]*

come doći *[dochee]*; **I come from London** ja sam iz Londona *[ya sam eez londona]*; **where do you come from?** odakle ste vi? *[odakle ste vee]*; **when are they coming?** kad dolaze?; **come here** dođite ovamo *[dodjeete]*; **come with me** pođite sa mnom *[podjeete]*; **come back!** vrati se! *[vratee]*; **I'll come back later** vratit ću se kasnije *[vrateet choo se kasneeye]*; **come in!** slobodno!; **he's coming on very well** (*improving*) vrlo dobro napreduje *[vurlo dobro napredooye]*; **come on!** ma hajde! *[hIde]*; **do you want to come out this evening?** želite li večeras izići? *[Jeleete lee vecheras eezeechee]*; **these two pictures didn't come out** ove dvije slike nisu izašle *[ove dvye sleeke neesoo eezashle]*; **the money hasn't come through yet** novac još nije stigao *[novats yosh neeye steegao]*

comfortable (*hotel etc*) udoban *[oodoban]*; **it's not veery comfortable** nije baš udoban *[neeye bash]*

Common Market Zajedničko evropsko tržište *[zIyedneechko evropsko turJeeshte]*

company (*firm*) kompanija *[kompaneeya]*

comparison: there's no comparison

(*S*) nema poređenja *[nema poredjenya]*; (*C*) nema poredbe
compartment (*train*) kupe (*m*) *[koope]*
compass kompas
compensation naknada
complain žaliti se *[Jaleetee]*; **I want to complain about my room** želim podnyeti žalbu u vezi sobe *[Jeleem podnyetee Jalboo oo vezee sobe]*
complaint pritužba *[preetooJba]*; **I have a complaint** imam pritužbu *[eemam preetooJboo]*
complete: the complete set komplet; **it's a complete disaster** potpuna katastrofa *[potpoona katastrofa]*
completely potpuno *[potpoono]*
complicated: it's very complicated vrlo je komplicirano *[vurlo ye kompleetseerano]*
compliment: my compliments to the chef moji komplimenti kuvaru (*S*)/ kuharu (*C*) *[moyee kompleementee koovaroo/kooharoo]*
comprehensive (*insurance*) kasko
compulsory obavezan
computer kompjuter *[kompyooter]*
concern: we are very concerned veoma smo zabrinuti *[veoma smo zabreenootee]*
concert koncert *[kontsert]*
concussion potres mozga
condenser (*in car*) kondenzator
condition: it's not in very good condition nije baš u dobrom stanju *[neeye bash oo dobrom stanyu]*
conditioner (*for hair*) regenerator
condom prezervativ *[prezervateev]*
conductor (*on train*) kondukter *[kondookter]*
conference konferencija *[konferentseeya]*
confirm: can you confirm the reservation? možete li potvrditi rezervaciju? *[moJete lee potvurdeetee rezervatseeyoo]*
confuse: it's very confusing vrlo je zamršeno *[vurlo ye zamursheno]*
congratulations! čestitam! *[chesteetam]*
conjunctivitis konjunktivitis *[konyoonkteeveetees]*
connection (*in travelling*) veza
connoisseur znalac *[znalats]*
conscious (*medically*) pri svijesti *[pree*

svyestee]
consciousness: he's lost consciousness izgubio je svijest *[eezgoobeeo ye svyest]*
constipation konstipacija *[konsteepatseeya]*
consul konzul *[konzool]*
consulate konzulat *[konzoolat]*
contact: how can I contact ...? kako mogu stupiti u vezu sa ...? *[kako mogoo stoopeetee oo vezoo]*; **I'm trying to contact ...** pokušavam da stupim u vezu sa ... *[pokooshavam da stoopeem]*
contact lenses (*S*) kontaktna sočiva *[socheeva]*; (*C*) kontaktne leće *[leche]*
continent: on the continent na kontinentu *[konteenentoo]*
contraceptive sredstvo za kontracepciju *[sredstvo za kontratseptseeyoo]*
convenient (*time, location*) pogodan; **that's not convenient** nije pogodno *[neeye pogodno]*
cook (*S*) kuvati *[koovatee]*; (*C*) kuhati *[koohatee]*; **it's not properly cooked** nije dobro skuvano/skuhano *[neeye dobro skoovano/skoohano]*; **it's beautifully cooked** prekrasno je skuvano/skuhano *[prekrasno ye]*; **he's a good cook** (*S*) on je dobar kuvar *[ye dobar koovar]*; (*C*) on je dobar kuhar *[koohar]*
cooker štednjak *[shtednyak]*
cookie keks
cool (*day, weather*) Hladan
corduroy (*S*) somot; (*C*) rebrasti samt *[rebrastee]*
Corfu Krf *[kurf]*
cork (*in bottle*) čep *[chep]*
corkscrew vadičep *[vadeechep]*
corn (*on foot*) žulj *[Jool-yuh]*
corner: on the corner na uglu *[oogloo]*; **in the corner** u uglu *[oo]*
cornflakes kukuruzne pahuljice *[kookooroozne pahoolyeetse]*
coronary (*noun*) infarkt *[eenfarkt]*
correct (*adjective*) ispravan *[eespravan]*; **please correct me if I make a mistake** ispravite me molim vas ako pogriješim *[eespraveete me moleem vas ako pogryesheem]*
corridor hodnik *[hodneek]*
corset steznik *[stezneek]*

cosmetics kosmetika *[kozmeteeka]*
cost: what does it cost? koliko košta?
[koleeko koshta]
cot *(for baby)* *(S)* krevetac *[krevetats]*;
(C) dječji krevetić *[dyechyee
chreveteech]*; *(camping)* poljski krevet
[polyskee]
cottage kućica *[koocheetsa]*
cotton pamuk *[pamook]*
cotton buds *(for make-up removal etc)*
loptice od vate *[lopteetse od vate]*
cotton wool vata
couch kauč *[kaooch]*
couchette kušet *[kooshet]*
cough *(noun)* kašalj *[kashal-yuh]*
cough medicine sirup za kašalj
[seeroop za kashal-yuh]
cough tablets tablete za kašalj
[kashal-yuh]
could: could you ...? da li biste mogli
... *[lee beeste moglee]*; **could I have
...?** mogu li dobiti ... *[mogoo lee
dobeetee]*; **I couldn't ...** ne bih
mogao ... *[beeн mogao]*
country *(nation)* zemlja *[zemlya]*; **in
the country** *(countryside)* na selu
[seloo]
countryside priroda *[preeroda]*
couple *(man and woman)* par; **a
couple of ...** nekoliko ... *[nekoleeko]*
courier turistički vodič
[tooreesteechkee vodeech]
course *(of meal)* jelo *[yelo]*; **of course**
naravno; **of course not** naravno ne
court *(law)* sud; *(tennis)* igralište
[eegraleeshte]
courtesy bus *(airport to hotel etc)* besplatan autobus *[besplatan aootoboos]*
cousin: my cousin moj rođak *[moy
rodjak]*
cover charge kuver *[koover]*
cow krava
crab rak
cracked: it's cracked *(plate etc)* napu-
kao je *[napookao ye]*
cracker *(biscuit)* slani keks *[slanee]*
craftshop narodna radinost
[radeenost]
cramp *(in leg etc)* grč *[gurch]*
crankshaft radilica *[radeeleetsa]*
crash: there's been a crash dogodio
se sudar *[dogodeeo se soodar]*
crash course intenzivni kurs
[eentenzeevnee koors]

crash helmet zaštitni šlem
[zashteetnee shlem]
crawl *(swimming)* kraul *[kraool]*
crazy lud *[lood]*
cream *(food)* vrhnje *[vurнnye]*;
(whipped) šlag *[shlag]*; *(for face)* krema
creche *(for babies)* jaslice *[yasleetse]*
credit card kreditna kartica
[kredeetna karteetsa]
crib *(baby's cot)* *(S)* krevetac *[krevetats]*;
(C) dječji krevetić *[dyechyee
kreveteech]*
crisis kriza *[kreeza]*
crisps čips *[cheeps]*
Croatia Hrvatska *[нrvatska]*
Croatian *(adjective, language)* hrvatski
[нrvatskee]; *(man)* Hrvat *[нrvat]*;
(woman) Hrvatica *[нurvateetsa]*
crockery zemljano posuđe *[zemlyano
posoodje]*
crook: he's a crook on je lopov *[ye]*
crossing *(by sea)* prijelaz *[pryelaz]*
crossroads raskrsnica *[raskursneetsa]*
crosswalk pješački prijelaz
[pyeshachkee pryelaz]
crowd gomila *[gomeela]*
crowded prepun *[prepoon]*
crown *(on tooth)* kruna *[kroona]*
crucial: it's absolutely crucial neo-
phodno je *[neop-нodno· ye]*
cruise krstarenje *[kurstarenye]*
crutch *(of body)* prijepone *[pryepone]*
crutches štake *[shtake]*
cry plakati *[plakatee]*; **don't cry** ne
plačite *[placheete]*
cucumber krastavac *[krastavats]*
cuisine kuhinja *[kooheenya]*
cultural kulturni *[kooltoornee]*
cup *(S)* šolja *[sholya]*; *(C)* šalica
[shaleetsa]; **a cup of coffee** šolja/
šalica kafe *[sholya/shaleetsa]*
cupboard ormar
**cure: have you got something to
cure it?** imate li nekakav lijek?
[eemate lee nekakav lyek]
curlers vikleri *[veekleree]*
current *(elec, in water)* struja *[strooya]*
curry kari *(m)* *[karee]*
curtains zavjese *[zavyese]*
curve *(noun: in road)* okuka *[okooka]*
cushion jastuk *[yastook]*
custom običaj *[obeechı]*
Customs carina *[tsareena]*
cut: I've cut myself posjekao sam se

[posyekao]; **could you cut a little off here?** možete li odsjeći malo odavde? *[moJete lee odsyechee]*; **we were cut off** *(tel)* prekinulo je *[prekeenoolo ye]*; **the engine keeps cutting out** motor stalno prekida *[prekeeda]*
cutlery pribor za jelo *[preebor za yelo]*
cutlets kotleti *[kotletee]*

cycle: can we cycle there? možemo li tamo biciklom? *[moJemo lee tamo beetseeklom]*
cyclist biciklista *(m)* *[beetseekleesta]*
cylinder *(of car)* cilindar *[tseeleendar]*
cylinder-head gasket zaptivka glave motora *[zapteevka glave motora]*
cynical ciničan *[tseeneechan]*
cystitis cistitis *[tseesteetees]*

D

Dalmatian *(adjective)* dalmatinski *[dalmateenskee]*
damage: you've damaged it oštetili ste to *[oshteteelee ste]*; **it's damaged** oštećeno je *[oshtecheno ye]*; **there's no damage** nema štete *[nema shtete]*
damn! do vraga!
damp *(adjective)* vlažan *[vlaJan]*
dance: a Yugoslav dance jugoslavenski ples *[yoogoslavenskee]*; **do you want to dance?** želite li plesati? *[Jeleete lee plesatee]*
dancer: he's a good dancer on je dobar plesač *[ye dobar plesach]*
dancing: we'd like to go dancing htjeli bismo ići na ples *[Htyelee beesmo eechee]*; **traditional (Yugoslav) dancing** narodni (jugoslavenski) ples *[narodnee (yoogoslavenskee)]*
dandruff perut *[peroot]*
dangerous opasan
dare: I don't dare ne usuđujem se *[oosoodjooyem]*
dark *(adjective)* taman; **dark blue** tamno plav; **when does it get dark?** kad se smrkava? *[smurkava]*; **after dark** noću *[nochoo]*
darling drag
dashboard vozačka tabla *[vozachka]*
date: what's the date? koji je datum? *[koyee ye datoom]*; **on what date?** kojeg datuma? *[koyeg datooma]*; **can we make a date?** *(romantic, business)* možemo li ugovoriti sastanak? *[moJemo lee oogovoreetee sastanak]*
dates *(to eat)* datule *[datoole]*
daughter: my daughter moja ćerka

[moya cherka]
daughter-in-law snaha
dawn *(noun)* zora; **at dawn** u zoru *[oo zoroo]*
day dan; **the day after** dan kasnije *[kasneeye]*; **the day before** dan ranije *[raneeye]*; **every day** svaki dan *[svakee]*; **one day** jedan dan *[yedan]*; **can we pay by the day?** možemo li plaćati prema broju dana? *[moJemo lee plachatee prema broyoo dana]*; **have a good day!** ugodan dan! *[oogodan]*
daylight robbery *(extortionate prices)* prava pljačka *[prava plyachka]*
day trip jednodnevni izlet *[eezlet]*
dead mrtav *[murtav]*
deaf *(S)* gluv *[gloov]*; *(C)* gluh *[glooн]*
deaf-aid *(S)* aparat za gluvoneme *[aparat za gloovoneme]*; *(C)* aparat za gluhonijeme *[gloohonyeme]*
deal *(business)* posao *(m)*; **it's a deal** ugovoreno *[oogovoreno]*; **will you deal with it?** da li biste se vi time pozabavili? *[lee beeste se vee teeme pozabaveelee]*
dealer *(agent)* posrednik *[posredneek]*
dear *(expensive)* skup *[skoop]*; **Dear Nikola** Dragi Nikola *[dragee]*; **Dear Sir** Poštovani gospodine *[poshtovanee gospodeene]*; **Dear Madam** Poštovana gospođo *[gospodjo]*
death smrt *(f)* *[smurt]*
decadent dekadentan
December *(S)* decembar *[detsembar]*; *(C)* prosinac *[proseenats]*
decent: that's very decent of you vrlo ljubazno od vas *[vurlo*

lyoobazno]
decide: we haven't decided yet još nismo odlučili *[yosh neesmo odloocheelee]*; **you decide for us** vi odlučite mjesto nas *[vee odloocheete myesto]*; **it's all decided** sve je odlučeno *[sve ye odloocheno]*
decision odluka *[odlooka]*
deck (*on ship*) paluba *[palooba]*
deckchair ležaljka *[leʒalyka]*
declare: I have nothing to declare nemam ništa za carinjenje *[nemam neeshta za tsareenyenye]*
decoration (*in room*) ukras *[ookras]*
deduct oduzeti *[odoozetee]*
deep dubok *[doobok]*; **is it deep?** je li duboko? *[ye lee dooboko]*
deep-freeze zamrzivač *[zamurzeevach]*
definitely definitivno *[defee-neeteevno]*; **definitely not** ni u kom slučaju *[nee oo kom sloochiyoo]*
degree (*university*) diploma *[dee-ploma]*; (*temperature*) (*S*) stepen; (*C*) stupanj *[stoopan-yuh]*
dehydrated (*medically*) dehidriran *[deheedreeran]*; (*very thirsty*) strašno žedan *[sturashno ʒedan]*
de-icer sprej za odleđivanje *[spray za odledjeevanye]*
delay: the flight was delayed let je kasnio *[ye kasneeo]*
deliberately namjerno *[namyerno]*
delicacy: a local delicacy lokalni specijalitet *[lokalnee spetseeyaleetet]*
delicious ukusan *[ookoosan]*
deliver: will you deliver it? da li biste ovo isporučili? *[lee beeste ovo eesporoocheelee]*
delivery: is there another mail delivery? dolazi li još jedna pošta? *[dolazee lee yosh yedna poshta]*
de luxe deluks *[delooks]*
denims (*S*) farmerke; (*C*) traperice *[trapereetse]*
Denmark Danska
dent: there's a dent in it udubljen je *[oodooblyen ye]*
dental floss konac za čišćenje zuba *[konats za cheeshchenye zooba]*
dentist zubar *[zoobar]*
dentures umjetna zubala *[oomyetna zoobala]*
deny: he denies it on to poriče *[poreeche]*

deodorant dezodorans
department store robna kuća *[koocha]*
departure (*S*) polazak; (*C*) odlazak
departure lounge čekaonica za odlaske *[chekaoneetsa za odlaske]*
depend: it depends zavisi *[zaveesee]*; **it depends on ...** zavisi od ...
deposit (*downpayment*) ulog *[oolog]*
depressed utučen *[ootoochen]*
depth dubina *[doobeena]*
description opis *[opees]*
deserted (*beach, area*) pust
dessert dezert
destination odredište *[odredeeshte]*
detergent deterdžent *[deterdjent]*
detour zaobilazni put *[zaobeelaznee poot]*
devalued devalviran *[devalveeran]*
develop: could you develop these films? možete li razviti ove filmove? *[moʒete lee razveetee ove feelmove]*
diabetic dijabetičar *[deeyabeteechar]*
diagram dijagram *[deeyagram]*
dialect dijalekt *[deeyalekt]*
dialling code pozivni broj *[pozeevnee broy]*
diamond dijamant *[deeyamant]*
diaper pelena
diarrh(o)ea proljev *[prolyev]*; **do you have something to stop diarrhoea?** imati li nešto za zaustavljanje proljeva? *[eematee lee neshto za zaoostavlyanye prolyeva]*
diary dnevnik *[dnevneek]*
dictionary rječnik *[ryechneek]*; **a Serbocroatian-English dictionary** srpskohrvatsko-engleski rječnik *[surpsko-Hurvatsko-engleskee]*
didn't *see* **not** *and pages* 114, 116
die umrijeti *[oomryetee]*; **I'm absolutely dying for a drink** umirem od žeđi *[oomeerem od ʒedjee]*
diesel (*fuel*) dizel *[deezel]*
diet dijeta *[deeyeta]*; **I'm on a diet** na dijeti sam *[deeyetee]*
difference razlika *[razleeka]*; **what's the difference between ...?** kakva je razlika između ...? *[kakva ye razleeka eezmedjoo]*; **I can't tell the difference** ne vidim razliku *[veedeem razleekoo]*; **it doesn't make any difference** ništa ne mijenja na stvar

[neeshta ne myenya]
different: they are different različiti su *[razleecheetee soo]*; **they are very different** vrlo su različiti *[vurlo]*; **it's different from this one** drukčiji je od ovog *[drookcheeyee ye]*; **may we have a different room?** možemo li dobiti drugu sobu *[moɹemo lee dobeetee droogoo soboo]*; **ah well, that's different** e, pa to je drugo *[ye droogo]*
difficult težak *[teɹak]*
difficulty teškoća *[teshkocha]*; **without any difficulty** bez ikakve teškoće *[eekakve teshkoche]*; **I'm having difficulties with ...** imam teškoća sa ... *[eemam]*
digestion varenje *[varenye]*
dinghy mali čamac *[malee chamats]*
dining car kola za ručavanje *[roochavanye]*
dining room (S) trpezarija *[turpezareeya]*; (C) blagovaonica *[blagovaoneetsa]*
dinner večera *[vechera]*
dinner jacket smoking
dinner party gosti na večeri *[gostee na vecheree]*
dipped headlights oborena svjetla *[oborena svyetla]*
dipstick mjerač nivoa ulja *[myerach neevoa oolya]*
direct (*adjective*) direktan *[deerektan]*; **does it go direct?** ide li direktno? *[eede lee deerektno]*
direction pravac *[pravats]*; **in which direction is it?** u kojem je to pravcu? *[oo koyem ye to pravtsoo]*; **is it in this direction?** je li to u ovom pravcu? *[lee to oo ovom]*
directory: telephone directory telefonski imenik *[telefonskee eemeneek]*
directory enquiries informacije *[eenformatseeye]*
dirt prljavština *[purlyavshteena]*
dirty prljav *[purlyav]*
disabled invalid *[eenvaleed]*
disagree: it disagrees with me (*food*) škodi mi *[shkodee]*
disappear nestati *[nestatee]*; **it's just disappeared** (*I've lost it*) prosto je nestalo *[prosto ye nestalo]*
disappointed: I was disappointed bio sam razočaran *[beeo sam razocharan]*

disappointing razočaravajući *[razocharavɪyoochee]*
disaster katastrofa
discharge (*pus*) gnoj *[gnoy]*
disc jockey disk-džokej *[deesk-djokay]*
disco disko (*m*) *[deesko]*
disco dancing disko-plesanje *[deesko-plesanye]*
discount (*noun*) popust *[popoost]*
disease bolest (*f*)
disgusting (*taste, food etc*) odvratan
dish (*meal*) jelo *[yelo]*; (*plate*) zdjela *[zdyela]*
dishcloth (S) krpa za pranje sudova *[kurpa za pranye soodova]*; (C) krpa za pranje suđa *[soodja]*
dishwashing liquid (S) tečnost za pranje sudova *[technost za pranye soodova]*; (C) tekućina za pranje suđa *[tekoocheena ... soodja]*
disinfectant (*noun*) dezinfekciono sredstvo *[dezeenfektseeono sredstvo]*
dislocated shoulder iščašeno rame *[eeshchasheno rame]*
dispensing chemist (S) apoteka; (C) ljekarna *[lyekarna]*
disposable nappies pelene koje se bacaju *[pelene koye se batsɪyoo]*
distance daljina *[dalyeena]*; **what's the distance from ... to ...?** kolika je daljina od ... do ...? *[koleeka ye]*; **in the distance** u daljini *[oo dalyeenee]*
distilled water destilirana voda *[desteeleerana voda]*
distributor (*in car*) razvodnik paljenja *[razvodneek palyenya]*
disturb: the disco is disturbing us disko nas uznemirava *[deesko nas ooznemeerava]*; **please do not disturb** molim ne uznemiravajte *[moleem ne ooznemeeravɪte]*
diversion (*traffic*) zaobilazni put *[zaobeelaznee poot]*
diving board daska za skokove u vodu *[daska za skokove oo vodoo]*
divorced razveden
dizzy: I feel dizzy hvata me vrtoglavica *[нvata me vurtoglaveetsa]*
dizzy spells povremena vrtoglavica *[povremena vurtoglaveetsa]*
do raditi *[radeete]*; **what shall I do?** šta da radim? *[shta da radeem]*; **what are you doing tonight?** šta radite večeras? *[radeete vecheras]*; **how do**

you do it? kako to radite? *[radeete]*;
will you do it for me? hoćete li mi
to uraditi? *[hochete lee mee to
ooradeetee]*; who did it? tko je to
uradio? *[tko ye to ooradeeo]*; the
meat's not done meso nije pečeno
[meso neeye pecheno]; what do you
do? (job) šta vi radite? *[vee radeete]*;
do you have ...? imate li ...? *[eemate]*
docks pristanište *[preestaneeshte]*
doctor doktor; he needs a doctor treba mu doctor *[treba moo]*; can you
call a doctor? da li biste pozvali
doktora? *[lee beeste pozvalee]*
document dokument *[dokooment]*
dog pas
doll lutka *[lootka]*
dollar dolar
donkey magarac *[magarats]*
don't! nemojte! *[nemoyte]*; see not and
page 114
door vrata
doorman vratar
dosage doza
double: double room dvokrevetna
soba; double bed bračni krevet
[brachnee]; double brandy dupli
brendi *[dooplee brendee]*; double r
(in spelling name) duplo r *[dooplo er]*;
it's all double Dutch to me to je
obično naklapanje za mene *[ye
obeechno naklapanye za mene]*
doubt: I doubt it sumnjam
[soomnyam]
douche (medical) ispiraljka
[eespeeralyka]
doughnut krofna
down: get down! silazite! *[seelazeete]*;
he's not down yet (is in room, bed)
još nije sišao *[yosh neeye seeshao]*;
further down the road niže cestom
[neeje tsestom]; I paid 20% down
platio sam 20% u gotovom *[plateeo
sam dvadeset protsenata oo gotovom]*
downmarket (restaurant, hotel) jevtin
[yevteen]
downstairs dolje *[dolye]*
dozen tuce *[tootse]*; half a dozen pola
tuceta *[pola tootseta]*
drain (in sink, street) odvodna cijev
[tsyev]
draughts (game) dame
draughty: it's rather draughty (S)
ima dosta promaje *[eema dosta*

promiye]*; (C) propuh je *[propooh ye]*
drawing pin (S) rajsnegla *[risnegla]*;
(C) čavlić *[chavleech]*
dreadful užasan *[oojasan]*
dream (noun) san; it's like a bad
dream ovo je kao ružan san *[ovo ye
kao roojan]*; sweet dreams lijepo
sanjajte! *[lyepo sanyite]*
dress (woman's) haljina *[halyeena]*; I'll
just get dressed odmah ću se obući
[odmah choo se aboochee]
dressing (for wound) zavoj *[zavoy]*;
(for salad) preliv *[preleev]*
dressing gown kućna haljina
[koochna halyeena]
drink (verb) piti *[peetee]*; (noun) piće
[peeche]; would you like a drink?
jesti li za piće? *[yeste lee]*; I don't
drink (alcohol) ne pijem *[peeyem]*; I
must have something to drink
moram nešto popiti *[neshto
popeetee]*; a long cool drink hladno
osvježavajuće piće *[hladno
osvyejaviyooche]*; may I have a
drink of water? mogu li dobiti čašu
vode? *[mogoo lee dobeetee chashoo
vode]*; drink up! ispijmo! *[eespeemo]*;
I had too much to drink previše
sam pio *[preveeshe sam peeo]*
drinkable: is the water drinkable? je
li voda za piće? *[ye lee voda za
peeche]*
drive: we drove here došli smo kolima *[doshlee smo koleema]*; I'll drive
you home odvešću vas kolima kući
[odveshchoo vas koleema koochee];
do you want to come for a drive?
želite li se provozati? *[jeleete lee se
provozatee]*; is it a very long drive?
je li vožnja jako duga? *[ye lee vojnya
yako dooga]*
driver (of car, bus) vozač *[vozach]*
driver's license vozačka dozvola
[vozachka dozvola]
drive shaft kardanska osovina
[osoveena]
driving licence vozačka dozvola
[vozachka dozvola]
drizzle: it's drizzling kiša rominja
[keesha romeenya]
drop: just a drop (of drink) samo
kapljicu *[kaplyeetsoo]*; I dropped it
ispustio sam *[eespoosteeo]*; drop in
some time svratite *[svrateete]*

drown: he's drowning davi se *[davee]*
drug (*medical*) lijek *[lyek]*; (*narcotic*)
droga
drugstore drogerija *[drogereeya]*
drunk (*adjective*) pijan *[peeyan]*
drunken driving vožnja u pijanom
stanju *[voJnya oo peeyanom stanyoo]*
dry (*adjective*) (*S*) suv *[soov]*; (*C*) suh
[sooH]
**dry-clean: can I get these dry-
cleaned?** (*S*) možete li mi ovo he-
mijski očistiti? *[moJete lee mee ovo
hemeeskee ocheesteetee]*; (*C*) možete
li mi ovo kemijski očistiti?
dry-cleaner (*S*) hemijska čistiona
[hemeeska cheesteeona]; (*C*) kemijska

čistionica *[kemeeska cheesteeoneetsa]*
duck patka
due: when is the bus due? kad stiže
autobus? *[steeJe aootoboos]*
dumb (*can't speak*) nijem *[nyem]*;
(*stupid*) glup *[gloop]*
dummy (*for baby*) cucla *[tsootsla]*
durex (*tm*) prezervativ *[prezervateev]*
during za vrijeme *[vryeme]*
dust prašina *[prasheena]*
dustbin kanta za smeće *[smeche]*
duty-free (*goods*) bescarinski
[bestsareenskee]
dynamo dinamo (*m*) *[deenamo]*
dysentery dizenterija *[deezentereeya]*

E

each: each of them svaki od njih
[svakee od nyeeH]; **one for each of
us** po jedan za svakog *[yedan za
svakog]*; **how much are they each?**
pošto je svaki? *[poshto ye]*; **each
time** svaki put *[poot]*; **we know each
other** znamo se
ear uho *[ooHo]*
earache: I have earache boli me uho
[bolee me ooHo]
early rano; **early in the morning**
rano ujutro *[ooyootro]*; **it's too early**
prerano je *[ye]*; **a day earlier** dan
ranije *[raneeye]*; **half an hour earlier**
pola sata ranije; **I need an early
night** treba rano da legnem
early riser: I'm an early riser ja sam
ranoranilac *[ya sam ranoraneelats]*
earring naušnica *[naooshneetsa]*
earth (*soil*) zemlja *[zemlya]*
earthenware grnčarija *[gurnchareeya]*
earwig uholaža *[ooHolaJa]*
east istok *[eestok]*; **to the east of ...**
istočno od ... *[eestochno]*; **in the east**
na istoku *[eestokoo]*
Easter Uskrs *[ooskurs]*
easy lako; **easy with the cream!**
manje šlaga! *[manye shlaga]*
eat jesti *[yestee]*; **something to eat**
nešto za jelo *[neshto za yelo]*; **we've
already eaten** već smo jeli *[vech smo*

yelee]
eau-de-Cologne kolonjska voda
[kolonyska voda]
eccentric ekscentričan *[ekstsentree-
chan]*
edible jestiv *[yesteev]*
efficient efikasan *[efeekasan]*
egg jaje *[yIye]*
eggplant plavi patlidžan *[plavee
patleedjan]*
Eire Irska *[eerska]*
either: either ... or ... ili ... ili ...
[eelee]; **I don't like either of them**
ne volim ni jednog ni drugog
[voleem nee yednog nee droogog]
elastic (*S*) lastiš *[lashteesh]*; (*C*)
elastika *[elasteeka]*
elastic band gumena vrpca *[goomena
vurptsa]*
Elastoplast (*tm*) flaster
elbow lakat
electric električan *[elektreechan]*
electric cooker električni štednjak
[elektreechnee shtednyak]
electric fire električna grijalica
[elektreechna greeyaleetsa]
electrician električar *[elektreechar]*
electricity (*S*) elektricitet
[elektreetseetet]; (*C*) struja *[strooya]*
electric outlet izvod struje *[eezvod
strooye]*

elegant elegantan
elevator lift *[leeft]*
else: something else nešto drugo
[neshto droogo]; **somewhere else**
negdje drugdje *[negdye droogdye]*;
let's go somewhere else hajdemo
negdje drugdje *[hɪdemo]*; **what else?**
šta još? *[shta yosh]*; **nothing else,
thanks** ništa više, hvala *[neeshta
veeshe Hvala]*
embarrassed: he's embarrassed
zbunjen je *[zboonyen ye]*
embarrassing nezgodan
embassy ambasada
emergency opasnost (*f*); **this is an
emergency!** ovo je hitan slučaj! *[ovo
ye Heetan sloochɪ]*
emery board šmirgla *[shmeergla]*
emotional (*person, time*) emocionalan
[emotseeonalan]
empty prazan
end (*noun*) kraj *[krɪ]*; **at the end of
the road** na kraju puta *[krɪyoo
poota]*; **when does it end?** kad
završava? *[zavurshava]*
energetic energičan *[energeechan]*
energy (*of person*) energija *[energeeya]*
engaged (*to be married*) vjeren
[vyeren]; (*toilet*) zauzet *[zaoozet]*
engagement ring vjerenički prsten
[vyereneechkee pursten]
engine motor
engine trouble kvar motora
England Engleska *[engleska]*
English (*adjective, language*) engleski
[engleskee]; **the English** Englezi
[englezee]; **I'm English** (*man*) ja sam
Englez *[ya sam englez]*; (*woman*) ja
sam Engleskinja *[engleskeenya]*
Englishman Englez *[englez]*
Englishwoman Engleskinja *[engles-
keenya]*
enjoy: I enjoyed it very much bilo
mi je lijepo *[beelo mee ye lyepo]*;
enjoy yourself! zabavite se!
[zabaveete]
enjoyable prijatan *[preeyatan]*
enlargement (*of photo*) povećanje
[povechanye]
enormous ogroman
enough dovoljno *[dovolyno]*; **there's
not enough** nema dovoljno; **it's not
big enough** nije dovoljno velik
[neeye dovolyno veleek]; **thank you,**

that's enough hvala, dosta je *[ye]*
entertainment zabava
enthusiastic oduševljen *[odooshev-
lyen]*
entrance (*noun*) ulaz *[oolaz]*
envelope (*S*) koverta; (*C*) kuverta
[kooverta]
epileptic epileptičar *[epeelepteechar]*
equipment oprema
eraser gumica za brisanje *[goomeetsa
za breesanye]*
erotic erotičan *[eroteechan]*
error pogreška *[pogreshka]*
escalator pokretne stepenice
[stepeneetse]
especially naročito *[narocheeto]*
espresso coffee espreso
essential: it is essential that ... bitno
je da ... *[beetno ye]*
estate agent trgovac nekretninama
[turgovats nekretneenama]
ethnic (*restaurant, clothes*) narodni
[narodnee]
Europe Evropa
European evropski *[evropskee]*
European plan polupansion
[poloopanseeon]
even: even the English čak i Englezi
[chak ee englezee]; **even if ...** čak
ako ...
evening veče *[veche]*; **good evening**
dobro veče; **this evening** večeras
[vecheras]; **in the evening** uveče
[ooveche]; **evening meal** večera
[vechera]
evening dress (*for man*) večernje odijelo *[vechernye odyelo]*; (*for woman*)
večernja haljina *[vechernya halyeena]*
eventually konačno *[konachno]*
ever: have you ever been to ...? da li
ste ikad bili u ...? *[lee ste eekad
beelee oo]*; **if you ever come to
Britain** ako ikad dođete u Britaniju
[ako eekad dodjete oo breetaneeyoo]
every svaki *[svakee]*; **every day** svaki
dan
everyone svako
everything sve
everywhere svuda *[svooda]*
exactly! (*S*) tačno! *[tachno]*; (*C*) točno!
[tochno]
exam ispit *[eespeet]*
example primjer *[preemyer]*; **for
example** na primjer

excellent odličan *[odleechan]*; **excellent!** odlično! *[odleechno]*

except osim *[oseem]*; **except Sunday** osim nedjelje *[nedyelye]*

exception izuzetak *[eezoozetak]*; **as an exception** izuzetno *[eezoozetno]*

excess baggage višak prtljaga *[veeshak purtlyaga]*

excessive pretjeran *[pretyeran]*; **that's a bit excessive** to je malo pretjerano *[ye malo pretyerano]*

exchange (*verb*: *money*) mijenjati *[myenyatee]*; **in exchange** u zamjenu *[oo zamyenoo]*

exchange rate: what's the exchange rate? kakav je kurs? *[kakav ye koors]*

exchange student student na razmjeni *[stoodent na razmyenee]*

exciting uzbudljiv *[oozboodlyeev]*

exclusive (*club*, *hotel*) ekskluzivan *[eskloozeevan]*

excursion izlet *[eezlet]*; **is there an excursion to ...?** ima li izlet u ...? *[eema lee eezlet oo]*

excuse me (*to get past, to get attention*) izvinite *[eezveeneete]*; (*pardon?*) molim? *[moleem]*; (*annoyed*) e, izvinite

exhaust (*on car*) (S) izduvna cijev *[eezvdoovna tsyev]*; (C) ispušna cijev *[eespooshna]*

exhausted (*tired*) premoren

exhibition izložba *[eezloJba]*

exist: does it still exist? da li još postoji? *[lee yosh postoyee]*

exit izlaz *[eezlaz]*

expect: I expect so očekujem da je tako *[ochekooyem da ye tako]*; **she's expecting** čeka bebu *[cheka beboo]*

expensive skup *[skoop]*

experience: an absolutely un- **forgettable experience** nesumnjivo nezaboravan doživljaj *[nesoomnyeevo nezaboravan doJeevlyı]*

experienced iskusan *[eeskoosan]*

expert stručnjak *[stroochnyak]*

expire: it's expired (*passport, etc*) istekao je *[eestekao ye]*

explain objasniti *[obyasneetee]*; **would you explain that to me?** da li biste mi to objasnili? *[lee beeste mee to obyasneelee]*

explore istraživati *[eestraJeevatee]*; **I just want to go and explore** želim malo istražiti okolinu *[Jeleem malo eestraJeetee okoleenoo]*

export (*verb*) izvoziti *[eezvozeetee]*

exposure meter svjetlomjer *[svyetlomyer]*

express (*mail, train*) ekspres

extra: can we have an extra chair? možemo li dobiti još jednu stolicu? *[moJemo lee dobeetee yosh yednoo stoleetsoo]*; **is that extra?** (*in cost*) da li je to doplata? *[lee ye to doplata]*

extraordinary (*very strange*) neobičan *[neobeechan]*

extremely krajnje *[krınye]*

extrovert ekstrovert

eye oko; **will you keep an eye on my bags for me?** da li biste mi pripazili torbe? *[lee beeste mee preepazeelee]*

eyebrow obrva *[oburva]*

eyebrow pencil olovka za obrve *[olovka za oburve]*

eye drops kapi za oči *[kapee za ochee]*

eyeliner ajlajner *[ılıner]*

eye shadow sjenka za oči *[syenka za ochee]*

eye witness očevidac *[ocheveedats]*

F

fabulous basnoslovan

face lice *[leetse]*

face cloth peškirić za pranje lica *[peshkeereech za pranye leetsa]*

face mask (*for diving*) maska

face pack (*cosmetic*) kozmetički prepa- rati za lice *[kozmeteechkee preparatee za leetse]*

facing: facing the sea s pogledom na more

fact činjenica *[cheenyeneetsa]*

factory (S) fabrika *[fabreeka]*; (C)

tvornica *[tvorneetsa]*
Fahrenheit *see page 121*
faint: she's fainted onesvijestila se *[onesvyesteela]*; **I'm going to faint** onesvijestit ću se *[onesvyesteet choo]*
fair *(fun-fair)* luna park; *(commercial)* sajam *[sayam]*; **it's not fair** to nije pošteno *[neeye poshteno]*; **OK, fair enough** sasvim u redu *[sasveem oo redoo]*
fake falsifikat *[falseefeekat]*
fall: he's had a fall pao je *[pao ye]*; **he fell off his bike** pao je sa bicikla *[beetseekla]*; **in the fall** *(autumn)* na jesen *[yesen]*
false lažan *[laʒan]*
false teeth *(S)* vještački zubi *[vyeshtachkee zoobee]*; *(C)* umjetni zubi *[oomyetnee]*
family *(S)* porodica *[porodeetsa]*; *(C)* obitelj *[obeetel-yuh]*
family hotel porodični hotel *[porodeechnee hotel]*
family name prezime *[prezeeme]*
famished: I'm famished umirem od gladi *[oomeerem od gladee]*
famous slavan
fan ventilator *[venteelator]*; *(hand-held)* lepeza; *(football etc)* navijač *[naveeyach]*
fan belt *(S)* kaiš ventilatora *[ka-eesh venteelatora]*; *(C)* remen ventilatora
fancy: he fancies you dopadate mu se *[dopadate moo]*
fancy dress party krabuljna zabava *[kraboolyna zabava]*
fantastic fantastičan *[fantasteechan]*
far dalek; **is it far?** je li daleko? *[ye lee]*; **how far is it to ...?** koliko je daleko do ...? *[koleeko]*; **as far as I'm concerned** što se mene tiče *[shto se mene teeche]*
fare vozarina *[vozareena]*; **what's he fare to ...?** pošto je karta do ...? *[poshto ye karta]*
farewell party oproštajna zabava *[oproshtɪna zabava]*
farm farma
farther dalje *[dalye]*; **farther than ...** dalje od ...
fashion *(in clothes etc)* moda
fashionable u modi *[oo modee]*
fast brz *[burz]*; **not so fast** ne tako brzo *[tako burzo]*

fastener *(on clothes)* kopča *[kopcha]*
fat *(person)* debeo; *(on meat)* masno meso
father: my father moj otac *[moy otats]*
father-in-law *(husband's father)* svekar; *(wife's father)* tast
fattening: it's fattening *(S)* od toga se goji *[toga se goyee]*; *(C)* od toga se deblja *[deblya]*
faucet slavina *[slaveena]*
fault greška *[greshka]*; **it was my fault** bila je moja greška *[beela ye moya]*; **it's not my fault** nije moja greška *[neeye]*
faulty *(equipment)* neispravan *[ne-eespravan]*
favo(u)rite omiljen *[omeelyen]*; **that's my favo(u)rite** to je moj omiljeni *[ye moy omeelyenee]*
fawn *(colour)* žućkastosmeđ *[ʒuch-kastosmedj]*
February *(S)* februar *[febrooar]*; *(C)* veljača *[velyacha]*
fed up: I'm fed up sit sam toga *[seet]*; **I'm fed up with ...** dozlogrdilo mi je ... *[dozlogurdeelo mee ye]*
feeding bottle bočica za hranjenje *[bocheetsa za ʜranyenye]*
feel: I feel hot/cold vruće/hladno mi je *[vrooche/ʜladno mee ye]*; **I feel like a drink** nešto mi se pije *[neshto mee se peeye]*; **I don't feel like it** nisam raspoložen za to *[neesam raspoloʒen]*; **how are you feeling today?** kako se danas osjećate? *[kako se danas osyechate]*; **I'm feeling a lot better** osjećam se mnogo bolje *[osyecham se mnogo bolye]*
felt-tip pen flomaster
fence ograda
fender *(of car)* branik *[braneek]*
ferry trajekt *[trayekt]*; **what time's the last ferry?** kad je posljednji trajekt? *[ye poslyednyee]*
festival festival *[festeeval]*
fetch: I'll go and fetch it otići ću i donijeti ga *[oteechee cho ee donyetee]*; **will you come and fetch me?** hoćete li doći po mene? *[hochete lee dochee po mene]*
fever groznica *[grozneetsa]*
feverish: I'm feeling feverish grozni-

ćavo se osijećan *[grozneechavo se oseeyechan]*

few: only a few samo nekoliko *[nekoleeko]*; **a few minutes** nekoliko minuta; **he's had a good few** (*to drink*) nacvrcao se *[natsvurtsao]*

fiancé: my fiancé (*S*) moj vjerenik *[moy vyereneek]*; (*C*) moj zaručnik *[zaroochneek]*

fiancée: my fiancée (*S*) moja vjerenica *[moya vyereneetsa]*; (*C*) moja zaručnica *[zaroochneetsa]*

fiasco: what a fiasco! kakav fijasko! *[feeyasko]*

field polje *[polye]*

fifty-fifty pola-pola

fight (*noun*) tuča *[toocha]*

figs smokve

figure (*of person*) stas; (*number*) broj *[broy]*; **I have to watch my figure** moram paziti na liniju *[pazeetee na leeneeyoo]*

fill ispuniti *[eespooneetee]*; **fill her up please** napunite rezervoar molim *[napooneete rezervo-ar moleem]*; **will you help me fill out this form?** da li biste mi pomogli da ispunim ovaj formular? *[lee beeste mee pomoglee da eespooneem ovi formoolar]*

fillet file (*m*) *[feele]*

filling (*in tooth*) plomba; **it's very filling** (*food*) jako je zasitno *[yako ye zaseetno]*

filling station benzinska pumpa *[benzeenska poompa]*

film film *[feelm]*; **do you have this type of film?** imate li ovu vrstu filma? *[eemate lee ovoo vurstoo feelma]*; **16mm film** film od 16 milimetara *[shesna-est meeleemetara]*; **35mm film** film od 35 milimetara *[treedeset pet]*

filter (*for camera, coffee*) filter *[feelter]*

filter-tipped sa filterom *[feelterom]*

filthy (*room etc*) prljav *[purlyav]*

find naći *[nachee]*; **I can't find it** ne mogu naći *[mogoo]*; **if you find it** ako nađete *[ako nadjete]*; **I've found a ...** našao sam ... *[nashao]*

fine: it's fine weather vrijeme je lijepo *[vryeme ye lyepo]*; **a 3,000 dinar fine** kazna od 3.000 dinara *[deenara]*; **how are you? — fine thanks** kako ste? — нvala dobro

finger prst *[purst]*

fingernail nokat

finish: I haven't finished nisam završio *[neesam zavursheeo]*; **when I've finished** kad završim *[zavursheem]*; **when does it finish?** kad se završava? *[zavurshava]*; **finish off your drink** popijte piće *[popeeyte peeche]*

Finland Finska *[feenska]*

fire: fire! (*something's on fire*) požar! *[poʒar]*; **may we light a fire here?** smijemo li ovdje ložiti vatru? *[smyemo lee ovdye loʒeetee vatroo]*; **it's on fire** gori *[goree]*; **it's not firing properly** (*car*) nema dobro paljenje *[palyenye]*

fire alarm požarna uzbuna *[poʒarna oozboona]*

fire brigade, fire department vatrogasna služba *[vatrogasna slooʒba]*

fire escape požarne stepenice *[poʒarne stepeneetse]*

fire extinguisher aparat za gašenje požara *[gashenye poʒara]*

firm (*company*) firma *[feerma]*

first prvi *[purvee]*; **I was first** bio sam prvi *[beeo]*; **at first** isprva *[eespurva]*; **this is the first time** ovo je prvi put *[ovo ye purvee poot]*

first aid prva pomoć *[purva pomoch]*

first aid kit pribor za prvu pomoć *[preebor za purvoo pomoch]*

first class (*S*) prva klasa *[purva]*; (*C*) prvi razred

first name ime *[eeme]*

fish (*noun*) riba *[reeba]*

fisherman ribar *[reebar]*

fishing ribolov *[reebolov]*

fishing boat ribarski brod *[reebarskee]*

fishing net ribarska mreža *[reebarska mreʒa]*

fishing rod štap za pecanje *[shtap za petsanye]*

fishing tackle pribor za pecanje *[preebor za petsanye]*

fishing village ribarsko selo *[reebarsko]*

fit (*healthy*) u formi *[oo formee]*; **I'm not very fit** nisam sasvim u formi *[neesam sasveem]*; **he's a keep fit fanatic** lud je za rekreacijom *[lood ye za rekre-atseeyom]*; **it doesn't fit** ne odgovara

fix: can you fix it? (*repair*) možete li
popraviti? *[moJete lee popraveetee]*;
(*arrange*) možete li srediti?
[sredeetee]; let's fix a time odredimo
vrijeme *[odredeemo vryeme]*; it's all
fixed up sve je dogovoreno *[ye]*; I'm
in a bit of a fix u maloj sam
neprilici *[oo maloy sam
nepreeleetsee]*
fizzy gaziran *[gazeeran]*
fizzy drink gazirano piće *[gazeerano
peeche]*
flab (*on body*) salo
flag zastava
flannel krpica za pranje lica
[kurpeetsa za pranye leetsa]
flash (*for camera*) fleš *[flesh]*
flashlight baterija *[batereeya]*
flashy (*clothes etc*) neukusan
[neookoosan]
flat (*adjective*) ravan; this beer is flat
ovo pivo nije dobro *[ovo peevo neeye
dobro]*; I've got a flat tyre/tire
spustila mi se guma *[spoosteela mee
se gooma]*; (*apartment*) stan
flatterer laskavac *[laskavats]*
flatware (*cutlery*) pribor za jelo
[preebor za yelo]; (*crockery*) zemljano
posuđe *[zemlyano posoodje]*
flavo(u)r ukus *[ookoos]*
flea (S) buva *[boova]*; (C) buha *[booha]*
flea bite ujed buve/buhe *[ooyed
boove/boohe]*
flea powder prašak protiv buva/buha
[prashak proteev boova/booha]
flexible (*material*) savitljiv *[saveet-
lyeev]*; (*plans*) fleksibilan
[flekseebeelan]
flies (*on trousers*) šlic *[shleets]*
flight let
flippers peraja *[peraya]*
flirt flertovati *[flertovatee]*
float ploviti *[ploveetee]*
flood poplava
floor (*of room*) pod; (*in hotel*) (S) sprat;
(C) kat; on the floor na podu
[podoo]; on the second floor (*UK*)
na drugom spratu/katu *[droogom
spratoo/katoo]*; (*US*) na trećem
spratu/katu *[trechem]*
floorshow program
flop (*failure*) neuspjeh *[neoospyeh]*
florist cvjećar *[tsvyechar]*
flour brašno *[brashno]*

flower cvijet *[tsvyet]*
flu gripa *[greepa]*
fluent: he speaks fluent Serbocroat
govori tečno srpskohrvatski *[govoree
techno surpsko-Hurvatskee]*
fly (*verb*) letjeti *[letyetee]*; can we fly
there? možemo li tamo letjeti?
[moJemo lee tamo]
fly (*insect*) (S) muva *[moova]*; (C) muha
[mooha]
fly spray sprej protiv muva/muha
[spray proteev moova/mooha]
foggy: it's foggy magla je *[ye]*
fog lights svjetla za maglu *[svyetla za
magloo]*
folk dancing narodni ples *[narodnee]*
folk music narodna muzika
[moozeeka]
follow pratiti *[prateetee]*; follow me
pratite me
fond: I'm quite fond of ... stvarno
volim ... *[stvarno voleem]*
food Hrana; the food's excellent hrana je odlična *[ye odleechna]*
food poisoning trovanje želuca
[trovanye Jelootsa]
food store samoposluga *[samopos-
looga]*
fool budala *[boodala]*
foolish glup *[gloop]*
foot noga; on foot pješke *[pyeshke]*;
see page 120
football (S) fudbal *[foodbal]*; (C)
nogomet
for: is that for me? je li to za mene?
[ye lee to za mene]; for me/her za
mene/nju *[nyoo]*; what's this for? za
šta je to? *[shta ye]*; for two days dva
dana; I've been here for a week
ovdje sam nedjelju dana *[ovdye sam
nedyelyoo]*; a bus for ... autobus
za ...
forbidden zabranjen *[zabranyen]*
forehead čelo *[chelo]*
foreign stran
foreigner stranac *[stranats]*
foreign exchange (*money*) devize
[deveeze]
forest šuma *[shooma]*
forget zaboraviti *[zaboraveetee]*; I
forget, I've forgotten zaboravio sam
[zaboraveeo]; dɔn't forget ne
zaboravite *[zaboraveete]*
fork (*for eating*) viljuška *[veelyooshka]*;

(*in road*) račvanje *[rachvanye]*
form (*in hotel etc*) formular *[formoolar]*
formal zvaničan *[zvaneechan]*
fortnight dvije nedjelje *[dvye nedyelye]*
fortunately srećom *[srechom]*
fortune-teller vračara *[vrachara]*
forward: could you forward my mail? možete li mi poslati poštu?
[moʃete lee mee poslatee poshtoo]
forwarding address adresa za slanje pošte *[adresa za slanye poshte]*
foundation cream podloga
fountain (*ornamental*) fontana; (*for drinking*) česma *[chesma]*
foyer (*of hotel, theatre*) foaje *[foa-ye]*
fracture (*noun*) fraktura *[fraktoora]*
fractured skull fraktura lobanje *[fraktoora lobanye]*
fragile krhak *[kurʜak]*
frame (*for picture*) okvir
France Francuska *[frantsooska]*
fraud prijevara *[pryevara]*
free (*at liberty*) slobodan; (*costing nothing*) besplatan; **admission free** besplatan ulaz *[oolaz]*
freezer zamrzivač *[zamurzeevach]*
freezing cold velika hladnoća *[veleeka ʜladnocha]*
French francuski *[frantsooskee]*
French fries pom frit *[freet]*
frequent čest *[chest]*
fresh (*weather, breeze, fruit*) svjež *[svyeʃ]*; (*cheeky*) drzak *[durzak]*; **don't get fresh with me** ne budite drski sa mnom *[boodeete durskee]*
fresh orange juice svjež sok od narandže *[svyeʃ sok od narandje]*
friction tape izolaciona traka *[eezolatseeona traka]*
Friday petak
fridge frižider *[freeʃeeder]*
fried egg prženo jaje *[purʃeno ʏɪye]*
fried rice pržena riža *[purʃena reeʃa]*
friend (*male*) prijatelj *[preeyatel-yuh]*; (*female*) prijateljica *[preeyatelyeetsa]*
friendly prijateljski *[preeyatelyskee]*
frog žaba *[ʃaba]*
from: I'm from London ja sam iz

Londona *[ya sam eez londona]*; **the next boat from ...** sljedeći brod iz ... *[slyedechee]*; **from here to the sea** odavde do mora; **as from Tuesday** od utorka *[ootorka]*
front prednji *[prednyee]*; **in front** naprijed *[napryed]*; **in front of us** ispred nas *[eespred]*; **at the front** na čelu *[cheloo]*
frozen zamrznut *[zamurznoot]*
frozen food zamrznuta hrana *[zamurznoota ʜrana]*
fruit voće *[voche]*
fruit juice voćni sok *[vochnee]*
fruit salad voćna salata *[vochna]*
frustrating: it's very frustrating čovjek se samo nervira *[chovyek se samo nerveera]*
fry pržiti *[purʃeetee]*; **nothing fried** ništa prženo *[neeshta purʃeno]*
frying pan (*S*) tiganj *[teegan-yuh]*; (*C*) tava
full pun *[poon]*; **it's full of ...** pun je ... (+*G*) *[ye]*; **I'm full** (*eating*) sit sam *[seet]*
full-board puni pansion *[poonee panseeon]*
full-bodied (*wine*) teško *[teshko]*
fun: it's fun zabavno je *[ye]*; **it was great fun** bilo je jako zabavno *[beelo ye yako]*; **just for fun** šale radi *[shale radee]*; **have fun** lijepo se provedite *[lyepo se provedeete]*
funeral pogreb
funny (*strange*) čudan *[choodan]*; (*amusing*) smiješan *[smyeshan]*
furniture namještaj *[namyeshtɪ]*
further dalje *[dalye]*; **2 kilometres further** dva kilometra dalje; **further down the road** niže cestom *[neeʃe tsestom]*
fuse (*noun*) osigurač *[oseegoorach]*; **the lights have fused** pregorio je osigurač *[pregoreeo ye]*
fuse wire žica za osigurač *[ʃeetsa za oseegoorach]*
future budućnost (*f*) *[boodoochnost]*; **in future** ubuduće *[ooboodooche]*

G

gale oluja *[olooya]*
gallon *see page 121*
gallstone žučni kamenac *[Joochnee kamenats]*
gamble kockati se *[kotskatee]*; **I don't gamble** ne kockam se *[kotskam]*
game igra *[eegra]*; (*meat*) divljač *[deevlyach]*
games room prostorija za igre *[prostoreeya za eegre]*
gammon šunka *[shoonka]*
garage (*petrol*) benzinska pumpa *[benzeenska poompa]*; (*repair*) auto-servis *[aooto-servees]*; (*for parking*) parking-garaža *[parkeeng-garaɹa]*
garbage (S) đubre *[djoobre]*; (C) smeće *[smeche]*
garden vrt *[vurt]*
garlic bijeli luk *[byelee look]*
gas plin *[pleen]*; (*gasoline*) benzin *[benzeen]*
gas cylinder (*for Calor gas etc*) plinska boca *[pleenska botsa]*
gasket zaptivač *[zapteevach]*
gas pedal pedala gasa
gas permeable lenses (S) porozna sočiva *[socheeva]*; (C) porozne leče *[leche]*
gas station benzinska stanica *[benzeenska staneetsa]*
gas tank benzinski rezervoar *[benzeenskee rezervo-ar]*
gastroenteritis gastroenteritis *[gastroentereetees]*
gate kapija *[kapeeya]*; (*at airport*) izlaz *[eezlaz]*
gauge mjerilo *[myerilo]*
gay (*homosexual*) homoseksualac *[homoseksoo-alats]*
gear brzina *[burzeena]*; (*equipment*) pribor *[preebor]*; **the gears keep sticking** zaglavljuje se mjenjač *[zaglavlyooye se myenyach]*
gearbox mjenjačka kutija *[myenyachka kooteeya]*; **I have gearbox trouble** imam problem s mjenjačem *[eemam problem s myenyachem]*

gear lever, gear shift ručica mjenjača *[roocheetsa myenyacha]*
general delivery post restant
generous: **that's very generous of you** vrlo velikodušno od vas *[vurlo veleekodushno]*
gentleman (*man*) gospodin *[gospodeen]*; **that gentleman over there** onaj gospodin tamo *[onɪ ... tamo]*; **he's such a gentleman** on je pravi gospodin *[ye pravee]*
gents (*toilet*) muški *[mooshkee]*
genuine pravi *[pravee]*
German measles rubeole *[roobeole]*
Germany Njemačka *[nyemachka]*
get: **have you got ...?** imate li ...? *[eemate lee]*; **how do I get to ...?** kako da dođem do ... (+G) *[dodjem]*; **where do I get it from?** gdje to mogu dobiti? *[gdye to mogoo dobeetee]*; **can I get you a drink?** mogu li vam naručiti piće? *[mogoo lee vam naroocheetee peeche]*; **will you get it for me?** hoćete li mi donijeti? *[hochete lee mee donyetee]*; **when do we get there?** kad tamo stižemo? *[steeɹemo]*; **I've got to ...** moram ...; **I've got to go** moram ići *[eechee]*; **where do I get off?** gdje silazim? *[gdye seelazeem]*; **its difficult to get to** teško je doći *[teshko ye dochee]*; **when I get up** (*in morning*) kad ustanem *[oostanem]*
ghastly grozan
ghost duh *[dooн]*
giddy: **it makes me giddy** od toga dobijem vrtoglavicu *[toga dobeeyem vurtoglaveetsoo]*
gift dar
gigantic divovski *[deevovskee]*
gin džin *[djeen]*; **a gin and tonic** džin i tonik *[ee toneek]*
girl djevojčica *[dyevoycheetsa]*
girlfriend djevojka *[dyevoyka]*
give dati *[datee]*; **will you give me ...?** hoćete li mi dati ...? *[hochete lee mee]*; **I'll give you 100 dinars** dat

ću vam 100 dinara *[dat choo vam sto deenara]*; **I gave it to him** dao sam mu *[dao sam moo]*; **will you give it back?** hoćete li to vratiti? *[hochete lee to vrateetee]*; **would you give this to ...?** da li biste ovo dali ... (+D)? *[lee beeste ovo dalee]*

glad radostan

glamorous (*woman*) zanosna

gland žlijezda *[Jlyezda]*

glandular fever upala žlijezda *[oopala Jlyezda]*

glass (*material*) staklo; (*drinking*) čaša *[chasha]*; **a glass of water** čaša vode

glasses (*spectacles*) naočale *[naochale]*

gloves rukavice *[rookavitse]*

glue ljepilo *[lyepeelo]*

gnat mušica *[moosheetsa]*

go ići *[eechee]*; **we want to go to ...** želimo ići u ... (+A) *[Jeleemo eechee oo]*; **I'm going there tomorrow** sutra idem tamo *[sootra eedem]*; **when does it go?** (*bus etc*) kad polazi? *[polazee]*; **where are you going?** kuda idete? *[kooda eedete]*; **let's go** hajdemo *[hidemo]*; **he's gone** otišao je *[oteeshao ye]*; **it's all gone** nema više *[nema veeshe]*; **I went there yesterday** juče sam otišao tamo *[yooche sam oteeshao]*; **a hotdog to go** hrenovka za ponijeti *[Hrenovka za ponyetee]*; **go away!** gubi se! *[goobee]*; **it's gone off** (*milk etc*) pokvareno je *[pokvareno ye]*; **we're going out tonight** večeras izlazimo *[vecheras eezlazeemo]*; **do you want to go out tonight?** zĕlite li večeras izići? *[Jeleete lee eezeechee]*; **has the price gone up?** je li poskupilo? *[ye lee poskoopeelo]*

goal (*sport*) gol

goat koza

goat's cheese kozji sir *[kozyee seer]*

god bog

goddess boginja *[bogeenya]*

gold zlato

golf golf

golf clubs štapovi za golf *[shtapovee]*

golf course igralište za golf *[eegraleeshte]*

good dobar; **good!** dobro!; **that's no good** to ne valja *[valya]*; **good heavens!** za boga miloga! *[meeloga]*

goodbye doviđenja *[doveedjenya]*

good-looking lijep *[lyep]*

gooey (*food etc*) gnjecav *[gnyetsav]*

goose guska *[gooska]*

gooseberries ogrozd

gorgeous (*meal, woman*) divan *[deevan]*

gourmet gurman *[goorman]*

government vlada

gradually postepeno

grammar gramatika *[gramatika]*

gram(me) gram; *see page 120*

granddaughter unuka *[oonooka]*

grandfather djed *[dyed]*

grandmother baka

grandson unuk *[oonook]*

grapefruit grejpfrut *[graypfroot]*

grapefruit juice sok od grejpfruta *[graypfroota]*

grapes grožđe *[groJdje]*

grass trava

grateful zaHvalan; **I'm very grateful to you** veoma sam van zahvalan

gravy umak *[oomak]*

gray siv *[seev]*

grease (*for car*) mazivo *[mazeevo]*; (*on food*) mast (*f*)

greasy (*food*) mastan

great velik *[veleek]*; **that's great!** divno! *[deevno]*

Great Britain Velika Britanija *[veleeka breetaneeya]*

Greece Grčka *[gurchka]*

Greek (*adjective, language*) grčki *[gurchkee]*; (*man*) Grk *[gurk]*; (*woman*) Grkinja *[gurkeenya]*

greedy poHlepan

green zelen

green card zeleni karton *[zelenee]*

greengrocer piljar *[peelyar]*

grey siv *[seev]*

grilled sa roštilja *[roshteelya]*

gristle hrskavica *[Hurskaveetsa]*

grocer (*S*) bakalin *[bakaleen]*; (*C*) špeceraj *[shpetserI]*

ground zemlja *[zemlya]*; **on the ground** na zemlji *[zemlyee]*; **on the ground floor** u prizemlju *[oo preezemlyoo]*

ground beef mljevena govedina *[mlyevena govedeena]*

group grupa *[groopa]*

group insurance grupno osiguranje *[groopno oseegooranye]*

group leader vođa grupe (*m*) *[vodja groope]*

guarantee (*noun*) garancija *[garantseeya]*; **is it guaranteed?** ima li garanciju? *[eema lee garantseeyoo]*

guardian (*of child*) staratelj *[staratelyuh]*

guest gost

guesthouse pansion *[panseeon]*

guest room gostinska soba *[gosteenska]*

guide (*noun*) vodič *[vodeech]*

guidebook vodič *[vodeech]*

guilty kriv *[kreev]*

guitar gitara *[geetara]*

gum desni *[desnee]*; (*chewing gum*) žvakaća guma *[Jvakacha gooma]*

gun puška *[pooshka]*

gymnasium gimnastička dvorana *[geemnasteechka dvorana]*

gyn(a)ecologist ginekolog *[geenekolog]*

H

hair kosa

hairbrush četka za kosu *[chetka za kosoo]*

haircut šišanje *[sheeshanye]*; **just an ordinary haircut please** samo obično šišanje, molim *[obeechno ... moleem]*

hairdresser frizer *[freezer]*

hairdryer fen za kosu *[kosoo]*

hair foam pjena za kosu *[pyena za kosoo]*

hair gel gel za kosu *[gel za kosoo]*

hair grip šnala za kosu *[shnala za kosoo]*

hair lacquer lak za kosu *[kosoo]*

half pola; **half an hour** pola sata; **a half portion** pola porcije *[portseeye]*; **half a litre/liter** pola litre *[leetre]*; **half as much** pola od toga; **half as much again** ponovo pola od toga; *see page 119*

halfway: halfway to Belgrade na pola puta do Beograda *[pola poota do]*

ham šunka *[shoonka]*

hamburger hamburger; (*Yugoslav variety*) pljeskavica *[plyeskaveetsa]*

hammer (*noun*) čekić *[chekeech]*

hand ruka *[rooka]*; **will you give me a hand?** hoćete li mi pomoći? *[hochete lee mee pomochee]*

handbag tašna *[tashna]*

hand baggage (*S*) ručni prtljag *[roochnee purtlyag]*; (*C*) ručna prtljaga *[roochna purtlyaga]*

handbrake ručna kočnica *[roochna kochneetsa]*

handkerchief maramica *[marameetsa]*

handle (*noun*) ručica *[roocheetsa]*; **will**

you handle it? hoćete li se vi time pozabaviti? *[hochete lee se vee teeme pozabaveetee]*

handmade ručna izrada *[roochna eezrada]*

handsome lijep *[lyep]*

hanger (*clothes*) vješalica *[vyeshaleetsa]*

hangover mamurluk *[mamoorlook]*; **I've got a terrible hangover** strašno sam mamuran *[strashno sam mamooran]*

happen dogoditi se *[dogodeetej]*; **how did it happen?** kako se to dogodilo? *[dogodeelo]*; **what's happening?** šta se događa? *[shta se dogadja]*; **it won't happen again** to se više neće dogoditi *[veeshe neche]*

happy sretan; **we're not happy with the room** nismo zadovoljni sobom *[neesmo zadovolynee sobom]*

harbo(u)r luka *[looka]*

hard tvrd *[tvurd]*; (*difficult*) težak *[teJak]*

hard-boiled egg (*S*) tvrdo bareno jaje *[tvurdo bareno yIye]*; (*C*) tvrdo kuhano jaje *[koohano]*

hard lenses (*S*) tvrda sočiva *[tvurda socheeva]*; (*C*) tvrde leće *[tvurde leche]*

hardly jedva *[yedva]*; **hardly ever** gotovo nikad *[gotovo neekad]*

hardware store (*S*) gvožđarska radnja *[gvoJdjarska radnya]*; (*C*) željezara *[Jelyezara]*

harm (*noun*) šteta *[shteta]*

hassle: it's too much hassle suviše je komplicirano *[sooveeshe ye*

kompleetseerano]; **a hassle-free trip**
putovanje bez neprilika *[pootovanye
bez nepreeleeka]*
hat šešir *[shesheer]*
hate: I hate ... mrzim ... *[murzeem]*
have imati *[eematee]*; **do you have ...?**
imate li? *[eemate lee]*; **can I have ...?**
molim vas ...? *[moleem]*; **can I have
some water?** molim vas malo vode?;
I have ... imam *[eemam]*; **I don't
have ...** nemam ...; **can we have
breakfast in our room?** možemo li
doručkovati u svojoj sobi? *[moJemo
lee doroochkovatee oo svoyoy sobee]*;
have another (*drink etc*) uzmite još
jedan *[oozmeete yosh yedan]*; **I have
to leave early** moram rano otići
[moram rano oteechee]; **do I have to
...?** moram li ...? *[lee]*; **I've got to ...**
moram ...; **do we have to ...?**
moramo li? *[moramo]*; *see page 114*
hay fever peludna groznica *[peloodna
grozneetsa]*
he on; **is he here?** je li on ovdje? *[ye
lee on ovdye]*; **where does he live?**
gdje živi? *[gdye Jeevee]*; *see page 111*
head glava; **we're heading for Dubrovnik** idemo u Dubrovnik *[eedemo
oo doobrovneek]*
headache glavobolja *[glavobolya]*
headlights farovi *[farovee]*
headphones slušalice *[slooshaleetse]*
head waiter šef sale *[shef sale]*
head wind čeoni vjetar *[cheonee
vyetar]*
health zdravlje (*n*) *[zdravlye]*; **your
health!** živjeli! *[Jeevyelee]*
healthy (*person, food, climate*) zdrav
hear: can you hear me? čujete li me?
[chooyete lee me]; **I can't hear you**
ne čujem vas *[chooyem]*; **I've heard
about it** čuo sam za to *[choo-o]*
hearing aid slušni aparat *[slooshnee]*
heart srce *[surtse]*
heart attack srčani napad *[surchanee]*
heat vrućina *[vroocheena]*; **not in this
heat!** ne po ovoj vrućini! *[ovoy
vroocheenee]*
heated rollers vrući vikleri *[vroochee
veekleree]*
heater (*in car*) grijač *[greeyach]*; (*in
room*) grijalica *[greeyaleetsa]*
heating grijanje *[greeyanye]*
heat rash osip od vrućine *[oseep od*

vroocheene]*
heat stroke toplotni udar *[toplotnee
oodar]*
heatwave toplotni talas *[toplotnee]*
heavy težak *[teJak]*
hectic grozničav *[grozneechav]*
heel (*of foot, of shoe*) peta; **could you
put new heels on these?** možete li
staviti na njih nove pete? *[moJete lee
staveetee na nyeeH nove pete]*
heelbar (*S*) obućar *[oboochar]*; (*C*)
postolar
height visina *[veeseena]*
helicopter helikopter *[heleekopter]*
hell: oh hell! do đavola! *[djavola]*; **go
to hell!** idi do đavola! *[eedee]*
hello zdravo; (*on phone*) halo
helmet (*for motorcycle*) kaciga
[katseega]
help (*verb*) pomoći *[pomochee]*; **can
you help me?** možete li mi pomoći?
[moJete lee mee]; **thanks for your
help** hvala vam na pomoći *[Hvala]*;
help! upomoć! *[oopomoch]*
helpful: he was very helpful bio je
od velike pomoći *[beeo ye od veleeke
pomochee]*; **that's helpful** to je
korisno *[ye koreesno]*
helping (*of food*) porcija *[portseeya]*
hepatitis hepatitis *[hepateetees]*
her: I don't know her ne poznajem je
[poznIyem ye]; **will you send it to
her?** hoćete li joj poslati? *[hochete
lee yoy poslatee]*; **it's her** to je ona;
with her s njom *[nyom]*; **for her** za
nju *[nyoo]*; **that's her suitcase** to je
njen kofer *[ye nyen]*; **who? — her**
ko? — ona; *see pages 109, 111*
herbs trave
here ovdje *[ovdye]*; **here you are**
(*giving something*) izvolite *[eezvoleete]*;
here he comes evo ga
hers njen *[nyen]*; **that's hers** to je
njeno *[ye nyeno]*; *see page 112*
hey! ej! *[ay]*
hi! (*hello*) zdravo!
hiccups štucanje *[shtootsanye]*
hide sakriti *[sakreetee]*
hideous (*taste, weather, journey*) grozan
high visok *[veesok]*
highbeam veliko svijetlo *[veleeko
svyetlo]*
highchair dječja stolica *[dyechya
stoleetsa]*

highlighter (*cosmetic*) hajlajter *[hılıter]*
highway autoput *[aootopoot]*
hiking pješačenje *[pyeshachenye]*
hill brdo *[burdo]*; **it's further up the hill** dalje uzbrdo *[dalye oozburdo]*
hillside padina *[padeena]*
hilly brdovit *[burdoveet]*
him: I don't know him ne poznajem ga *[poznıyem]*; **will you send it to him?** hoćete li mu poslati? *[hochete lee moo poslatee]*; **it's him** to je on *[ye]*; **with him** s njim *[nyeem]*; **for him** za njega *[nyega]*; **who? — him ko? — on**; *see page 111*
hip kuk *[kook]*
hire iznajmiti *[eeznımeetee]*; **can I hire a car?** mogu li iznajmiti kola? *[mogoo lee]*; **do you hire them out?** da li ih iznajmljujete? *[lee eeн eeznımlyooyete]*
his: it's his drink to je njegovo piće *[ye nyegovo peeche]*; **it's his** njegov je *[nyegov ye]*; *see pages 109, 112*
history: the history of Belgrade (*S*) istorija Beograda *[eestoreeya]*; (*C*) povijest Beograda *[povyest]*
hit udariti *[oodareetee]*; **he hit me** udario me je *[oodareeo me ye]*; **I hit my head** udario sam se u glavu *[oodareeo sam se oo glavoo]*
hitch: is there a hitch? postoji li tu neki problem? *[postoyee lee too nekee problem]*
hitch-hike stopirati *[stopeeratee]*
hitch-hiker autostoper *[aootostoper]*
hit record ploča s top-liste *[plocha s top-leeste]*
hole rupa *[roopa]*
holiday odmor; **I'm on holiday** na odmoru sam *[odmoroo]*
home dom; (*house*) kuća *[koocha]*; **at home** (*in my house etc*) kod kuće *[kooche]*; (*in my country*) u domovini *[oo domoveenee]*; **I go home tomorrow** sutra idem kući *[sootra eedem koochee]*
home address kućna adresa *[koochna]*
homemade domaći *[domachee]*
homesick: I'm homesick čeznem za domom *[cheznem]*
honest pošten *[poshten]*
honestly? časna riječ? *[chasna ryech]*
honey med

honeymoon medeni mjesec *[medenee myesets]*; **it's our honeymoon** sada je naš medeni mjesec *[sada ye nash]*
honeymoon suite apartman za mladence *[apartman za mladentse]*
hood (*of car*) hauba *[haooba]*
hoover (*tm*) usisivač *[ooseeseevach]*
hope nadati se *[nadatee]*; **I hope so** nadam se da je tako *[ye]*; **I hope not** nadam se da nije tako *[neeye]*
horn (*of car*) truba *[trooba]*
horrible užasan *[ooжasan]*
hors d'oeuvre predjelo *[predyelo]*
horse konj *[kon-yuh]*
horse riding jahanje *[yahanye]*
hose (*for car radiator*) gumeno crijevo *[goomeno tsuryevo]*
hospital bolnica *[bolneetsa]*
hospitality gostoprimstvo *[gostopreemstvo]*; **thank you for your hospitality** hvala vam na gostoprimstvu *[нvala vam na gostopreemstvoo]*
hostel hostel
hot vruć *[vrooch]*; (*curry*) ljut *[lyoot]*; **I'm hot** vruće mi je *[vrэoche mee ye]*; **something hot to eat** nešto toplo za jelo *[neshto toplo za yelo]*; **it's so hot today** danas je tako vruće *[ye]*
hotdog нrenovka
hotel hotel; **at my hotel** u mom hotelu *[oo mom hoteloo]*
hotel clerk službenik na recepciji *[slooжbeneek na retseptseeyee]*
hotplate (*on cooker*) (*S*) plotna; (*C*) kuhalo *[koohalo]*
hot-water bottle termofor
hour sat; **on the hour** svakog sata
house kuća *[koocha]*
housewife domaćica *[domacheetsa]*
house wine domaće vino *[domache veeno]*
hovercraft hoverkraft
how kako; **how many?** koliko? *[koleeko]*; **how much?** pošto? *[poshto]*; **how often?** kako često? *[chesto]*; **how are you?** kako ste?; **how do you do?** (*on being introduced*) drago mi je! *[drago mee ye]*; **how about a beer?** jeste li za pivo? *[yeste lee za peevo]*; **how nice!** baš lijepo! *[bash lyepo]*; **would you show me how to?** da li biste mi pokazali kako?

[lee beeste me pokazalee]
humid vlažan *[vlaɹan]*
humidity vlaga
humo(u)r: where's your sense of humo(u)r? gdje vam je smisao za humor? *[gdye vam ye smeesao za hoomor]*
hundredweight *see page 121*
Hungarian *(adjective, language)* mađarski *[madjarskee]*; *(man)* Mađar; *(woman)* Mađarica *[madjareetsa]*
Hungary Mađarska *[madjarska]*

hungry: I'm hungry gladan sam; **I'm not hungry** nisam gladan *[neesam]*
hurry: I'm in a hurry žurim se *[ɹooreem]*; **hurry up!** požurite! *[poɹooreete]*; **there's no hurry** nije hitno *[neeye heetno]*
hurt: it hurts boli *[bolee]*; **my back hurts** bole me leđa *[bole me ledja]*
husband: my husband moj muž *[moy mooɹ]*
hydrofoil hidrogliser *[heedrogleeser]*

I

I ja *[ya]*; **I am English** *(man)* ja sam Englez *[englez]*; *(woman)* ja sam Engleskinja *[engleskeenya]*; **I live in Manchester** živim u Mančesteru *[jeeveem oo]*; *see page 111*
ice led; **with ice** sa ledom; **with ice and lemon** sa ledom i limunom *[ee leemoonom]*
ice cream sladoled
ice-cream cone kornet sladoleda
iced coffee ajskafe *[ɪskafe]*
ice lolly sladoled no štapiću *[na shtapeechoo]*
idea ideja *[eedeya]*; **good idea!** dobra ideja!
ideal *(solution, time)* idealan *[eedealan]*
identity papers lični dokumenti *[leechnee dokoomentee]*
idiot idiot *[eedeeot]*
idyllic idiličan *[eedeeleechan]*
if ako; **if you could** ako biste mogli *[beeste moglee]*
ignition paljenje *[palyenye]*
ill bolestan; **I feel ill** osjećam se bolestan *[osyecham]*
illegal ilegalan *[eelegalan]*
illegible nečitak *[necheetak]*
illness bolest
imitation imitacija *[eemeetatseeya]*; **imitation leather** umjetna koža *[oomyetna koɹa]*
immediately odmaн
immigration imigracija *[eemeegratseeya]*
import *(verb)* uvesti *[oovestee]*

important važan *[vaɹan]*; **it's very important** veoma je važno *[veoma ye vaɹno]*; **it's not important** nije važno *[neeye]*
impossible nemoguć *[nemogooch]*
impressive impresivan *[eempreseevan]*
improve: it's improving poboljšava se *[pobolyshava]*; **I want to improve my Serbocroat** želim da poboljšam svoj srpskohrvatski *[ɹeleem da pobolysham svoy surpsko-ʜurvatskee]*
improvement poboljšanje *[pobolyshanye]*
in: in my room u mojoj sobi *[oo moyoy sobee]*; **in the town centre** u centru grada *[tsentroo]*; **in London** u Londonu *[londonoo]*; **in one hour's time** za jedan sat *[yedan]*; **in August** u avgustu; **in English** na engleskom; **in Serbocroat** na srpskohrvatskom *[surpsko-ʜurvatskom]*; **is he in?** je li kod kuće *[ye lee kod kooche]*
inch *see page 120*
include uključiti *[ooklyoocheetee]*; **is that included in the price?** je li to uključeno u cijenu? *[ye lee to ooklyoocheno oo tsyenoo]*
incompetent nesposoban
inconvenient nezgodan
increase *(noun)* povećanje *[povechanye]*
incredible *(very good, amazing)* nevjerojatan *[nevyeroyatan]*
indecent nepristojan *[nepreestoyan]*
independent *(adjective)* nezavisan

[nezaveesan]
India Indija *[eendeeya]*
Indian (*adjective*) indijski *[eendeey-skee]*; (*man*) Indijac *[eendeeyats]*; (*woman*) Indijka *[eendeeyka]*
indicator (*on car*) (*S*) migavac *[meegavats]*; (*C*) žmigavac *[Jmeegavats]*
indigestion loša probava *[losha]*
indoor pool zatvoreni bazen *[zatvorenee bazen]*
indoors unutra *[oonootra]*
industry industrija *[eendoostreeya]*
inefficient neefikasan *[ne-efeekasan]*
infection infekcija *[eenfektseeya]*
infectious (*S*) infektivan *[eenfekteevan]*; (*C*) zarazan
inflammation (*S*) zapaljenje *[zapalyenye]*; (*C*) upala *[oopala]*
inflation inflacija *[eenflatseeya]*
informal neformalan
information informacije *[eenform-atseeye]*
information desk šalter za informacije *[shalter za eenformatseeye]*
information office šalter za informacije *[shalter za eenformatseeye]*
injection injekcija *[eenyektseeya]*
injured povrijeđen *[povryedjen]*; **she's been injured** povrijeđena je *[povryedjena ye]*
injury povreda
in-law: my in-laws (*said by wife*) porodica mog muža *[porodeetsa mog mooJa]*; (*said by husband*) porodica moje žene *[moye Jene]*
innocent nevin *[neveen]*
inquisitive radoznao
insect insekt *[eensekt]*
insect bite ujed insekta *[ooyed eensekta]*
insecticide insekticid *[eensekteetseed]*
insect repellent sredstvo za zaštitu od insekata *[sredstvo za zashteetoo od eensekata]*
inside: inside the tent u šatoru *[oo shatoroo]*; **let's sit inside** sjednimo unutra *[syedneemo oonootra]*
insincere neiskren *[ne-eeskren]*
insist: I insist inšistiram *[eenseest-eeram]*
insomnia nesanica *[nesaneetsa]*
instant coffee nes-kafa
instead umjesto *[oomyesto]*; **I'll have**

that one instead uzet ću taj umjesto *[oozet choo tI]*; **instead of ...** umjesto ... (+G)
insulating tape izolaciona traka *[eezolatseeona traka]*
insulin insulin *[eensooleen]*
insult (*noun*) uvreda *[oovreda]*
insurance osiguranje *[oseegooranye]*; **write the name and address of your insurance company here** napišite ovdje ime i adresu vašeg osiguravajućeg društva *[napeesheete ovdye eeme ee adresoo vasheg oseegooravIyoocheg drooshtva]*
insurance policy polica osiguranja *[poleetsa oseegooranya]*
intellectual (*noun*) intelektualac *[eentelektooalats]*
intelligent inteligentan *[eentelee-gentan]*
intentional: it wasn't intentional nije bilo namjerno *[neeye beelo namyerno]*
interest: places of interest znamenitosti *[znameneetostee]*
interested: I'm very interested in ... veoma sam zainteresiran za ... *[veoma sam za-eentereseeran]*
interesting zanimljiv *[zaneemlyeev]*; **that's very interesting** to je veoma zanimljivo *[ye veoma zaneemlyeevo]*
international međunarodni *[medjoonarodnee]*
international driving licence/driver's license međunarodna vozačka dozvola *[medjoonarodna vozachka]*
interpret prevoditi *[prevodeetee]*; **would you interpret?** da li biste vi prevodili? *[lee beeste vee prevodeelee]*
interpreter prevodilac *[prevodeelats]*
intersection raskrsnica *[raskursneetsa]*
interval interval *[eenterval]*
into u *[oo]*; **I'm not into that** (*don't like*) nisam ja za to *[neesam ya]*
introduce: may I introduce ...? mogu li predstaviti ...? *[mogoo lee predstaveetee]*
introvert introvert *[eentrovert]*
invalid invalid *[eenvaleed]*
invalid chair invalidska kolica *[eenvaleedska koleetsa]*
invitation poziv *[pozeev]*; **thank you**

for the invitation hvala vam na pozivu *[Hvala vam na pozeevoo]*
invite pozvati *[pozvatee]*; **can I invite you out?** mogu li vas pozvati da iziđemo? *[mogoo lee vas ... da eezeedjemo]*
involved: I don't want to get involved in it ne želim da se uplićem *[Jeleem da se oopleechem]*
iodine jod *[yod]*
Ireland Irska *[eerska]*
Irish irski *[eerskee]*
Irishman Irac *[eerats]*
Irishwoman Irkinja *[eerkeenya]*
iron (*material*) (*S*) gvožđe *[gvoJdje]*; (*C*) željezo *[Jelyezo]*; (*for clothes*) (*S*) pegla; (*C*) glačalo *[glachalo]*; **can you iron these for me?** možete li mi ovo ispeglati? *[moJete lee mee ovo eespeglatee]*

ironmonger (*S*) gvožđar *[gvoJdjar]*; (*C*) željezarnica *[Jelyezarneetsa]*
is je *[ye]*; *see page 114*
island otok
isolated izoliran *[eezoleeran]*
it to; **is it ...?** je li ...? *[ye lee]*; **where is it?** gdje je to? *[gdye ye]*; **it's her** to je ona *[ona]*; **it was ...** bilo je to ... *[beelo]*; **that's just it** (*just the problem*) upravo je u tome stvar *[oopravo ye oo tome]*; **that's it** (*that's right*) tako je; *see page 111*
Italian (*adjective, language*) (*S*) italijanski *[eetaleeyanskee]*; (*man*) Italijan *[eetaleeyan]*; (*woman*) Italijanka; (*C*) talijanki *[taleeyankee]*; talijan *[taleeyan]*; talijanka *[taleeyanka]*
Italy Italija *[eetaleeya]*
itch: it itches svrbi *[svurbee]*
itinerary itinerer *[eeteenerer]*

J

jack (*for car*) dizalica *[deezaleetsa]*
jacket sako (*m*)
jam džem *[djem]*; **a traffic jam** saobraćajna gužva *[saobrachJna gooJva]*; **I jammed on the brakes** naglo sam pritisnuo kočnice *[naglo sam preeteesnoo-o kochneetse]*
January (*S*) januar *[yanooar]*; (*C*) siječanj *[syechan-yuh]*
jaundice žutica *[Jooteetsa]*
jaw vilica *[veeleetsa]*
jazz džez *[djez]*
jazz club džez klub *[djez kloob]*
jealous ljubomoran *[lyoobomoran]*; **he's jealous** ljubomoran je *[ye]*
jeans (*S*) farmerke; (*C*) traperice *[trapereetse]*
jellyfish meduza *[medooza]*
jetlag: I'm/he's suffering from jetlag osjećam/osjeća posljedice džetlega *[osyecham/osyecha poslyedeetse djetlega]*
jet-set džet-set *[djet-set]*
jetty molo
Jew (*S*) Jevrejin *[yevreyeen]*; (*C*) Židov *[Jeedov]*
jewel(le)ry nakit *[nakeet]*

Jewish (*S*) jevrejski *[yevrayskee]*; (*C*) židovski *[Jeedovskee]*
jiffy: just a jiffy samo tren
job posao (*m*); **just the job!** baš što se traži! *[bash shto se traJee]*; **it's a good job you told me!** dobro je što ste mi rekli! *[ye shto ste mee reklee]*
jog: I'm going for a jog idem na trčanje *[eedem na turchanye]*
jogging trčanje *[turchanye]*
join: I'd like to join želio bih da pristupim *[Jeleeo beeH da preestoopeem]*; **can I join you?** (*go with*) mogu li poći s vama? *[mogoo lee pochee]*; (*sit with*) mogu li vam se pridružiti? *[preedrooJeetee]*; **do you want to join us?** (*go with*) želite li poći s nama? *[Jeleete lee pochee]*; (*sit with*) želite li nam se pridružiti?
joint (*in body*) zglob; (*to smoke*) marihuana *[mareeHooana]*
joke šala *[shala]*; **you've got to be joking!** ma vi se šalite! *[vee se shaleete]*; **it's no joke** nema šale *[shale]*
jolly: it was jolly good bilo je vrlo dobro *[beelo ye vurlo dobro]*; **jolly**

good! vrlo dobro!
journey putovanje *[pootovanye]*; **have a good journey!** sretan put! *[poot]*
jug (S) krčag *[kurchag]*; (C) bokal; **a jug of water** krčag vode
July (S) jul *[yool]*; (C) srpanj *[surpanyuh]*
jump: you made me jump preplašili ste me *[preplasheelee]*; **jump in!** (to car) uskačite! *[ooskacheete]*
jumper džemper *[djemper]*
jump leads, jumper cables kabl za punjenje akumulatora *[poonyenye akoomoolatora]*
junction raskrsnica *[raskursneetsa]*
June (S) jun *[yoon]*; (C) lipanj *[leepan-yuh]*
junior: Mr Jones junior Gospodin Džons mlađi *[gospodeen djons mladjee]*
junk (rubbish) (S) đubre *[djoobre]*; (C) smeće *[smeche]*
just: just one samo jedan *[yedan]*; **just me** samo ja *[ya]*; **just for me** samo za mene; **just a little** samo malo; **just here** upravo ovdje *[oopravo ovdye]*; **not just now** ne baš sad *[bash]*; **that's just right** upravo tako; **it's just as good** dobro je i tako *[ye ee]*; **he was here just now** sad je bio ovdje *[ye beeo]*; **I've only just arrived** tek sam stigao *[steegao]*

K

kagul laka vjetrovka *[laka vyetrovka]*
keen: I'm not keen nisam željan *[neesam Jelyan]*
keep: can I keep it? mogu li zadržati? *[mogoo lee zadurJatee]*; **please keep it** molim vas zadržite *[moleem vas zadurJeete]*; **keep the change** zadržite kusur *[koosoor]*; **will it keep?** (food) da li će se održati? *[lee che se odurJatee]*; **it's keeping me awake** ne da mi da spavam *[mee da]*; **it keeps on breaking** stalno se lomi *[lomee]*; **I can't keep anything down** (food) ništa ne mogu zadržati *[neesta]*
kerb (S) ivičnjak *[eeveechnyak]*; (C) rub pločnika *[roob plochneeka]*
kerosene (for lamps etc) petrolej *[petrolay]*
ketchup kečap *[kechap]*
key ključ *[klyooch]*
kid: the kids klinci *[kleentsee]*; **I'm not kidding** ne šalim se *[shaleem]*
kidneys bubrezi *[boobrezee]*
kill ubiti *[oobeetee]*; **my feet are killing me** strašno me bole noge *[sturashno]*
kilo kilogram *[keelogram]*; see page 120
kilometre, kilometer kilometar *[keelometar]*; see page 120

kind: that's very kind to je veoma ljubazno *[ye veoma lyoobazno]*; **this kind of ...** ova vrsta ... (+G) *[vursta]*
kiosk kiosk *[keeosk]*
kiss (noun) poljubac *[polyoobats]*; (verb) poljubiti *[polyoobeetee]*
kitchen kuhinja *[kooHeenya]*
kitchenette čajna kuhinja *[chIna kooHeenya]*
Kleenex (tm) papirna maramica *[papeerna marameetsa]*
knee koljeno *[kolyeno]*
kneecap patella
knickers ženske gaće *[Jenske gache]*
knife nož *[noJ]*
knitting (act) plentenje *[pletenye]*; (material) pletivo *[pleteevo]*
knitting needles pletaće igle *[pletache eegle]*
knock: there's a knocking noise from the engine nešto lupa u motoru *[neshto loopa oo motoroo]*; **he's had a knock on the head** udario se u glavu *[oodareeo se oo glavoo]*; **he's been knocked over** bio je oboren *[beeo ye]*
knot (in rope) čvor *[chvor]*
know znati *[znatee]*; **I don't know** ne znam; **do you know a good restaurant?** znate li dobar restoran?;

who knows? ko zna?; **I didn't know that** nisam to znao *[neesam to znao]*;

I don't know him ne znam ga

L

label etiketa *[eteeketa]*
laces (*for shoes*) pertle
lacquer (*for hair*) lak
ladies (room) ženski *[Jenskee]*
lady gospođa *[gospodja]*; **ladies and gentlemen!** dame i gospodo! *[ee]*
lager pivo *[peevo]*
lake jezero *[yezero]*
lamb jagnje *[yagnye]*
lamp lampa
lamppost stup za uličnu rasvjetu *[stoop za ooleechnoo rasvyetoo]*
lampshade (S) abažur *[abaJoor]*; (C) sjenilo *[syeneelo]*
land (*not sea*) kopno; **when does the plane land?** kad se avion spušta? *[aveeon spooshta]*
landscape (S) pejzaž *[payzaJ]*; (C) krajolik *[krIyoleek]*
lane (*on motorway*) traka; **a country lane** seoski put *[se-oskee poot]*
language jezik *[yezeek]*
language course (S) jezički kurs *[yezeechkee koors]*; (C) jezični tečaj *[yezeechnee techI]*
large velik *[veleek]*
laryngitis laringitis *[lareengeetees]*
last prošli *[proshlee]*; **last year** prošla godina *[proshla godeena]*; **last Wednesday** prošla srijeda *[sryeda]*; **last night** sinoć *[seenoch]*; **when's the last bus?** kad je posljednji autobus? *[ye poslyednyee aootoboos]*; **one last drink** posljednje piće *[poslyednye peeche]*; **when were you last in London?** kad ste bili posljednji put u Londonu? *[beelee poslyednyee poot oo londonoo]*; **at last!** konačno! *[konachno]*; **how long does it last?** koliko traje? *[koleeko trIye]*
last name prezime *[prezeeme]*
late kasno; **we'll be back late** vratit ćemo se kasno *[vrateet chemo]*; **it's getting late** vrijeme je odmaklo

[vryeme ye]; **is it that late!** zar je tako kasno! *[ye]*; **it's too late now** sad je prekasno; **I'm a late riser** kasno ustajem *[oostIyem]*; **sorry I'm late** izvinite što sam zakasnio *[eezveeneete shto sam zakasneeo]*; **don't be late** nemojte zakasniti *[nemoyte zakasneetee]*; **the bus was late** autobus je zakasnio *[aootoboos ye]*
lately nedavno
later kasnije *[kasneeye]*; **later on** kasnije; **I'll come back later** vratit ću se kasnije *[vrateet choo]*; **see you later** vidimo se kasnije *[veedeemo]*; **no later than Tuesday** najkasnije do utorka *[nIkasneeye do ootorka]*
latest: the latest news najnovija vijest *[nInoveeya vyest]*; **at the latest** najkasnije *[nIkasneeye]*
laugh smijati se *[smeeyatee]*; **don't laugh** nemojte se smijati *[nemoyte]*; **it's no laughing matter** nije smiješno *[neeye smyeshno]*
launderette, laundromat (S) perionica rublja *[pereeoneetsa rooblya]*; (C) praonica rublja *[praoneetsa]*
laundry (*clothes*) rublje *[rooblye]*; (*place*) (S) perionica *[pereeoneetsa]*; (C) praonica *[praoneetsa]*; **could you get the laundry done?** možete li dati da se opere rublje? *[moJete lee datee]*
lavatory (S) klozet; (C) заход
law zakon; **against the law** protivzakonito *[proteevzakoneeto]*
lawn travnjak *[travnyak]*
lawyer advokat
laxative laksativ *[laksateev]*
lay-by prostor za parkiranje pokraj ceste *[parkeeranye pokrI tseste]*
laze around: I just want to laze around želim samo da ljenčarim *[Jeleem samo da lyenchareem]*
lazy lijen *[lyen]*; **don't be lazy** ne

budite lijeni *[boodeete lyenee]*; **a nice lazy holiday** divan lijen odmor *[deevan]*

lead *(electric)* vod; **where does this road lead?** kuda vodi ovaj put? *[kooda vodee ovɪ poot]*

leaf list *[leest]*

leaflet prospekt; **do you have any leaflets on ...?** imate li prospekte o ...? *[eemate lee]*

leak curiti *[tsooreetee]*; **the roof leaks** krov prokišnjava *[prokeeshnyava]*

learn: I want to learn ... želim učiti ... *[ʒeleem oocheetee]*

learner: I'm just a learner ja tek učim *[ya tek oochem]*

lease *(verb)* iznajmiti *[eeznɪmeetee]*

least: not in the least nimalo *[neemalo]*; **at least 50** bar 50

leather koža *[koʒa]*

leave: when does the bus leave? kad polazi autobus? *[polazee aootoboos]*; **I leave tomorrow** odlazim sutra *[odlazeem sootra]*; **he left this morning** otišao je jutros *[oteeshao ye yootros]*; **may I leave this here?** mogu li ovo ostaviti ovdje? *[mogoo lee ovo ostaveetee ovdye]*; **I left my bag in the bar** ostavio sam torbu u kafiću *[ostaveeo sam torboo oo kafeechoo]*; **she left her bag here** ostavila je torbu ovdje *[ostaveela ye]*; **leave the window open please** ostavite otvoren prozor, molim vas *[ostaveete ... moleem]*; **there's not much left** nije mnogo ostalo *[neeye]*; **I've hardly any money left** gotovo sam ostao bez novca *[novtsa]*; **I'll leave it up to you** prepustit ću tebi *[propoosteet choo tebee]*

lecherous razvratan

left lijevo *[lyevo]*; **on the left** s lijeve strane *[lyeve strane]*

left-hand drive vozilo s volanom na lijevoj strani *[vozeelo s volanom na lyevoy stranee]*

left-handed ljevak *[lyevak]*

left luggage office garderoba

leg noga

legal *(allowed)* dopušten *[dopooshten]*

lemon limun *[leemon]*

lemonade limunada *[leemoonada]*

lemon tea čaj sa limunom *[chɪ sa leemoonom]*

lend: would you lend me your ...? da li biste mi posudili svoj ... *[lee beeste mee posoodeelee svoy]*

lens *(of camera)* objektiv *[obyekteev]*; *(contact)* (S) sočivo *[socheevo]*; (C) leća *[lecha]*

lens cap poklopac za objektiv *[poklopats za obyekteev]*

Lent (S) veliki post *[veleekee]*; (C) Korizma *[koreezma]*

lesbian lezbijka *[lezbeeyka]*

less: less than an hour manje od sata *[manye]*; **less than that** manje od toga; **less hot** manje vruće *[vrooche]*

lesson poduka *[podooka]*; **do you give lessons?** podučavate li? *[podoochavate lee]*

let: would you let me use it? da li biste mi dozvolili da ga upotrebim? *[lee beeste mee dozvoleelee da ga oopotrebeem]*; **will you let me know?** hoćete li me obavijestiti *[hochete lee me obavyesteetee]*; **I'll let you know** obavijestit ću vas *[obavyesteet choo]*; **let me try** dozvolite mi da pokušam *[dozvoleete mee da pokoosham]*; **let me go!** pustite me *[poosteete]*; **let's leave now** hajdemo sada *[hɪdemo]*; **let's not go yet** nemojmo još ići *[nemoymo yosh eechee]*; **will you let me off at ...?** da li biste stali da iziđem u ...? *[stalee da eezeedjem oo]*; **rooms to let** sobe za izdavanje *[eezdavanye]*

letter pismo *[peesmo]*; *(of alphabet)* slovo; **are there any letters for me?** ima li pošte za mene? *[eema lee poshte]*

letterbox (S) poštansko sanduče *[poshtansko sandooche]*; (C) poštanski sanduk *[sandook]*

lettuce zelena salata

level crossing rampa

lever *(noun)* ručica *[roocheetsa]*

liable *(responsible)* odgovoran

liberated: a liberated woman emancipovana žena *[emantseepovana ʒena]*

library biblioteka *[beebleeoteka]*

licence, license dozovola

license plate *(on car)* registarska tablica *[regeestarska tableetsa]*

lid poklopac *[poklopats]*

lie *(untruth)* laž *[laʒ]*; **can he lie down**

for a while? može li malo da legne? *[moJe lee]*; **I want to go and lie down** želim otići i leći *[Jeleem oteechee ee lechee]*

lie-in: I'm going to have a lie-in tomorrow sutra ću se naspavati *[sootra choo se naspavatee]*

life život *[Jeevot]*; **not on your life!** ni za živu glavu! *[nee za Jeevo glavoo]*; **that's life!** to je život! *[ye]*

lifebelt pojas za spasavanje *[poyas za spasavanye]*

lifeboat čamac za spasavanje *[chamats za spasavanye]*

lifeguard spasilac *[spaseelats]*

life insurance životno osiguranje *[Jeevotno oseegooranye]*

life jacket prsluk za spasavanje *[purslook za spasavanye]*

lift (*in hotel etc*) lift *[leeft]*; **could you give me a lift?** možete li me povesti? *[moJete lee me povestee]*; **do you want a lift?** želite li da vas povezem? *[Jeleete lee]*; **thanks for the lift** hvala na vožnji *[Hvala na voJnyee]*; **I got a lift** neko me dovezao

light (*noun*) svijetlo *[svyetlo]*; (*not heavy*) lak; **the light was on** svijetlo je bilo upaljeno *[ye beelo oopalyeno]*; **do you have a light?** (*for cigarette*) imate li šibicu? *[eemate lee sheebeetsoo]*; **a light meal** lak obrok; **light blue** svijetlo plav

light bulb (*S*) sijalica *[seeyaleetsa]*; (*C*) žarulja *[Jaroolya]*

lighter (*cigarette*) upaljač *[oopalyach]*

lighthouse svjetionik *[svyeteeoneek]*

light meter svjetlomjer *[svyetlomyer]*

lightning munja *[moonya]*

like: I'd like a ... želio bih ... *[Jeleeo beeH]*; **I'd like to ...** želio bih da ...; **would you like a ...?** da li biste željeli ...? *[lee beeste Jelyelee]*; **would you like to come too?** da li biste i vi željeli doći? *[ee vee Jelyelee dochee]*; **I'd like to** želio bih; **I like it** dopada mi se *[mee]*; **I like you** dopadate mi se; **I don't like it** ne dopada mi se; **he doesn't like it** ne dopada mu se *[moo]*; **do you like ...?** volite li ...? *[voleete lee]*; **I like swimming** volim plivati *[voleem pleevatee]*; **OK, if you like** u redu, ako želite *[oo redoo ako Jeleete]*; **what's it like?** kakvo je?

[ye]; **do it like this** ovako uradite *[ooradeete]*; **one like that** jedan ovakav *[yedan]*

lilo (*S*) dušek za naduvavanje *[dooshek za nadoovavanye]*; (*C*) zračni madrac *[zrachnee madrats]*

line (*tel*) linija *[leeneeya]*; (*on road etc*) crta *[curta]*; (*of people*) red; **would you give me a line?** (*tel*) da li biste mi dali vezu? *[lee beeste mee dalee vezoo]*

linen (*for beds*) posteljina *[postelyeena]*

linguist lingvist *[leengveest]*; **I'm no linguist** nisam baš neki jezičar *[neesam bash nekee yezeechar]*

lining postava

lip usna *[oosna]*

lip brush četkica za usne *[chetkeetsa za oosne]*

lip gloss sjaj za usne *[syI za oosne]*

lip pencil krejon za usne *[kreyon za oosne]*

lip salve krema za usne *[oosne]*

lipstick ruž za usne *[rooJ za oosne]*

liqueur liker *[leeker]*

liquor alkoholno piće *[peeche]*

list spisak *[speesak]*

listen: I'd like to listen to ... želio bih da slušam ... *[Jeleeo beeH da sloosham]*; **listen!** slušajte! *[slooshIte]*

litre, liter litar *[leetar]*; *see page 121*

litter (*rubbish*) (*S*) đubre *[djoobre]*; (*C*) smeće *[smeche]*

little malo; **just a little, thanks** samo malo, Hvala; **just a very little** sasvim malo *[sasveem]*; **a little milk** malo mlijeka *[mlyeka]*; **a little more** još malo *[yosh]*; **a little better** malo bolje *[bolye]*; **that's too little** (*not enough*) to je premalo *[ye]*

live živjeti *[Jeevyetee]*; **I live in ...** živim u ... *[Jeeveem oo]*; **where do you live?** gdje živite? *[gdye Jeeveete]*; **where does he live?** gdje živi? *[Jeevee]*; **we live together** živimo zajedno *[Jeeveemo zIyedno]*

lively (*person*) živahan *[Jeevahan]*; (*town*) živ *[Jeev]*

liver (*in body, food*) jetra *[yetra]*

lizard gušter *[gooshter]*

loaf (*S*) hljeb *[Hlyeb]*; (*C*) kruh *[krooH]*

lobby (*of hotel*) predvorje *[predvorye]*

lobster jastog *[yastog]*

local: a **local wine** lokalno vino
[veeno]; a **local newspaper** lokalne
novine *[noveene]*; a **local restaurant**
lokalni restoran *[lokalnee]*
lock *(noun)* brava; **it's locked** zaklju-
čano je *[zaklyoochano ye]*; **I locked
myself out of my room** zaboravio
sam ključ u sobi a vrata su se
zaključala *[zaboraveeo sam klyooch
oo sobee a vrata soo se zaklyoochala]*
locker *(for luggage)* pretinac
[preteenats]
log: I slept like a log spavao sam kao
klada
lollipop lilihip *[leeleeheep]*
lonely usamljen *[oosamlyen]*; **are you
lonely?** da li ste usamljeni? *[lee ste
oosamlyenee]*
long dugo *[doogo]*; **how long does it
take?** koliko dugo traje? *[koleeko
doogo trıye]*; **is it a long way?** je li
daleko? *[ye lee]*; **a long time** dugo
vremena; **I won't be long** neću se
dugo zadržati *[nechoo se doogo
zadurɹatee]*; **don't be long** nemojte
dugo ostati *[nemoyte doogo ostatee]*;
that was long ago to je bilo davno
[ye beelo]; **I'd like to stay longer**
želio bih duže ostati *[ɹeleeo beeн
dooɹe]*; **long time no see!** dugo se
nismo vidjeli! *[neesmo veedyelee]*; **so
long!** do viđenja! *[doveedjenya]*
long distance call međugradski
razgovor *[medjoogradskee]*
loo: where's the loo? gdje je WC?
[gdye ye ve tse]; **I want to go to the
loo** želim ići u WC *[ɹeleem eechee
oo]*
look: that looks good to dobro izgle-
da *[eezgleda]*; **you look tired**
izgledate umorni *[eezgledate
oomornee]*; **I'm just looking, thanks**
samo gledam, нvala; **you don't look
your age** ne izgledate kao da vam je
toliko godina *[eezgledate kao da vam
ye toleeko godeena]*; **look at him**
pogledajte ga *[pogledɪte]*; **I'm
looking for ...** tražim ... *[traɹeem]*;
look out! pazite! *[pazeete]*; **can I
have a look?** mogu li pogledati?
[mogoo lee pogledatee]; **can I have a
look around?** mogu li razgledati?
[razgledatee]
loose *(button, handle etc)* labav

loose change sitan novac *[seetan
novats]*
lorry kamion *[kameeon]*
lorry driver vozač kamiona *[vozach
kameeona]*
lose izgubiti *[eezgoobeetee]*; **I've lost
my ...** izgubio sam svoj ...
[eezgoobeeo sam svoy]; **I'm lost**
izgubio sam se
lost property office, lost and found
biro za izgubljene stvari *[beero za
eezgooblyene stvaree]*
lot: a lot, lots mnogo; **not a lot** ne
mnogo; **a lot of money** mnogo
novca *[novtsa]*; **a lot of women**
mnogo žena *[ɹena]*; **a lot cooler**
mnogo hladnije *[нladneeye]*; **I like it
a lot** mnogo mi se dopada *[mee]*; **is
it a lot further?** je li mnogo dalje
[ye ... dalye]; **I'll take the (whole)
lot** uzet ću sve *[oozet choo]*
lotion losion *[loseeon]*
loud glasan; **the music is rather loud**
muzika je dosta glasna *[moozeeka ye]*
lounge *(in house)* salon; *(in hotel)*
predvorje *[predvorye]*
lousy *(weather etc)* užasno *[ooɹasno]*
love: I love you volim te *[voleem]*;
he's fallen in love zaljubio se
[zalyoobeeo]; **I love Yugoslavia**
volim Jugoslaviju *[yoogoslaveeyoo]*;
let's make love hajde da vodimo
ljubav *[нɪde da vodeemo lyoobav]*
lovely divan *[deevan]*
low *(price, bridge)* nizak *[neezak]*
low beam oboreno svijetlo *[svyetlo]*
LP LP ploča *[long-play plocha]*
luck sreća *[srecha]*; **hard luck!** loša
sreća! *[losha]*; **good luck!** srećno!
[srechno]; **just my luck!** takve sam
sreće *[sreche]*; **it was pure luck** bila
je to puka sreća *[beela ye to pooka]*
lucky: that's lucky! kakva sreća!
[srecha]
lucky charm amajlija *[amıleeya]*
luggage *(S)* prtljag *[purtlyag]*; *(C)*
prtljaga *[purtlyaga]*
lumbago lumbago *(m)* *[loombago]*
lump *(medical)* izraslina *[eezrasleena]*
lunch ručak *[roochak]*
lungs pluća *[ploocha]*
luxurious luksuzan *[looksoozan]*
luxury luksuz *[looksooz]*

M

macho mačo *[macho]*
mad lud *[lood]*
madam gospođa *[gospodja]*
magazine časopis *[chasopees]*
magnificent   veličanstven *[veleechanstven]*
maid sobarica *[sobareetsa]*
maiden   name djevojačko   ime *[dyevoyachko eeme]*
mail (*noun*) pošta *[poshta]*; **is there any mail for me?** ima li za mene pošte? *[eema lee za mene poshte]*; **where can I mail this?** gdje mogu ovo predati na poštu? *[gdye mogoo ovo predatee na poshtoo]*
mailbox   (S)   poštansko   sanduče *[poshtansko sandooche]*; (C) poštanski sanduk *[sandook]*
main glavni *[glavnee]*; **where's the main post office?** gdje je glavna pošta? *[gdye ye glavna poshta]*
main road glavni put *[glavnee poot]*
make praviti *[praveetie]*; **do you make them yourself?** da li ih sami pravite? *[lee eeн samee praveete]*; **it's very well made** veoma dobro je napravljen *[veoma dobro ye napravlyen]*; **what does that make altogether?** na šta to ukupno izlazi? *[shta to ookoopno eezlazee]*; **I make it only 500 dinars** po meni je to samo 500 dinara *[menee ye to samo pet stoteena deenara]*
make-up šminka *[shmeenka]*
make-up remover mlijeko za skidanje šminke *[mlyeko za skeedanye shmeenke]*
male chauvinist pig seksist *[sekseest]*
man čovjek *[chovyek]*
manager direktor *[deerektor]*; **may I see   the   manager?**   mogu   li razgovarati sa direktorom? *[mogoo lee razgovaratee sa deerektorom]*
manicure manikiranje *[maneekeeranye]*
many mnogi *[mnogee]*
map: a map of ... karta ... (+*G*); **it's**

not on this map nije na ovoj karti *[neeye na ovoy kartee]*
marble (*noun*) mramor
March (S) mart; (C) ožujak *[oлooyak]*
marijuana marihuana *[mareeнooana]*
mark: there's a mark on it isflekano je *[eesflekano ye]*; **could you mark it on the map for me?** možete li mi to obilježiti na karti? *[moлete lee mee to obeelyeлeetee na kartee]*
market (*noun*) (S) pijaca *[peeyatsa]*; (C) tržnica *[turлneetsa]*
marmalade džem od naranče *[djem od naranche]*
married: are you married? (*woman*) jeste li udati? *[yeste lee oodatee]*; (*man*) jeste li oženjeni? *[oлenyenee]*; **I'm married** udata sam/oženjen sam *[oodata/oлenyen]*
mascara maskara
mass: I'd like to go to mass želim ići na misu *[лeleem eechee na meesoo]*
mast jarbol *[yarbol]*
masterpiece   remek-djelo   *[remek-dyelo]*
matches šibice *[sheebeetse]*
material (*cloth*) tkanina *[tkaneena]*
matter: it doesn't matter nije važno *[neeye vaлno]*; **what's the matter?** u čemu je stvar? *[oo chemo ye]*
mattress (S) dušek *[dooshek]*; (C) madrac *[madrats]*
maximum maksimum *[makseemoom]*
May (S) maj *[mı]*; (C) svibanj *[sveeban-yuh]*
may: may I have another bottle? molim vas još jednu bocu *[moleem vas yosh yednoo botsoo]*; **may I?** mogu li? *[mogoo lee]*
maybe možda *[moлda]*; **maybe not** možda ne
mayonnaise majoneza *[mıyoneza]*
me: come with me dođite sa mnom *[dodjeete]*; **it's for me** za mene je *[mene ye]*; **it's me** to sam ja *[ya]*; **me too** i ja *[ee]*; *see page 111*
meal objed *[obyed]*; **that was an**

excellent meal bio je to odličan objed *[beeo ye to odleechan]*; **does that include meals?** da li je uključeno jelo? *[lee ye ooklyoocheno yelo]*

mean: what does this word mean? šta znači ova riječ *[shta znachee ova ryech]*; **what does he mean?** šta hoće da kaže? *[shta hoche da kaje]*

measles male boginje *[bogeenye]*

measurements dimenzije *[deemenzeeye]*

meat meso

mechanic: do you have a mechanic here? imate li ovdje mehaničara? *[eemate lee ovdye meнaneechara]*

medicine lijek *[lyek]*

medieval srednjovjekovni *[srednyovyekovnee]*

Mediterranean Mediteran *[medeeteran]*

medium *(adjective)* srednji *[srednyee]*

medium-dry srednje suho *[srednye sooнo]*

medium-rare srednje pečeno *[srednye pecheno]*

medium-sized srednje veličine *[srednye veleecheene]*

meet: pleased to meet you drago mi je *[drago mee ye]*; **where shall we meet?** gdje ćemo se naći? *[gdye chemo se nachee]*; **let's meet up again** nađimo se ponovo *[nadjeemo]*

meeting sastanak

meeting place mjesto sastanka *[myesto]*

melon dinja *[deenya]*

member član *[chlan]*; **I'd like to become a member** želio bih postati član *[jeleeo beeн postatee]*

men ljudi *[lyoodee]*

mend: can you mend this? možete li ovo popraviti? *[moлete lee ovo popraveetee]*

men's room muški klozet *[mooshkee]*

mention: don't mention it nema na čemu *[nema na chemoo]*

menu jelovnik *[yelovneek]*; **may I have the menu please?** molim vas jelovnik *[moleem]*

mess zbrka *[zburka]*

message: are there any messages for me? ima li poruka za mene? *[eema lee porooka za mene]*; **I'd like to**

leave a message for ... želio bih ostaviti poruku za ... *(+A) [jeleeo beeн ostaveetee porookoo]*

metal *(noun)* metal

metre, meter metar; *see page 120*

midday: at midday u podne *[oo]*

middle: in the middle u sredini *[oo sredeenee]*; **in the middle of the road** usred puta *[oosred poota]*

midnight: at midnight u ponoć *[oo ponoch]*

might: I might want to stay another 3 days mogao bih odlučiti da ostanem još 3 dana *[mogaoo beeн odloocheetee da ostanem yosh tree dana]*; **you might have warned me!** mogli ste me upozoriti! *[moglee ste me oopozoreetee]*

migraine migrena *[meegrena]*

mild *(taste, weather)* blag

mile milja *[meelya]*; **that's miles away!** to je veoma daleko! *[ye]*

mileometer kilometar-sat

military *(adjective)* vojni *[voynee]*

milk mlijeko *[mlyeko]*

milkshake frape

millimetre, millimeter milimetar *[meeleemetar]*

minced meat mljeveno meso *[mlyeveno meso]*

mind: I don't mind svejedno mi je *[sveyedno mee ye]*; **would you mind if I ...?** imate li nešto protiv ako ... *[eemate lee neshto proteev ako]*; **never mind** ništa za to *[neeshta]*; **I've changed my mind** predomislio sam se *[predomeesleeo]*

mine: it's mine moje je *[moye ye]*; *see page 112*

mineral water mineralna voda *[meeneralna voda]*

minimum minimalan *[meeneemalan]*

mint *(sweet)* pepermint *[pepermeent]*

minus minus *[meenoos]*; **minus 3 degrees** *(S)* minus 3 stepena *[tree stepena]*; *(C)* minus 3 stupnja *[stoopnya]*

minute minuta *[meenoota]*; **in a minute** odmaн; **just a minute** samo trenutak *[samo trenootak]*

mirror *(S)* ogledalo; *(C)* zrcalo *[zurtsalo]*

Miss gospođica *[gospodjeetsa]*; **miss!** gospođice! *[gospodjeetse]* miss: I miss you nedostajete mi [nedostɪyete mee]; there's a ... missing nedostaje ... [nedostɪye]; we missed the bus nismo uhvatili autobus [neesmo ooнvateelee aootoboos]

mist magla

mistake greška [greshka]; I think there's a mistake here mislim da je ovo greška [meesleem da ye ovo]

misunderstanding nesporazum [nesporazoom]

mixture mješavina [myeshaveena]

mix-up: there's been some sort of mix-up with ... došlo je do nekakve zbrke sa ... [doshlo ye do nekakve zburke]

modern moderan

modern art moderna umjetnost [moderna oomyetnost]

moisturizer hidrantna krema [heedrantna krema]

moment: I won't be a moment odmah se vraćam [odmaн se vracham]

monastery (S) manastir [manasteer]; (C) samostan

Monday ponedjeljak [ponedyelyak]

money novac [novats]; I don't have any money nemam novca [nemam novtsa]; do you take English/American money? primate li engleski/američki novac? [preemate lee engleskee/amereechkee]

month mjesec [myesets]

monument spomenik [spomeneek]

moon mjesec [myesets]

moorings sidrište [seedreeshte]

moped moped

more više [veeshe]; may I have some more? molim vas još malo [moleem vas yosh malo]; more water, please još malo vode, molim [vode]; no more, thanks ne mogu više, hvala [mogoo veeshe, нvala]; more expensive skuplji [skooplyee]; more than 50 više od 50 [veeshe od pedeset]; more than that više od toga; a lot more mnogo više; not any more ne više; I don't stay there any more ne odsijedam više tamo [odsyedam veeshe]

morning jutro [yootro]; good morning dobro jutro; this morning jutros [yootros]; in the morning ujutro [ooyootro]

mosquito komarac [komarats]

most: I like this one most najviše mi se sviđa ovaj [nɪveeshe mee se sveedja ovɪ] most of the time najveći dio vremena [nɪvechee deeo]; most hotels većina hotel [vecheena]

mother: my mother moja majka [moya mɪka]

motif (in pattern) motiv [moteev]

motor motor

motorbike motocikl [mototseekl]

motorboat motorni čamac [motornee chamats]

motorist automobilist [aootomobeeleest]

motorway autoput [aootopoot]

motor yacht motorna jahta [motorna yahta]

mountain planina [planeena]; up in the mountains gore u planinama [gore oo planeenama]; a mountain village planinsko selo [planeensko]

mouse miš [meesh]

moustache brkovi [burkovee]

mouth usta [oosta]

move: he's moved to another hotel prešao je u drugi hotel [preshao ye oo droogee]; could you move your car? da li biste mogli pomaknuti kola? [lee beeste moglee pomaknutee]

movie film [feelm]; let's go to the movies (S) hajdemo u bioskop [hɪdemo oo beeoskop]; (C) idemo u kino [eedemo oo keeno]

movie camera filmska kamera [feelmska]

movie theater (S) bioskop [beeoskop]; (C) kino [keeno]

moving: a very moving tune dirljiva melodija [deerlyeeva melodeeya]

Mr gospodin [gospodeen]

Mrs gospođa [gospodja]

Ms no equivalent in Yugoslavia

much mnogo; much better mnogo bolje [bolye]; much cooler mnogo hladnije [hladneeye]; not much ne mnogo; not so much ne toliko [toleeko]

muffler prigušivač [preegooheevach]

mug: I've been mugged napali su me i opljačkali [napalee soo me ee oplyachkali]

muggy (*weather*) sparan
mule mazga
mumps zauške *[zaooshke]*
murals zidne slike *[zeedne sleeke]*
muscle mišić *[meesheech]*
museum muzej *[moozay]*
mushrom gljiva *[glyeeva]*
music muzika *[moozeeka]*; **accordion music** muzika na harmonici *[harmoneetsee]*; **do you have the sheet music for ...?** imate li note za ...? *[eemate lee note]*
musician muzičar *[moozeechar]*

mussels mušule *[mooshoole]*
must: I must ... moram ...; **I mustn't drink ...** ne smijem piti ... *[smyem peetee]*; **you mustn't forget** ne smijete zaboraviti *[smyete zaboraveetee]*
mustache brkovi *[burkovee]*
mustard senf
my: my room moja soba *[moya soba]*; see page 109
myself: I'll do it myself uradit ću sam *[ooradeet choo]*

N

nail (*of finger*) nokat; (*in wood*) (S) ekser; (C) ćavao (m) *[chavao]*
nail clippers spravica za sječenje noktiju *[spraveetsa za syechenye nokteeyoo]*
nailfile turpija za nokte *[toorpeeya]*
nail polish lak za nokte
nail polish remover aceton *[atseton]*
nail scissors (S) makaze za nokte; (C) škare za nokte *[shkare]*
naked (S) go; (C) gol
name ime *[eeme]*; **what's your name?** kako se zovete?; **what's its name?** kako se to zove?; **my name is ...** zovem se ...
nap: he's having a nap malo je prilegao *[malo ye preelegao]*
napkin (*serviette*) salveta
nappy pelena
narrow (*road*) uzak *[oozak]*
nasty (*taste, person, weather, cut*) gadan
national narodni *[narodnee]*
nationality državljanstvo *[durjavlyanstvo]*
natural prirodan *[preerodan]*
naturally (*of course*) (S) prirodno *[preerodno]*; (C) naravno
nature (*trees etc*) priroda *[preeroda]*
nausea mučnina *[moochneena]*
near blizu *[bleezoo]*; **is it near here?** je li blizu? *[ye lee]*; **near the window** blizu prozora; **do you go near ...?** prolazite li blizu ...? *[prolazeete lee]*; **where is the nearest ...?** gdje je

najbliži ...? *[gdye ye nıbleejee]*
nearby blizu *[bleezoo]*
nearly gotovo
neat (*room etc*) uredan *[ooredan]*; (*drink*) čist *[cheest]*
necessary potreban; **is it necessary to ...?** je li potrebno ... *[ye lee]*; **it's not necessary** nije potrebno *[neeye]*
neck (*of body*) vrat; (*of dress, shirt*) okovratnik *[okovratneek]*
necklace ogrlica *[ogurleetsa]*
necktie kravata
need: I need a ... treba mi ... *[mee]*; **do I need a ...?** da li trebam ...? *[lee]*; **it needs more salt** treba dosoliti *[dosoleetee]*; **there's no need** nema potrebe; **there's no need to shout!** zašto vičete! *[zashto veechete]*
needle igla *[eegla]*
negative (*film*) negativ *[negateev]*
neighbo(u)r susjed *[soosyed]*
neighbo(u)rhood susjedstvo *[soosyedstvo]*
neither: neither of us nijedan od nas *[neeyedan]*; **neither one (of them)** nijedan (od njih) *[neeyedan (od nyeeн)]*; **neither ... nor ...** ni ... ni ... *[nee]*; **neither do I** ni ja *[ya]*; **neither does he** ni on
nephew: my nephew moj nećak *[moy nechak]*
nervous nervozan
net (*fishing, tennis*) mreža *[mreja]*
nettle kopriva *[kopreeva]*

neurotic neurotičan *[neooroteechan]*
neutral (*gear*) prazan hod
never nikad *[neekad]*
new nov
news vijest (*f*) *[vyest]*; **is there any news?** ima li ikakvih vijesti? *[eema lee eekakveeн vyestee]*
newspaper novine (*always in plural*) *[noveene]*; **do you have any English newspapers?** imate li kakve engleske novine? *[eemate lee kakve engleske]*
newstand kiosk za prodaju novina *[keeosk za prodɪyoo noveena]*
New Year Nova godina *[godeena]*; **Happy New Year** sretna Nova godina *[sretna]*
New Year's Eve Stara godina *[stara godeena]*
New York Njujork *[nyooyork]*
New Zealand Novi Zeland *[novee zeland]*
New Zealander Novozelanđanin *[novozelandjaneen]*
next sljedeći *[slyedechee]*; **it's at the next corner** na slijedećem uglu *[slyedechem oogloo]*; **next week/Monday** slijedeći tjedan/ponedjeljak; **next to the post office** pored pošte *[poshte]*; **the one next to that** onaj pored *[onɪ]*
next door susjedni *[soosyednee]*
next of kin najbliži rod *[nɪbleeɹee]*
nice (*person, town, day*) prijatan *[preeyatan]*; (*meal*) krasan; **that's very nice of you** to je veoma ljubazno od vas *[ye veoma lyoobazno]*; **a nice cold drink** hladan napitak
nickname nadimak *[nadeemak]*
niece: my niece moja nećakinja *[moya nechakeenya]*
night noć (*f*) *[noch]*; **for one night** za jednu noć *[yednoo]*; **for three nights** za tri noći *[tree nochee]*; **good night** laku noć *[lakoo]*; **at night** noću *[nochoo]*
nightcap (*drink*) prije spavanja napitak *[pureeye spavanya napeetak]*
nightclub bar, noćni lokal *[nochnee]*
nightdress spavaćica *[spavacheetsa]*
night flight noćni let *[nochnee]*
nightie spavaćica *[spavacheetsa]*
night-life noćni život *[nochnee ɹeevot]*
nightmare mora
night porter noćni portir *[nochnee porteer]*
nits (*bugs in hair etc*) gnjide *[gnyeede]*
no ne; **I've no money** nemam novca *[novtsa]*; **there's no more** nema više *[veeshe]*; **no more than ...** ne više od ...; **oh no!** (*upset*) nije valjda! *[neeye valyda]*
nobody niko *[neeko]*
noise buka *[booka]*
noisy bučan *[boochan]*; **it's too noisy** previše je bučno *[preveeshe ye boochno]*
non-alcoholic (*drink*) bezalkoholan
none nijedan *[neeyedan]*; **none of them** nijedan od njih *[nyeeн]*
nonsense besmislica *[besmeesleetsa]*
non-smoking (*compartment etc*) za nepušače *[nepooshache]*
non-stop (*travel*) direktan *[deerektan]*
noodles rezanci *[rezantsee]*
no-one niko *[neeko]*
nor: nor do I ni ja *[nee ya]*; **nor does he** ni on
normal normalan
north sjever *[syever]*; **to the north of ...** sjeverno od ... *[syeverno]*; **in the north** na sjeveru *[syeveroo]*
northeast sjeveroistok *[syevero-eestok]*; **to the northeast of ...** sjeveroistočno od ... *[syevero-eestochno]*
Northern Ireland Sjeverna Irska *[syeverna eerska]*
northwest sjeverozapad *[syevero-zapad]*; **to the northwest of ...** sjeverozapadno od ... *[syevero-zapadno]*
Norway Norveška *[norveshka]*
nose nos; **my nose is bleeding** nos mi krvari *[mee kurvaree]*
not ne; **I don't smoke** ne pušim *[poosheem]*; **he didn't arrive** nije stigao *[neeye steegao]*; **he didn't say anything** nije ništa rekao *[neeye neeshta]*; **it's not important** nije važno *[vaɹno]*; **not that one** ne taj *[tɪ]*; **not for me** ne za mene; *see pages 114-116*
note (*bank note*) novčanica *[novchaneetsa]*; (*written message etc*) poruka *[porooka]*
notebook bilježnica *[beelyeɹneetsa]*
nothing ništa *[neeshta]*
November (*S*) novembar; (*C*) studeni

[stoodenee]
now sada; **not now** ne sada
nowhere nigdje *[neegdye]*
nudist nudist *[noodist]*
nudist beach nudistička plaža *[noodeesteechka plaJa]*
nuisance: he's being a nuisance on gnjavi *[gnyavee]*
numb (*limb etc*) utrnuo *[ooturnoo-o]*
number (*figure*) broj *[broy]*; **what number?** koji broj? *[koyee]*

number plates registarske tablice *[regeestarske tableetse]*
nurse bolničarka *[bolneecharka]*; (*male*) bolničar *[bolneechar]*
nursery (*at airport etc, for children*) prostorija za majke sa djecom *[prostoreeya za mIke sa dyetsom]*
nut (*for bolt*) navrtanj *[navurtan-yuh]*
nutter: he's a nutter on je ćaknut *[ye chaknoot]*

O

oar veslo
obligatory obavezan
oblige: much obliged (*thank you*) veliko hvala *[veleeko Hvala]*
obnoxious (*person*) odvratan
obvious: that's obvious to je očigledno *[ye ocheegledno]*
occasionally povremeno
o'clock see page 119
October (*S*) oktobar; (*C*) listopad *[leestopad]*
octopus hobotnica *[hobotneetsa]*
odd (*strange*) čudan *[choodan]*; (*number*) neparan
odometer kilometar-sat
of od; **the name of the hotel** ime hotela *[eeme hotela]*; **have one of mine** uzmite jedan moj *[oozmeete yedan moy]*; **he is a friend of mine** on je moj prijatelj *[preeyatel-yuh]*; **of no value** nikakve vrijednosti *[neekakve vryednostee]*; see page 104
off: 20% off 20% popusta *[dvadeset posto popoosta]*; **the lights were off** svjetla su bila isključena *[svyetla soo beela eesklyoochena]*; **just off the main road** malo izvan glavnog puta *[malo eezvan glavnog poota]*
offend: don't be offended nemojte se uvrijediti *[nemoyte se oovryedeetee]*
office (*place of work*) (*S*) kancelarija *[kantselareeya]*; (*C*) ured *[oored]*
officer (*to policeman*) druže *[drooJe]*
official (*noun*) službenik *[slooJbeneek]*; **is that official?** je li to zvanično? *[ye lee to zvaneechno]*

off-season mrtva sezona *[murtva]*
often često *[chesto]*; **not often** ne često
oil ulje *[oolye]*; **it's losing oil** gubi ulje *[goobee]*; **will you change the oil?** da li biste promjenili ulje? *[lee beeste promyeneelee]*; **the oil light's flashing** pali se svjetlo za ulje *[palee se svyetlo]*
oil painting uljana slika *[oolyana sleeka]*
oil pressure pritisak ulja *[preeteesak oolya]*
ointment mast
OK u redu *[oo redoo]*; **are you OK?** jeste li u redu? *[yeste lee]*; **that's OK thanks** u redu, hvala *[Hvala]*; **that's OK by me** u redu što se mene tiče *[shto se mene teeche]*
old star; **how old are you?** koliko imate godina? *[koleeko eemate godeena]*
old-age pensioner penzioner *[penzeeoner]*
old-fashioned staromodan
old town stari grad *[staree]*
olive maslina *[masleena]*
olive oil maslinovo ulje *[masleenovo oolye]*
omelet(t)e omlet
on na; **on the roof** na krovu *[krovoo]*; **on the beach** na plaži *[plaJee]*; **on Friday** u petak *[oo]*; **on television** na televiziji *[televeezeeyee]*; **I don't have it on me** nemam kod sebe; **this drink's on me** ja plaćam ovo piće

[ya placham ovo peeche]; **a book on Belgrade** knjiga o Beogradu *[knyeega o beogradoo]*; **the warning light comes on** pali se signalno svijetlo *[palee se seegnalno svyetlo]*; **the light was on** svijetlo je bilo uključeno *[svyetlo ye beelo ooklyoocheno]*; **what's on in town?** šta se dešava u gradu? *[shta se deshava oo gradoo]*; **it's just not on!** (*not acceptable*) ne može to tako! *[moje]*

once (*one time*) jednom *[yednom]*; (*formerly*) nekad; **at once** (*immediately*) odman

one jedan *[yedan]*; **that one** taj *[ti]*; **the green one** onaj zeleni *[oni zelenee]*; **the one with the black skirt on** ona u crnoj suknji *[oona oo tsurnoy sooknyee]*; **the one in the blue shirt** onaj u plavoj košulji *[oo plavoy koshoolyee]*

onion luk *[look]*

only samo; **only one** samo jedan *[yedan]*; **only once** samo jednom *[yednom]*; **it's only 9 o'clock** tek je 9 sati *[ye devet satee]*; **I've only just arrived** tek sam stigao *[steegao]*

open (*adjective*) otvoren; **when do you open?** kad otvarate?; **in the open** (*in open air*) napolju *[napolyoo]*; **it won't open** neće da se otvori *[neche da se otvoree]*

opening times radno vrijeme *[vryeme]*

open top (*car*) kabriolet *[kabreeolet]*

opera opera

operation (*med*) operacija *[operatseeya]*

operator (*telephone*) (*woman*) telefonistkinja *[telefoneestkeenya]*; (*man*) telefonista *[telefoneesta]*

opportunity prilika *[preeleeka]*

opposite: opposite the church prekoputa crkve *[prekopoota tsurkve]*; **it's directly opposite** tačno prekoputa *[tachno]*

oppressive (*heat*) težak *[tejak]*

optician optičar *[opteechar]*

optimistic optimistički *[opteemeesteechkee]*

optional opcionalan *[optseeonalan]*

or ili *[eelee]*

orange (*fruit*) narandža *[narandja]*; (*colour*) narandžast *[narandjast]*

orange juice (*fresh*) sok od narandže *[narandje]*; (*fizzy, diluted*) oranžada *[oranjada]*

orchestra orkestar

order: could we order now? (*in restaurant*) možemo li sada naručiti? *[mojemo lee sada naroocheetee]*; **I've already ordered** već sam naručio *[vech sam naroocheeo]*; **I didn't order that** nisam to naručio *[neesam]*; **it's out of order** (*lift etc*) u kvaru je *[oo kvaroo ye]*

ordinary običan *[obeechan]*

organization (*company*) organizacija *[organeezatseeya]*

organize organizirati *[organeezeeratee]*; **could you organize it?** da li biste mogli to organizirati? *[lee beeste moglee]*

original (*adjective*) originalan *[oreegeenalan]*; **is it an original?** je li original? *[ye lee]*

ornament ukras *[ookras]*

ostentatious raskošan *[raskoshan]*

other drugi *[droogee]*; **the other waiter** drugi konobar; **the other one** onaj drugi *[oni]*; **do you have any others?** imate li drugih? *[eemate lee droogeen]*; **some other time, thanks** drugi put, hvala *[poot nvala]*

otherwise inače *[eenache]*

ouch! jao! *[yao]*

ought: he ought to be here soon uskoro treba stići *[ooskoro treba steechee]*

ounce *see page 121*

our: our hotel naš hotel *[nash hotel]*; **our suitcases** naši koferi *[nashee koferee]*; *see page 109*

ours naš *[nash]*; **that's ours** to je naše *[ye]*; *see page 112*

out: he's out izišao je *[eezeeshao ye]*; **get out!** izlazite! *[eezlazeete]*; **I'm out of money** nemam novca; **a few kilometres out of town** nekoliko kilometara izvan grada *[nekoleeko keelometara eezvan grada]*

outboard (**motor**) vanbrodski *[vanbrodskee]*

outdoors napolju *[napolyoo]*

outlet (*elec*) izvod

outside vani *[vanee]*; **can we sit outside?** možemo li sjediti vani?

[moJemo lee syedeetee]
outskirts: on the outskirts of ... na periferiji ... *[pereefereeyee]*
oven pećnica *[pechneetsa]*
over: over here ovdje *[ovdye]*; **over there** tamo; **over 100** preko 100; **I'm burnt all over** sav sam izgorio *[eezgoreeo]*; **the holiday's over** odmor je prošao *[ye proshao]*
overcharge: you've overcharged me previše ste mi naplatili *[preveeshe ste mee naplateelee]*
overcoat ogrtač *[ogurtach]*
overcooked *(S)* prekuvan *[prekoovan]*; *(C)* prekuhan
overexposed *(photograph)* preosvijetljen *[preosvyetlyen]*
overheat: it's overheating *(car)* pre-

grijava se *[pregreeyava]*
overland *(travel)* kopneni *[kopnenee]*
overlook: overlooking the sea s pogledom na more
overnight *(travel)* noćni *[nochnee]*
oversleep: I overslept zaspao sam
overtake preticati *[preteetsatee]*
overweight pretežak *[preteJak]*
owe: how much do I owe you? koliko vam dugujem? *[koleeko vam doogooyem]*
own: my own ... moj vlastiti ... *[moy vlasteetee]*; **are you on your own?** da li ste sami? *[lee ste samee]*; **I'm on my own** sam sam
owner vlasnik *[vlasneek]*
oyster kamenica *[kameneetsa]*

P

pack: a pack of cigarettes kutija cigareta *[kooteeya tseegareta]*; **I'll go and pack** idem se spakovati *[eedem se spakovatee]*
package *(at post office etc)* paket
package holiday turistički aranžman *[tooreesteechkee aranJman]*
package tour paket aranžman *[paket aranJman]*
packed lunch spakovani ručak *[spakovanee roochak]*
packed out: the place was packed out bilo je prepuno *[beelo ye prepoono]*
packet paket; **a packet of cigarettes** kutija cigareta *[kooteeya tseegareta]*
paddle *(noun)* veslo
padlock *(noun)* katanac *[katanats]*
page *(of book)* strana; **could you page Mr ...?** da li biste mogli pozvati gospodina ... preko razglasa? *[lee beeste moglee pozvatee gospodeena]*
pain bol *(f)*; **I have a pain here** ovdje me boli *[ovdye me bolee]*
painful bolan
painkillers sredstvo za umirenje bolova *[sredstvo za oomeerenye bolova]*
paint *(noun)* boja *[boya]*; **I'm going to do some painting** *(artist)* malo ću

slikati *[malo choo sleekatee]*
paintbrush *(artist's)* kist *[keest]*
painting slika *[sleeka]*
pair: a pair of ... par ...
pajamas pidžama *[peedjama]*
Pakistan Pakistan *[pakeestan]*
Pakistani *(adjective)* pakistanski *[pakeestanskee]*; *(man)* Pakistanac *[pakeestanats]*; *(woman)* Pakistanka *[pakeestanka]*
pal prijatelj *[preeyatel-yuh]*
palace *(S)* palata; *(C)* palača *[palacha]*
pale blijed *[blyed]*; **pale blue** svijetlo plav *[svyetlo]*
palm tree palma
palpitations palpitacije *[palpeetatseeye]*
pancake palačinka *[palacheenka]*
panic: don't panic ne paničarite *[paneechareete]*
panties gaćice *[gacheetse]*
pants *(trousers)* *(S)* pantalone; *(C)* hlače *[Hlache]*; *(underpants)* gaće *[gache]*
panty girdle mider-gaćice *[meedergacheetse]*
pantyhose hulahopke *[hoolahopke]*
paper papir *[papeer]*; *(newspaper)* novine *[noveene]*; **a piece of paper** komad papira *[komad papeera]*

paper handkerchiefs papirnate maramice *[papeernate marameetse]*
paraffin petrolej *[petrolay]*
parallel: parallel to ... paralelan sa ...
parasol suncobran *[soontsobran]*
parcel paket
pardon (me)? (*didn't understand*) molim? *[moleem]*
parents: my parents moji roditelji
[moyee rodeetelyee]
parents-in-law (*man's*) tast i tašta *[ee
tashta]*; (*woman's*) svekar i svekrva
[svekar ee svekurva]
park (*noun*) park; **where can I park?**
gdje mogu parkirati? *[gdye mogoo
parkeeratee]*; **there's nowhere to
park** nema se gdje parkirati *[gdye]*
parka parka
parking lights poziciona svjetla
[pozeetseeona svyetla]
parking lot parkiralište *[parkeera-
leeshte]*
**parking place: there's a parking
place!** eno mjesta za parkiranje! *[eno
myesta za parkeeranye]*
part (*noun*) dio (*m*) *[deeo]*
partner (*boyfriend, girlfriend etc*)
partner; (*in business*) ortak
party (*group*) grupa *[groopa]*;
(*celebration*) zabava *[zabava]*; **let's
have a party** priredimo zabavu
[preeredeemo]
pass (*in mountains*) klanac *[klanats]*;
(*verb: overtake*) preteći *[pretechee]*; **he
passed out** onesvijestio se
[onesvyesteeo]; **he made a pass at
me** pokušao mi se udvarati
[pokooshao mee se oodvaratee]
passable (*road*) prohodan
passenger putnik *[pootneek]*
passport pasoš *[pasosh]*
past: in the past u prošlosti *[oo
proshlostee]*; **just past the bank**
odmah pored banke *[odmaн]*
pastry (*dough*) tijesto *[tyesto]*; (*small
cake*) kolač *[kolach]*
**patch: could you put a patch on
this?** da li biste mogli ovo zakrpiti?
[lee beeste moglee ovo zakurpeetee]
pâté pašteta *[pashteta]*
path staza
patient: be patient budite strpljivi
[boodeete sturplyeevee]
patio terasa

pattern uzorak *[oozorak]*; **a dress
pattern** kroj za haljinu *[kroy za
halyeenoo]*
paunch trbuh *[turbooh]*
pavement (*sidewalk*) pločnik
[plochneek]
pay (*verb*) platiti *[plateetee]*; **can I
pay, please?** mogu li platiti, molim?
[mogoo lee ... moleem]; **it's already
paid for** za mene je već plaćeno *[ye
vech placheno]*; **I'll pay for this** ja
ću platiti ovo *[ya choo ...]*
pay phone telefonska govornica
[telefonska govorneetsa]
peace and quiet mir i tišina *[meer ee
teesheena]*
peach breskva
peanuts kikiriki *[keekeereekee]*
pear kruška *[krooshka]*
pearl biser *[beeser]*
peas grašak *[grashak]*
peculiar čudan *[choodan]*
pedal (*noun*) pedala
pedalo bicikl za vodu *[beetseekl za
vodoo]*
pedestrian pješak *[pyeshak]*
pedestrian crossing pješački prelaz
[pyeshachkee prelaz]
pedestrian precinct pješačka zona
[pyeshachka]
pee: I need to go for a pee piški mi
se *[peeshkee mee]*
peeping Tom voajer *[vo-iyer]*
peg (*washing*) štipaljka *[shteepalyka]*;
(*tent*) kočić *[kocheech]*
pen pero; **do you have a pen?** imate
li pero? *[eemate lee]*
pencil olovka
penfriend prijatelj za dopisivanje
[preeyatel-yuh za dopeeseevanye];
shall we be penfriends? hoćemo li
se dopisivati? *[hochemo lee se
dopeeseevatee]*
penicillin penicilin *[peneetseeleen]*
penis penis *[penees]*
penknife džepni nož *[djepnee noj]*
pen pal prijatelj za dopisivanje
[preeyatel-yuh za dopeeseevanye]
pensioner penzioner *[penzeeoner]*
people narod; **a lot of people** mnogo
naroda; **the Croatian people**
hrvatski narod *[нurvatskee]*
pepper (*spice*) biber *[beeber]*; **green
pepper** zelena paprika *[papreeka]*;

red pepper crvena paprika
[tsurvena]
peppermint (sweet) pepermint
[pepermeent]
per: per night za noć [noch]; **how
much per hour?** pošto za sat?
[poshto]
per cent posto
perfect savršen [savurshen]
perfume parfem
perhaps možda [moJda]
period (of time) period [pereeod];
(menstruation) menstruacija
[menstrooatseeya]
perm trajna [trɪna]
permit (noun) dozvola
person osoba
pessimistic pesimističan [peseemeest-
eechan]
petrol benzin [benzeen]
petrol can kanta za benzin [benzeen]
petrol station benzinska stanica
[benzeenska staneetsa]
petrol tank (in car) rezervoar za
benzin [rezervo-ar za benzeen]
pharmacy (S) apoteka; (C) ljekarna
[lyekarna]
phone see **telephone**
photogenic fotogeničan [fotogen-
eechan]
photograph (noun) fotografija
[fotografeeya]; **would you take a
photograph of us?** da li biste nas
uslikali? [lee beeste nas oosleekalee]
photographer fotograf
phrase: a useful phrase koristan izraz
[koreestan eezraz]
phrasebook rječnik fraza [ryechneek]
pianist klavirist [klaveereest]
piano klavir [klaveer]
pickpocket džeparoš [djeparosh]
pick up: where can I pick them up?
(clothes from laundry etc) kad ih mogu
podići? [eeн mogoo podeechee]; **will
you come and pick me up?** hoćete li
doći po mene? [hochete lee dochee]
picnic (noun) piknik [peekneek]
picture slika [sleeka]
pie (meat, fruit) pita [peeta]
piece komad; **a piece of ...** komad ...
(+G)
pig prase
pigeon golub [goloob]
piles (medical) hemoroidi [hemoro-

eedee]
pile-up (crash) višestruki sudar
[veeshestrookee soodar]
pill pilula [peeloola]; **I'm on the pill**
uzimam pilule za kontracepciju
[oozeemem peeloole za
kontratseptseeyoo]
pillarbox poštansko sanduče
[poshtansko sandooche]
pillow jastuk [yastook]
pillow case jastučnica [yastooch-
neetsa]
pin (noun) pribadača [preebadacha]
pineapple ananas
pineapple juice sok od ananasa
pink ružičast [rooJeechast]
pint see page 121
pipe (for smoking) lula [loola]; (for
water) cijev [tsyev]
pipe cleaner pribor za čišćenje lule
[preebor za cheeshchenye loole]
pipe tobacco (S) duvan za lulu
[doovan za looloo]; (C) duhan za lulu
[doohan]
pity: it's a pity šteta [shteta]
pizza pica [peetsa]
place (noun) mjesto [myesto]; **is this
place taken?** je li ovo mjesto
zauzeto? [ye lee ovo ... zaoozeto];
would you keep my place for me?
hoćete li mi čuvati mjesto? [hochete
lee mee choovatee]; **at my place** kod
mene; **at Marko's place** kod Marka
place mat podmetač [podmetach]
plain (food) jednostavan [yednostavan];
(no pattern) jednobojan [yednoboyan]
plane avion [aveeon]
plant biljka [beelyka]
plaster cast gips [geeps]
plastic plastičan [plasteechan]
plastic bag najlon-kesa [nɪylon-kesa]
plate (S) tanjir [tanyeer]; (C) tanjur
[tanyoor]
platform peron; **which platform,
please?** koji peron, molim vas?
[koyee ... moleem]
play (verb) igrati se [eegratee]; (theatre)
kazališni komad [kazaleeshnee]
playboy plejboj [playboy]
playground igralište [eegraleeshte]
pleasant prijatan [preeyatan]
please molim [moleem]; **yes please** da
molim; **could you please ...?** da li
biste mogli molim vas ...? [lee beeste

moglee]
pleasure: with pleasure sa zado-
voljstvom *[zadovolystvom]*
plenty: plenty of ... mnogo ... (+G);
that's plenty, thanks dosta je, hvala
[dosta ye Hvala*]*
pleurisy pleuritis *[pleooreetees]*
pliers kliješta *[klyeshta]*
plonk (*wine*) vino *[veeno]*; (*cheap wine*)
jevtino vino *[yevteeno]*
plug (*elec*) utikač *[ooteekach]*; (*for car*)
svjećica *[svyecheetsa]*; (*in sink*) čep
[chep]
plughole otvor za odliv vode *[odleev]*
plum šljiva *[shlyeeva]*
plumber vodoinstalater *[vodo-
eenstalater]*
plus plus *[ploos]*
p.m. popodne; **at 2 p.m.** u 2 popodne
[oo]; **at 10 p.m.** u 10 popodne; *see
page 119*
pneumonia upala pluća *[oopala
ploocha]*
poached egg poširano jaje
[posheerano yIye]
pocket džep *[djep]*; **in my pocket** u
mom džepu *[oo mom djepoo]*
pocketbook (*handbag*) tašna *[tashna]*
pocketknife džepni nož *[djepnee noJ]*
podiatrist pediker *[pedeeker]*
point: could you point to it? da li biste mogli to pokazati? *[lee beeste
moglee to pokazatee]*; **four point six**
četiri zarez šest; **there's no point**
nema svrhe *[svurhe]*
points (*in car*) platine *[plateene]*
poisonous otrovan
police milicija *[meeleetseeya]*; **call the
police!** zovite miliciju! *[zoveete
meeleetseeyoo]*
policeman milicajac *[meeleetsIyats]*
police station milicijska stanica
[meeleetseeyska staneetsa]
polish (*noun*) laštilo *[lashteelo]*; **will
you polish my shoes?** hoćete li mi
očistiti cipele? *[hochete lee mee
ocheesteetse tseepele]*
polite učtiv *[oochteev]*
politician političar *[poleeteechar]*
politics politika *[poleeteeka]*
polluted zagađen *[zagadjen]*
pond jezero *[yezero]*
pony poni (*m*) *[ponee]*
pool (*for swimming*) bazen; (*game*) bili-

jar *[beeleeyar]*
pool table sto za bilijar *[beeleeyar]*
poor (*not rich*) siromašan
[seeromashan]; (*quality*) loš *[losh]*;
poor old Nikola! jadni Nikola!
[yadnee neekola]
Pope papa (*m*)
pop music pop muzika *[moozeeka]*
popsicle (*tm*) sladoled na štapiću
[sladoled na shtapeechoo]
pop singer pop pjevač *[pyevach]*
popular popularan *[popoolaran]*
population stanovništvo *[stanov-
neeshtvo]*
pork svinjetina *[sveenyeteena]*
port luka *[looka]*; (*drink*) porto
porter (*in hotel*) portir *[porteer]*; (*at
station etc*) nosač *[nosach]*
portrait portret
Portugal (*S*) Portugalija
[portoogaleeya]; (*C*) Portugal
poser (*phoney person*) pozer
posh otmjen *[otmyen]*
possibility mogućnost (*f*)
[mogoochnost]
possible moguć *[mogooch]*; **is it
possible to ...?** je li moguće ...? *[ye
lee mogooche]*; **as ... as possible** što
... moguće *[shto]*; **as much as
possible** što je više moguče *[ye
veeshe]*
post (*noun: mail*) pošta *[poshta]*; **could
you post this for me?** da li biste mi
ovo mogli predati na poštu? *[lee
beeste mee ovo moglee predatee na
poshtoo]*
postbox poštansko sanduče
[poshtansko sandooche]
postcard razglednica *[razgledneetsa]*
poster plakat
poste restante poste restant
post office pošta *[poshta]*
pot lonac *[lonats]*; **a pot of tea for
two** lončić čaja za dvoje *[loncheech
chIya za dvoye]*; **pots and pans** lonci
i šerpe *[lontsee ee sherpe]*
potato (*S*) krompir *[krompeer]*; (*C*)
krumpir *[kroompeer]*
potato chips čips *[cheeps]*
potato salad (*S*) krompir salata
[krompeer salata]; (*C*) krumpir salata
[kroompeer]
pottery (*S*) grnčarija *[gurnchareeya]*;
(*C*) keramika *[kerameeka]*; (*workshop*)

pound 53 push-chair

(S) grnčarska radionica *[gurncharska
radeeoneetsa]*; (C) keramičarska
radiona *[kerameecharska radeeona]*
pound (*money, weight*) funta *[foonta]*;
see page 121
pour: it's pouring down pljušti
[plyooshtee]
powder (*for face*) puder *[pooder]*
powdered milk mlijeko u prahu (*n*)
[mlyeko oo prahoo]
power cut prekid struje *[prekeed
strooye]*
power point šteker *[shteker]*
power station električna centrala
[elektreechna tsentrala]
practise, practice: I need to practise
treba da vježbam *[treba da vyeɪbam]*
pram dječja kolica *[dyechya koleetsa]*
prawn cocktail salata òd račića
[salata od racheecha]
prawns račići *[racheechee]*
prefer: I prefer white wine više volim bijelo vino *[veeshe voleem byelo
veeno]*
preferably: preferably not tomorrow
radije ne sutra *[radeeye ne sootra]*
pregnant trudna *[troodna]*
prescription (*for chemist*) recept
[retsept]
present (*gift*) poklon; here's a present
for you ovo je poklon za vas *[ovo
ye]*; at present sada
president predsjednik *[predsyedneek]*
press: can you press these? možete li
ih ispeglati? *[moɪete lee eeн
eespeglatee]*
pretty ljepuškast *[lyepooshkast]*; it's
pretty expensive prilično je skupo
[preeleechno ye skoopo]
price cijena *[tsyena]*
prickly heat osip *[oseep]*
priest (S) sveštenik *[sveshteneek]*; (C)
svećenik *[svecheneek]*
prime minister premijer *[premeeyer]*
print (*noun: picture*) grafika *[grafeeka]*
printed matter tiskanica *[teeskan-
eetsa]*
priority (*driving*) prednost (*f*)
prison zatvor
private privatan *[preevatan]*; private
bath (S) privatno kupatilo *[preevatno
koopateelo]*; (C) privatna kupaonica
[preevatna koopaoneetsa]
prize nagrada

probably vjerojatno *[vyero-yatno]*
problem problem; I have a problem
imam problem *[eemam]*; no
problem! nema problema!
product proizvod *[proeezvod]*
program(me) (*noun*) program
promise: I promise obećavam
[obechavam]; is that a promise?
obećavate li? *[obechavate lee]*
pronounce: how do you pronounce
this? kako ovo izgovarate?
[eezgovarate]; I can't pronounce it
ne mogu izgovoriti *[mogoo
eezgovoreetee]*
properly: it's not repaired properly
nije dobro popravljeno *[neeye dobro
popravlyeno]*
prostitute prostitutka *[prosteetootka]*
protect štititi *[shteeteetee]*
protection factor faktor zaštite
[zashteete]
protein remover (*for contact lenses*) (S)
sredstvo za čišćenje kontaktnih sočiva *[sredstvo za cheesh-chenye
кontaktneeн socheeva]*; (C) sredstvo
za čišćenje kontaktnih leća *[lecha]*
Protestant protestant
proud ponosan
prunes (S) suve šljive *[soove shlyeeve]*;
(C) suhe šljive *[soohe]*
public (*adjective*) javni *[yavnee]*
public convenience javni toalet
[yavnee to-alet]
public holiday državni praznik
[durɪavnee prazneek]
pudding (*dessert*) dezert
pull vući *[voochee]*; he pulled straight
out without indicating krenuo je
bez migavca *[krenoo-o ye bez
meegavtsa]*
pullover pulover *[poolover]*
pump (*noun*) pumpa *[poompa]*
punctual (S) tačan *[tachan]*; (C) točan
puncture (*noun*) probušena guma
[probooshena gooma]
pure (*silk etc*) čist *[cheest]*
purple ljubičast *[lyoobeechast]*
purse (*for money*) novčanik
[novchaneek]; (*handbag*) tašna
[tashna]
push gurati *[gooratee]*; don't push in!
ne gurajte se preko reda! *[goorɪte]*
push-chair kolica za bebu *[koleetsa za
beboo]*

put staviti *[staveetee]*; **where did you put ...?** gdje ste stavili ...? *[gdye ste staveelee]*; **where can I put ...?** gdje mogu staviti ...? *[mogoo]*; **could you put the lights on?** da li biste upalili svijetlo? *[lee beeste oopaleelee svyetlo]*; **will you put the light out?** hoćete li ugasiti svijetlo? *[hochete lee*

oogaseetee]; **you've put the price up** podigli ste cijene *[podeeglee ste tsyene]*; **could you put us up for the night?** da li bismo mogli kod vas prenoćiti? *[li beesmo moglee kod vas prenocheetee]*
pyjamas pidžama *[peedjama]*

Q

quality kvalitet *[kvaleetet]*; **poor quality** loš kvalitet *[losh]*; **good quality** dobar kvalitet
quarantine karantena
quart *see page 121*
quarter četvrt *[chetvurt]*; **quarter of an hour** četvrt sata
quay kej *[kay]*
quayside: on the quayside na keju *[kayoo]*
question pitanje *[peetanye]*; **that's out of the question** ni govora *[nee]*
queue *(noun)* red; **there was a big queue** bio je veliki red *[beeo ye*

veleekee]
quick brz *[burz]*; **that was quick** to je bilo brzo *[ye beelo burzo]*; **which is the quickest way?** koje je najbrži put? *[koye ye nıburjee poot]*
quickly brzo *[burzo]*
quiet *(place, hotel)* tih *[teeн]*; **be quiet!** tišina! *[teesheena]*
quinine kinin *[keeneen]*
quite: it's quite different sasvim je drukčije *[sasveem ye drookcheeye]*; **I'm not quite sure** nisam sasvim siguran *[neesam ... seegooran]*

R

rabbit kunić *[kooneech]*
rabies bjesnilo *[byesneelo]*
race *(for horses, cars)* trka *[turka]*; **I'll race you there** tamo ćemo vidjeti ko će stići prvi *[tamo chemo veedyetee ko che steechee purvee]*
racket *(sport)* reket
radiator *(of car)* hladnjak *[нladnyak]*; *(in room)* radijator *[radeeyator]*
radio radio *(m)* *[radeeo]*; **on the radio** na radiju *[radeeyoo]*
rag *(for cleaning)* krpa *[kurpa]*
rail: by rail željeznicom *[jelyez-neetsom]*
railroad, railway željeznica *[jelyez-neetsa]*
railroad crossing ukrštanje u nivou *[ookurshtanye oo neevo-oo]*

rain *(noun)* kiša *[keesha]*; **in the rain** na kiši *[keeshee]*; **it's raining** pada kiša
rain boots gumene čizme *[goomene cheezme]*
raincoat kišni mantil *[keeshnee manteel]*
rape *(noun)* silovanje *[seelovanye]*
rare *(object etc)* rijedak *[ryedak]*; *(steak)* manje pečen *[manye pechen]*
rash *(on skin)* osip *[oseep]*
raspberry malina *[maleena]*
rat *(S)* pacov *[patsov]*; *(C)* štakor *[shtakor]*
rate *(for money)* kurs *[koors]*; **what's the rate for the pound?** koji je kurs za funtu? *[koyee ye koors za foontoo]*; **what are your rates?** kakve

su vam cijene? *[kakve soo vam
tsyene]*
rather: it's rather late prilično je
kasno *[preeleechno ye]*; **I'd rather ...**
radije bih ... *[radeeye beeн]*; **I'd
rather have peas** radije bih volio
grašak *[voleeo grashak]*
raw (*meat*) prijesan *[pryesan]*
razor (*dry*) britva *[breetva]*; (*electric*)
aparat za brijanje *[breeyanye]*
razor blades žileti *[Jeeletee]*
reach: within easy reach na dohvatu
[doнvatoo]
read čitati *[cheetatee]*; **I can't read it**
ne mogu to pročitati *[mogoo to
procheetatee]*; **could you read it out?**
da li biste to mogli glasno pročitati?
[lee beeste to moglee glasno]
ready gotov; **when will it be ready?**
kada će biti gotovo? *[kada che
beetee]*; **I'll go and get ready** idem
da se spremim *[eedem da se
spremeem]*; **I'm not ready yet** još
nisam spreman *[yosh neesam]*
real stvaran
really stvarno; **I really must go**
stvarno moram ići *[moram eechee]*;
is it really necessary? je li to
stvarno potrebno? *[ye lee]*
realtor trgovac nekretninama
[turgovats nekretneenama]
rear: at the rear pozadi *[pozadee]*;
rear wheels stražnji točkovi
[straлnyee tochkovee]
rearview mirror retrovizor
[retroveezor]
reasonable (*prices etc*) umjeren
[oomyeren]; **be reasonable** budite
razumni *[boodeete razoomnee]*
receipt priznanica *[preeznaneetsa]*
recently nedavno
reception (*hotel*) recepcija
[retseptseeya]; (*for guests*) prijem
[preeyem]
reception desk recepcija *[retsept-
seeya]*
receptionist (*man*) službenik na recepciji *[slooлbeneek na retseptseeyee]*;
(*woman*) službenica na recepciji
[slooлbeneetsa]
recipe recept *[retsept]*; **can you give
me the recipe for this?** možete li mi
dati recept za ovo? *[moлete lee mee
datee ...]*

recognize prepoznati *[prepoznatee]*; **I
didn't recognize it** nisam prepoznao
[neesam]
**recommend: could you recommend
...?** da li biste mogli preporučiti ...?
[lee beeste moglee preporoocheetee]
record (*music*) ploča *[plocha]*
record player gramofon
red crven *[tsurven]*
red wine crno vino *[tsurno veeno]*
reduction (*price*) sniženje *[sneeлenye]*
refreshing osvježavajući *[osvyeлavı-
yoochee]*
refrigerator frižider *[freeлeeder]*
refund povraćay novca *[povrachay
novtsa]*; **do I get a refund?** hoće li
mi biti vraćen novac? *[hoche lee mee
beetee vrachen novats]*
region kraj *[krı]*
registered: by registered mail prepo-
ručeno *[preporoocheno]*
registration number registarski broj
[regeestarskee broy]
relative: my relatives moji rođaci
[moyee rodjatsee]
relaxing: it's very relaxing to je veoma relaksirajuće *[ye veoma
relakseerıyoochee]*
reliable pouzdan *[po-oozdan]*
religion religija *[releegeeya]*
remains ostaci *[ostatsee]*
remember: I don't remember ne sjećam se *[syecham]*; **I remember**
sjećam se; **do you remember?** sjećate
li se? *[syechate lee]*
remote (*village etc*) udaljen *[oodalyen]*
rent (*noun*) najamnina *[nıyamneena]*;
(*for apartment*) stanarina *[stanareena]*;
(*verb: car etc*) iznajmiti *[eeznımeetee]*;
I'd like to rent a bike/car želio bih
iznajmiti bicikl/kola *[Jeleeo beeн]*
rental car kolaza iznajmljivanje
[kolaza eeznımlyeevanye]
repair popraviti *[popraveetee]*; **can
you repair it?** možete li popraviti?
[moлete lee]
repeat ponoviti *[ponoveetee]*; **could
you repeat that?** da li biste mogli to
ponoviti? *[lee beeste moglee]*
representative (*noun: of company*)
predstavnik *[predstavneek]*
request (*noun*) molba
rescue (*verb*) spasiti *[spaseetee]*
reservation rezervacija *[rezervats-*

eeya]; **I have a reservation** imam
rezervaciju *[eemam rezervatseeyoo]*
reserve (S) rezervisati *[rezerveesatee]*;
(C) rezervirati *[rezerveeratee]*; **I
reserved a room in the name of ...**
rezervisao/rezervirao sam sobu na
ime ... *[rezerveesao/rezerveerao sam
soboo na eeme]*; **can I reserve a
table for tonight?** mogu li
rezervisati/rezervirati stol za večeras?
*[mogoo lee rezerveesatee/
rezerveeratee stol za vecheras]*
rest *(repose)* **odmor**; *(remainder)*
ostatak; **I need a rest** potreban mi je
odmor *[potreban mee ye]*; **the rest of
the group** ostatak grupe *[groope]*
restaurant restoran
rest room toalet
retired: I'm retired u penziji sam *[oo
penzeeyee]*
return: a return to Dubrovnik
povratnu (kartu) za Dubrovnik
[povratnoo (kartoo) za doobrovneek];
I'll return it tomorrow sutra ću
vratiti *[sootra choo vrateetee]*
reverse charge call telefonski razgovor na račun broja koji se zove
*[telefonskee razgovor na rachoon
broya koyee se zove]*
reverse gear brzina za vožnju unazad
[burzeena za voJnyoo oonazad]
revolting odvratan
rheumatism reumatizam *[re-
oomateezam]*
rib rebro; **a cracked rib** slomljeno rebro *[slomlyeno]*
ribbon *(for hair)* vrpca *[vurptsa]*
rice (S) pirinač *[peereenach]*; (C) riža
[reeJa]
rich *(person)* bogat; *(food)* mastan; **it's
too rich** prezasitno je *[prezaseetno
ye]*
**ride: can you give me a ride into
town?** možete li me povesti do grada? *[moJete lee me povestee do
grada]*; **thanks for the ride** hvala na
vožnji *[Hvala na voJnyee]*
ridiculous: that's ridiculous to je
smiješno *[ye smyeshno]*
right *(correct)* ispravan *[eespravan]*;
(not left) desno; **you're right** u pravu
ste *[oo pravoo ste]*; **you were right**
bili ste u pravu *[beelee]*; **that's right**
tačno *[tachno]*; **that can't be right** to

ne može biti tačno *[moJe beetee]*;
right! dobro!; **is this the right road
for ...?** je li ovo pravi put za ...? *[ye
lee ovo pravee poot]*; **on the right**
desno; **turn right** skrenite desno
[skreneete]; **not just right now** ne
sada
right-hand drive vozilo s volanom na
desnoj strani *[vozeelo s volanom na
desnoy stranee]*
ring *(on finger)* prsten *[pursten]*; **I'll
ring you** telefonirat ću vam
[telefoneerat choo]
ring road kružni put *[krooJnee poot]*
ripe *(fruit)* zreo
rip-off: it's a rip-off to je prevara
[ye]; **rip-off prices** previsoke cijene
[preveesoke tsyene]
risky riskantan *[reeskantan]*; **it's too
risky** previše je riskantno *[preveeshe
ye reeskantno]*
river rijeka *[ryeka]*; **by the river**
pored rijeke *[ryeke]*
road put *[poot]*; **is this the road to
...?** je li ovo put za ...? *[ye lee ovo]*;
further down the road niže putem
[neeJe pootem]
road accident saobraćajna nesreća
[saobrachJna nesrecha]
road hog siledžija za volanom
[seeledjeeya]
road map putna karta *[pootna]*
roadside by the roadside kraj puta
[krJ poota]
roadsign saobraćajni znak
[saobrachJnee]
roadwork(s) radovi na putu *[radovee
na pootoo]*
roast beef goveđe pečenje *[govedje
pechenye]*
rob: I've been robbed pokraden sam
robe *(housecoat)* kućni mantil
[koochnee manteel]
rock *(stone)* stijena *[styena]*; **on the
rocks** *(with ice)* s ledom
rocky *(coast etc)* stjenovit *[styenoveet]*
roll *(bread)* žemlja *[Jemlya]*
Roman Catholic rimokatolik
[reemokatoleek]
romance romansa
Romania (S) Rumunija
[roomooneeya]; (C) Rumunjska
[roomoon-yuh-ska]
Romanian *(adjective, language)* ru-

munjski *[roomoon-yuh-skee]*; (*man*)
Rumunj *[roomoon-yuh]*; (*woman*)
Rumunjka *[roomoon-yuh-ka]*; **the**
Romanians Rumunji *[roomoonyee]*
Rome: when in Rome ... kad ste u
Rimu ... *[oo reemoo]*
roof krov; **on the roof** na krovu
[krovoo]
roof rack krovni prtljažnik *[krovnee*
purtlyaɹneek]
room soba; **do you have a room?**
imate li sobu? *[eemate lee soboo]*; **a**
room for two people soba za dvije
osobe *[dveeye osobe]*; **a room for**
three nights soba za tri noći *[tree*
nochee]; **in my room** u mojoj sobi
[oo moyoy sobee]; **there's no room**
nema mjesta *[myesta]*
room service posluga u sobi
[poslooga oo sobee]
rope uže *[ooɹe]*
rose ruža *[rooɹa]*
rosé (*wine*) ružica *[rooɹeetsa]*
rotary kružni tok *[krooɹnee]*
rough (*sea*) uzburkan *[oozboorkan]*;
(*crossing*) neugodan *[ne-oogodan]*; **the**
engine sounds a bit rough motor
zvuči malo ispresjecano *[zvoochee*
malo eespresyetsano]; **I've been**
sleeping rough spavam na
otvorenom
roughly (*approximately*) otprilike
[otpreeleeke]
roulette rulet *[roolet]*
round (*adjective*) okrugao *[okroogao]*;
it's my round ja plaćam ovu rundu
[ya placham ovoo roondoo]
roundabout (*traffic*) kružni tok
[krooɹnee]

round-trip: a round-trip ticket to ...
povratnu kartu za ... *[povratnoo*
kartoo]
route pravac *[pravats]*; **what's the best**
route? koji je najbolji pravac? *[koyee*
ye ntbolyee]
rowboat, rowing boat čamac na vesla
[chamats]
rubber (*material*) guma *[gooma]*;
(*eraser*) gumica za brisanje
[goomeetsa za breesanye]
rubber band lastiš *[lasteesh]*
rubbish (*S*) đubre *[djoobre]*; (*C*)
smeće *[smeche]*; **that's rubbish!**
(*nonsense*) to je glupost! *[ye gloopost]*
rucksack ruksak *[rooksak]*
rude neuljudan *[neoolyoodan]*; **he was**
very rude bio je veoma neuljudan
[beeo ye veoma]
rug ćilim *[cheeleem]*
ruins ruševine *[roosheveene]*
rum rum *[room]*
rum and coke rum i koka-kola *[room*
ee]
run (*person*) trčati *[turchatee]*; **I go**
running redovito trčim *[redoveeto*
turcheem]; **quick, run!** brzo, trk!
[burzo turk]; **how often do the buses**
run? kako su česti autobusi? *[soo*
chestee aootoboosee]; **he's been run**
over pregažen je *[pregaɹen ye]*; **I've**
run out of gas/petrol ostao sam bez
benzina *[benzeena]*
rupture (*medical*) kila *[keela]*
Russia Rusija *[Rooseeya]*
Russian (*adjective, language*) ruski
[rooskee]; (*man*) Rus *[roos]*; (*woman*)
Ruskinja *[rooskeenya]*

S

saccharine saharin *[sahareen]*
sad tužan *[tooɹan]*
saddle (*for bike, horse*) sedlo
safe (*not in danger*) siguran
[seegooran]; (*not dangerous*)
bezopasan; **will it be safe here?**
hoće li ovdje biti sigurno? *[hoche lee*
ovdye beetee seegoorno]; **is it safe to**

drink? je li bezopasno piti? *[ye lee*
bezopasno peetee]; **is it a safe beach**
for swimming? je li to sigurna plaža
za plivanje? *[ye lee to seegoorna*
plaɹa za pleevanye]; **could you put**
this in your safe? da li biste ovo
stavili u svoj sef? *[lee beeste ovo*
staveelee oo svoy]

safety pin ziherica *[zeehereetsa]*
sail (*noun*) jedro *[yedro]*; **can we go sailing?** možemo li na jedrenje? *[moJemo lee na yedrenye]*
sailboard daska za jedrenje *[yedrenye]*
sailboarding: I like sailboarding volim jedrenje na dasci *[voleem yedrenye na dastsee]*
sailor mornar
salad salata
salad cream majonez *[mIyonez]*
salad dressing preliv za salatu *[preleev za salatoo]*
sale: is it for sale? je li za prodaju? *[ye lee za prodIyoo]*; **it's not for sale** nije za prodaju *[neeye]*
sales clerk (*male*) trgovački pomoćnik *[turgovachkee pomochneek]*; (*female*) trgovačka pomoćnica *[turgovachka pomochneetsa]*
salmon losos
salt (*S*) so (*f*); (*C*) sol (*f*)
salty: it's too salty preslano je *[ye]*
same isti *[eestee]*; **one the same as this** još jedan ovakav *[yosh yedan]*; **the same again, please** ponovo isto, molim *[eesto, moleem]*; **have a good time — same to you** lijepo se provedite — vi takođe *[vee takodje]*; **it's all the same to me** meni je svejedno *[menee ye sveyedno]*; **thanks all the same** ipak hvala *[eepak Hvala]*
sand pijesak *[pyesak]*
sandals sandale; **a pair of sandals** par sandala
sandwich sendvič *[sendveech]*; **a chicken sandwich** sendvič sa piletinom *[peeleteenom]*
sandy pjeskovit *[pyeskoveet]*; **a sandy beach** pjeskovita plaža *[pyeskoveeta plaJa]*
sanitory napkin/towel higijenski uložak *[heegeeyenskee ooloJak]*
sarcastic sarkastičan *[sarkasteechan]*
sardines sardine *[sardeene]*
satisfactory zadovoljavajući *[zadovolyava-yoochee]*; **this is not satisfactory** ovo nije zadovoljavajuće *[ovo neeye zadovolyava-yooche]*
Saturday subota *[soobota]*
sauce umak *[oomak]*
saucepan (*S*) tiganj *[teegan-yuh]*; (*C*) lonac *[lonats]*

saucer tanjirić *[tanyeereech]*
sauna sauna *[saoona]*
sausage kobasica *[kobaseetsa]*
sauté potatoes (*S*) restani krompir *[restanee krompeer]*; (*C*) restani krumpir *[kroompeer]*
save (*life*) spasiti *[spaseetee]*
savo(u)ry slan
say: how do you say ... in Serbo-croat? kako se na srpskohrvatskom kaže ...? *[surpsko-Hurvatskom kaJe]*; **what did you say?** šta ste rekli? *[shta ste reklee]*; **what did he say?** šta je rekao? *[ye]*; **I said ...** rekao sam ...; **he said ...** rekao je ...; **I wouldn't say no** neću reći ne *[nechoo rechee]*
scald: he's scalded himself opario se *[opareeo]*
scarf (*for neck*) šal *[shal]*; (*for head*) marama
scarlet grimizan *[greemeezan]*
scenery pejzaž *[payzaJ]*
scent (*perfume*) miris *[meerees]*
schedule raspored
scheduled flight redovan let
school škola *[shkola]*; (*university*) univerzitet *[ooneeverzeetet]*; **I'm still at school** još idem u školu *[yosh eedem oo shkoloo]*
science (*S*) nauka *[naooka]*; (*C*) znanost (*f*)
scissors: a pair of scissors (*S*) makaze; (*C*) škare *[shkare]*
scooter (*motor scooter*) skuter *[skooter]*
scorching: it's really scorching (*weather*) zaista je strašno vruće *[zaeesta ye strashno vrooche]*
score: what's the score? kakav je rezultat? *[kakav ye rezooltat]*
scotch (*whisky*) škotski viski *[shkotskee veeskee]*
Scotch tape (*tm*) selotejp *[selotayp]*
Scotland Škotska *[shkotska]*
Scottish škotski *[shkotskee]*
scrambled eggs kajgana *[kIgana]*
scratch (*noun*) ogrebotina *[ogreboteena]*; **it's only a scratch** to je obična ogrebotina *[ye obeechna]*
scream (*verb*) vrisnuti *[vreesnootee]*
screw (*noun*) zavrtanj *[zavurtan-yuh]*
screwdriver odvrtač *[odvurtach]*
scrubbing brush (*for hands*) četka za ruke *[chetka za rooke]*; (*for floors*) četka za ribanje *[reebanye]*

scruffy otrcan *[oturtsan]*
scuba diving ronjenje *[ronyenye]*
sea more; **by the sea** kraj mora *[krɪ]*
sea air (S) morski vazduh *[morskee vazdooн]*; (C) morski zrak
seafood morski specijaliteti *[morskee spetseeyaleetetee]*
seafood restaurant riblji restoran *[reeblyee]*
seafront morska obala; **on the seafront** na morskoj obali *[morskoy obalee]*
seagull galeb
search (*verb*) tražiti *[traɪeetee]*; **I searched everywhere** svugdje sam tražio *[svoogdye sam traɪeeo]*
search party potraga
seashell morska školjka *[shkolyka]*
seasick: I feel seasick imam morsku bolest *[eemam morskoo]*; **I get seasick** dobijem morsku bolest *[dobeeyem]*
seaside: by the seaside kraj mora *[krɪ]*; **let's go to the seaside** hajdemo na more *[hɪdemo]*
season sezona; **in the high season** u punoj sezoni *[oo poonoy sezonee]*; **in the low season** van sezone
seasoning začin *[zacheen]*
seat sjedište *[syedeeshte]*; **is this anyone's seat?** je li ovo nečije sjedište? *[ye lee ovo necheeye syedeeshte]*
seat belt sigurnosni pojas *[seegoornosnee poyas]*; **do you have to wear a seat belt?** morali se staviti sigurnosni pojas? *[moralee se staveetee]*
sea urchin morski jež *[morskee yeɪ]*
seaweed morska trava
secluded osamljen *[osamlyen]*
second (*adjective*) drugi *[droogee]*; (*of time*) sekunda *[sekoonda]*; **just a second!** samo trenutak! *[trenootak]*; **can I have a second helping?** mogu li se po drugi put poslužiti? *[mogoo lee se po droogee poot poslooɪetee]*
second class drugi razred *[droogee]*
second-hand polovan
secret (*noun*) tajna *[tɪna]*
security check sigurnosna kontrola *[seegoornosna]*
sedative sedativ *[sedateev]*
see vidjeti *[veedyetee]*; **I didn't see it**

nisam vidio *[neesam veedeeo]*; **have you seen my husband?** jesti li vidjeli mog muža? *[yeste lee veedyelee mog mooɪa]*; **I saw him this morning** vidio sam ga jutros *[veedeeo sam ga yootroos]*; **can I see the manager?** mogu li razgovarati sa direktorom? *[mogoo lee razgovaratee sa deerektorom]*; **see you tonight!** vidimo se večeras! *[veedeemo se vecheras]*; **can I see?** mogu li vidjeti?; **oh, I see** o, shvaćam *[sнvacham]*; **will you see to it?** (*arrange it*) hoćete li se brinuti za to? *[hochete lee se breenootee]*
seldom rijetko *[ryetko]*
self-catering apartment stan
self-service samoposluga *[samoposlooga]*
sell prodavati *[prodavatee]*; **do you sell ...?** prodajete li ...? *[prodɪyete lee]*; **will you sell it to me?** hoćete li mi prodati? *[hochete lee mee prodatee]*
sellotape (*tm*) selotejp *[selotayp]*
send poslati *[poslatee]*; **I want to send this to England** želim poslati ovo u Englesku *[ɪeleem ... ovo oo engleskoo]*; **I'll have to send this food back** morat ću vratiti ovu hranu *[morat choo vrateetee ovoo нranoo]*
senior: Mr Jones senior Gospodin Džons stariji *[gospodeen djons stareeyee]*
senior citizen penzioner *[penzeeoner]*
sensational (*holiday, experience etc*) senzacionalan *[senzatseeonalan]*
sense: I have no sense of direction nemam osjećanja pravca *[nemam osyechanya pravtsa]*; **it doesn't make sense** nema smisla *[nema smeesla]*
sensible razuman *[razooman]*
sensitive osjetljiv *[osyetlyeev]*
sentimental sentimentalan *[senteementalan]*
separate odvojen *[odvoyen]*; **can we have separate bills?** možemo li platiti odvojeno? *[moɪemo lee plateetee odvoyeno]*
separated: I'm separated rastavljen sam *[rastavlyen]*
separately odvojeno *[odvoyeno]*
September (S) septembar; (C) rujan

[rooyan]
septic septičan *[septeechan]*
Serb (*man*) Srbin *[surbeen]*; (*woman*)
Srpkinja *[surpkeenya]*
Serbia Srbija *[surbeeya]*
Serbian (*adjective, language*) srpski
[surpskee]
Serbocroat (*adjective, language*)
srpskohrvatski *[surpsko-Hurvatskee]*
serious ozbiljan *[ozbeelyan]*; **I'm
serious** ozbiljno mislim *[ozbeelyno
meesleem]*; **you can't be serious!** ne
mislite to ozbiljno! *[meesleete to
ozbeelyno]*; **is it serious, doctor?** je li
ozbiljno, doktore? *[ye lee]*
seriously: seriously ill ozbiljno bolestan *[ozbeelyno bolestan]*
service: the service was excellent
usluga je bila odlična *[ooslooga ye
beela odleechna]*; **could we have
some service, please!** molim vas,
možete li nas poslužiti? *[moleem vas,
moɹete lee nas poslooɹeetee]*;
(church) service služba *[slooɹba]*;
(*Catholic*) misa *[meesa]*; **the car needs
a service** kolima je potreban servis
[koleema ye potreban servees]
service charge servis *[servees]*
service station benzinska stanica
[benzeenska staneetsa]
serviette salveta
set: it's time we were setting off vrijeme je da krenemo *[vryeme ye]*
set menu meni
settle up: can we settle up now? možemo li sad podmiriti račun? *[mo-
ɹemo lee sad podmeereetee rachoon]*
several nekoliko *[nekoleeko]*
sew šiti *[sheetee]*; **could you sew this
back on?** da li biste mogli ovo zašiti?
[lee beeste moglee ovo zasheetee]
sex (*sexual intercourse*) seks
sexist (*noun*) seksist *[sekseest]*
sexy seksi *[seksee]*
shade: in the shade u hladu *[oo
Hladoo]*
shadow sjenka *[syenka]*
shake: let's shake hands hajde da se
rukujemo *[hɪde da se rookooyemo]*
shallow (*water*) plitak *[pleetak]*
shame: what a shame! šteta! *[shteta]*
shampoo (*noun*) šampon *[shampon]*;
can I have a shampoo and set?
molim vas pranje i vodenu? *[moleem*

vas pranye ee vodenoo]
shandy, shandy-gaff pivo sa limuna-
dom *[peevo sa leemoonadom]*
share (*verb: room, table etc*) dijeliti
[dyeleetee]; **let's share the cost**
podijelimo troškove *[podyeleemo
troshkove]*
shark (*S*) ajkula *[ɪkoola]*; (*C*) morski
pas *[morskee]*
sharp (*knife, pain*) oštar *[oshtar]*; (*taste*)
izoštren *[eezoshtren]*
shattered: I'm shattered (*tired*) gotov
sam
shave: I need a shave treba da se
obrijem *[obreeyem]*; **can you give
me a shave?** možete li me obrijati?
[moɹete lee me obreeyatee]
shaver aparat za brijanje *[breeyanye]*
shaving brush četka za brijanje
[chetka za breeyanye]
shaving foam pjena za brijanje
[pyena za breeyanye]
shaving point utikač za brijanje
[ooteekach za breeyanye]
shaving soap sapun za brijanje
[sapoon za breeyanye]
shawl šal *[shal]*
she ona; **is she here?** je li ona ovdje?
[ye lee ona ovdye]; **she's not English**
nije Engleskinja *[neeye
engleskeenya]*; *see page 111*
sheep ovca *[ovtsa]*
sheet (*for bed*) plaHta
shelf polica *[poleetsa]*
shell školjka *[shkolyka]*
shellfish školjke *[shkolyke]*
sherry šeri *[sheree]*
ship brod: **by ship** brodom
shirt košulja *[koshoolya]*
shit! sranje! *[sranye]*
shock (*surprise*) šok *[shok]*; **I got an
electric shock from the ...** uhvatila
me struja na ... (+*P*) *[ooHvateela me
strooya]*
shock-absorber amortizer *[amortee-
zer]*
shocking skandalozan
shoe cipela *[tseepela]*; **my shoes** moje
cipele *[moye tseepele]*; **a pair of
shoes** par cipela
shoelaces pertle
shoe polish pasta za obuću
[oboochoo]
shoe repairer (*S*) obućar *[oboochar]*;

(C) postolar

shop (S) prodavnica [*prodavneetsa*]; (C) prodavaonica [*prodavaoneetsa*]

shopping: I'm going shopping idem u kupovinu [*eedem oo koopoveenoo*]

shop window izlog [*eezlog*]

shore (*of sea, lake*) obala

short (*person*) nizak [*neezak*]; (*time, journey*) kratak; **it's only a short distance** to je blizu [*ye bleezoo*]

short-change: you've short-changed me vratili ste mi manje [*vrateelee ste mee manye*]

short circuit kratki spoj [*kratkee spoy*]

shortcut prečica [*precheetsa*]

shorts kratke pantalone; (*underwear*) gaće [*gache*]

should: what should I do? šta da radim? [*shta da radeem*]; **he shouldn't be long** ne bi trebalo da se dugo zadrži [*bee trebalo da se doogo zadurJee*]; **you should have told me** trebali ste mi reći [*trebalee ste mee rechee*]

shoulder rame

shoulder blade lopatica [*lopateetsa*]

shout (*verb*) vikati [*veekatee*]

show: could you show me? možete li mi pokazati? [*moJete lee mee pokazatee*]; **does it show?** vidi li se? [*veedee*]; **we'd like to go to a show** htjeli bismo ići na predstavu [*Htyelee beesmo eechee na predstavoo*]

shower (*in bathroom*) tuš [*toosh*]; **with shower** s tušem [*tooshem*]

showercap kapa za tuširanje [*toosheeranye*]

show-off: don't be a show-off nemojte se praviti važni [*nemoyte se praveetee vaJnee*]

shrimps račići [*racheechee*]

shrine (*place of worship*) Hram; (*holy place*) svetište [*sveteeshte*]

shrink: it's shrunk skupilo se [*skoopeelo*]

shut (*verb*) zatvarati [*zatvaratee*]; **when do you shut?** kad zatvarate?; **when do they shut?** kad zatvaraju? [*zatvarIyoo*]; **it was shut** bilo je zatvoreno [*beelo ye*]; **I've shut myself out** zalupio sam vrata a ključ je ostao unutra [*zaloopeeo sam vrata a klyooch ye ostao oonootra*]; **shut**

up! zaveži! [*zaveJee*]

shutter (*camera*) blenda; (*window*) kapak

shutter release okidač [*okeedach*]

shy stidljiv [*steedlyeev*]

sick (*ill*) bolestan; **I think I'm going to be sick** (*vomit*) mislim da ću povraćati [*meesleem da choo povrachatee*]

side strana; (*in game*) (S) tim [*teem*]; (C) momčad [*momchad*]; **at the side of the road** pored puta [*poota*]; **the other side of town** druga strana grada [*drooga*]

side lights poziciona svjetla [*pozeetseeona svyetla*]

side salad salata

side street sporedna ulica [*ooleetsa*]

sidewalk pločnik [*plochneek*]

sidewalk café kafana sa terasom

siesta popodnevni odmor [*popodnevnee*]

sight: the sights of ... znamenitosti ... (+G) [*znameneetostee*]

sightseeing: sightseeing tour razgledanje [*razgledanye*]; **we're going sightseeing** idemo u razgledanje [*eedemo oo*]

sign (*roadsign etc*) saobraćajni znak [*saobrachInee*]; **where do I sign?** gdje da potpišem? [*gdye da potpeeshem*]

signal: he didn't give a signal (*driver, cyclist*) nije dao znak [*neeye dao*]

signature potpis [*potpees*]

signpost putokaz [*pootokaz*]

silence tišina [*teesheena*]

silencer prigušivač [*preegoosheevach*]

silk svila [*sveela*]

silly (*person, thing etc*) glup [*gloop*]; **that's silly!** to je glupo! [*ye gloopo*]

silver srebro; (*adjective*) srebren

silver foil aluminijumska folija [*aloomeeneeyoomska foleeya*]

similar sličan [*sleechan*]

simple (*easy*) jednostavan [*yednostavan*]

since: since yesterday od juče [*yooche*]; **since we got here** otkada smo stigli ovamo [*steeglee*]

sincere iskren [*eeskren*]

sing pjevati [*pyevatee*]

singer pjevač [*pyevach*]

single: a single room jednokrevetna

soba *[yednokrevetna]*; **a single to ...**
kartu za ... *[kartoo]*; **I'm single**
(*man*) ja sam neoženjen *[ya ...
neoJenyen]*; (*woman*) ja sam neudata
[neoodata]
sink (*in kitchen*) sudoper *[soodoper]*; **it
sank** potonuo je *[potonoo-o ye]*
sir gospodine *[gospodeene]*; **excuse
me, sir** izvinite, gospodine
[eezveeneete]
sirloin bubrežnjak *[boobreJnyak]*
sister: my sister moja sestra *[moya]*
sister-in-law (*brother's wife*) snaha;
(*husband's sister*) zaova; (*wife's sister*)
(*S*) svastika; (*C*) šogorica
[shogoreetsa]; (*wife of husband's
brother*) jetrva *[yeturva]*
sit: may I sit here? mogu li ovdje sje-
sti? *[mogoo lee ovdye syestee]*; **is
anyone sitting here?** sjedi li neko
ovdje? *[syedee lee neko ovdye]*
sitting: the second sitting for lunch
druga smjena za ručak *[drooga
symena za roochak]*
situation situacija *[seetooatseeya]*
size veličina *[veleecheena]*; **do you
have any other sizes?** imate li u
drugim veličinama? *[eemate lee oo
droogeem veleecheenama]*
sketch (*noun*) skica *[skeetsa]*
ski (*noun*) skija *[skeeya]*; (*verb*) skijati
se *[skeeyatee]*; **a pair of skis** skije
[skeeye]
ski boots skijaške cipele *[skeeyashke
tseepele]*
skid: I skidded okliznuo sam se
[okleeznoo-o]
skiing skijanje *[skeeyanye]*; **we're
going skiing** idemo na skijanje
[eedemo]
ski instructor instruktor skijanja
[eenstrooktor skeeyanya]
ski-lift uspinjača *[oospeenyacha]*
skin koža *[koJa]*
skin-diving ronjenje *[ronyenye]*; **I'm
going skin-diving** idem na ronjenje
[eedem]
skinny mršav *[murshav]*
ski-pants skijaške hlače *[skeeyashke
Hlache]*
ski pass skijaška propusnica
[skeeyashka propoosneetsa]
ski pole skijaški štap *[skeeyashkee
shtap]*

skirt suknja *[sooknya]*
ski run skijaška staza *[skeeyashka]*
ski slope pista za skijanje *[peesta za
skeeyanye]*
ski wax vosak za skije *[skeeye]*
skull lubanja *[loobanya]*
sky nebo
sleep spavati *[spavatee]*; **I can't sleep**
ne mogu spavati *[mogoo]*; **did you
sleep well?** jeste li dobro spavali?
[yeste lee dobro spavalee]; **I need a
good sleep** potrebno mi je da se
dobro ispavam *[potrebno mee ye da
se dobro eespavam]*
sleeper (*rail*) spavaća kola *[spavacha]*
sleeping bag vreća za spavanje
[vrecha za spavanye]
sleeping car spavača kola *[spavacha]*
sleeping pill pilula za spavanje
[peeloola za spavanye]
sleepy (*person*) pospan; (*weather, day*)
dremovan; (*town*) uspavan
[oospavan]; **I'm feeling sleepy**
pospan sam
sleeve rukav *[rookav]*
slice (*noun*) kriška *[kreeshka]*
slide (*phot*) dijapozitiv *[deeyapozee-
teev]*
slim (*adjective*) vitak *[veetak]*; **I'm
slimming** na dijeti sam *[deeyetee]*
slip (*under dress*) kombinezon
[kombeenezon]; **I slipped** (*on
pavement etc*) okliznuo sam se
[okleeznoo-o]
slipped disc iščašenje pršljena
[eeshchashenye purshlyena]
slippery klizav *[kleezav]*; **it's slippery**
klizavo je *[kleezavo ye]*
slivovitz šljivovica *[shleevoveetsa]*
slow spor; **slow down!** (*driving, speaking*) sporije! *[sporeeye]*
slowly sporo; **could you say it
slowly?** da li biste to mogli reći sporije? *[lee beeste to moglee rechee
sporeeye]*; **very slowly** veoma sporo
small mali *[malee]*
small change sitan novac *[seetan
novats]*
smallpox velike boginje *[veleeke
bogeenye]*
smart (*clothes*) elegantan
smashing izvanredan *[eezvanredan]*
smell: there's a funny smell ima neki
čudan miris *[eema nekee choodan*

meerees]; **what a lovely smell!**
kakav krasan miris!; **it smells** (*bad*)
smrdi *[smurdee]*
smile (*verb*) smiješiti se *[smyesheetee]*
smoke (*noun*) dim *[deem]*; **do you**
smoke? pušite li? *[poosheete lee]*; **do**
you mind if I smoke? imate li nešto
protiv ako pušim? *[eemate lee neshto*
proteev ako pooshem]; **I don't smoke**
ne pušim
smoothe (*surface*) gladak
snack: I'd just like a snack ja bih
nesto sasvim malo da pojedem *[ya*
beeн neshto sasveem malo da
poyedem]
snackbar snek-bar
snake zmija *[zmeeya]*
sneakers (*S*) patike *[pateeke]*; (*C*)
tenisice *[teneeseetse]*
snob snob
snorkel cijev za disanje *[tsyev za*
deesanye]
snow (*noun*) snijeg *[snyeg]*
so: it's so hot tako je vruče *[tako ye*
vrooche]; **it was so beautiful!** bilo je
tako lijepo *[beelo ye tako lyepo]*; **not**
so fast ne tako brzo *[burzo]*; **thank**
you so much veliko vam hvala
[veleeko vam Hvala]; **it wasn't — it**
was so! nije tako bilo — kako da
nije! *[neeye — kako da neeye]*; **so**
am I i ja sam *[ee ya]*; **so do I** i ja;
how was it? — so-so kako je bilo?
— tako-tako
soaked: I'm soaked sav sam mokar
soaking solution (*for contact lenses*)
rastvor za potapanje *[potapanye]*
soap sapun *[sapoon]*
soap-powder sapun u prahu *[sapoon*
oo prahoo]
sober trijezan *[tryezan]*
soccer (*S*) fudbal *[foodbal]*; (*C*)
nogomet
sock čarapa *[charapa]*
socket (*elec*) utikač *[ooteekach]*
soda (water) soda
sofa sofa
soft (*material etc*) mekan
soft drink bezalkoholno piće *[peeche]*
soft lenses (*S*) meka sočiva *[meka*
socheeva]; (*C*) meke leće *[meke leche]*
soldier vojnik *[voyneek]*
sole (*of shoe*) đon *[djon]*; (*of foot*)
taban; **could you put new soles on**

these? možete li ih pođoniti? *[mojete*
lee eeн podjoneetee]
solid solidan *[soleedan]*
some: may I have some water? mogu
li dobiti malo vode? *[mogoo lee*
dobeetee]; **do you have some**
matches? imate li šibica? *[eemate lee*
sheebeetsa]; **that's some drink!** to se
zove piće! *[peeche]*; **some of them**
neki od njih *[nekee od nyeeн]*; **can I**
have some? mogu li i ja dobiti?
somebody, someone neko
something nešto *[neshto]*; **something**
to drink nešto za popiti *[popeetee]*
sometime: sometime this afternoon u
toku današnjeg poslijepodneva *[oo*
tokoo danashnyeg poslyepodneva]
sometimes ponekad
somewhere negdje *[negdye]*
son: my son moj sin *[moy seen]*
song pjesma *[pyesma]*
son-in-law: my son-in-law moj zet
[moy]
soon uskoro *[ooskoro]*; **I'll be back**
soon brzo ću se vratiti *[burzo choo*
se vrateetee]; **as soon as you can** što
brže možete *[shto burje mojete]*
sore: it's sore boli me *[bolee]*
sore throat: I have a sore throat boli
me grlo *[bolee me gurlo]*
sorry: (I'm) sorry oprostite!
[oprosteete]; **sorry?** (*didn't understand*)
molim? *[moleem]*
sort: what sort of ...? kakva vrsta ...?
[kakva vursta]; **a different sort of ...**
drukčija vrsta ... *[drookcheeya]*; **will**
you sort it out? hoćete li to srediti?
[hochete lee to sredeetee]
soup (*S*) supa *[soopa]*; (*C*) juha
[yooha]
sour (*taste*) kiseo *[keeseo]*
south jug *[yoog]*; **to the south of**
južno od *[yoojno]*; **in the south** na
jugu *[yoogoo]*
South Africa Južna Afrika *[yoojna*
afreeka]
South African (*adjective*) južnoafrički
[yoojnoafreechkee]; (*man*) Južno-
afrikanac *[yoojnoafreekanats]*;
(*woman*) Južnoafrikanka *[yoojno-*
afreekanka]
southeast jugoistok *[yoogo-eestok]*; **to**
the southeast jugoistočno *[yoogo-*
eestochno]

southwest jugozapad *[yoogozapad]*; **to the southwest** jugozapadno
souvenir suvenir *[sooveneer]*
spa (*S*) banja *[banya]*; (*C*) toplice *[topleetse]*
space heater grijalica *[greeyaleetsa]*
spade lopata
Spain (*S*) Španija *[shpaneeya]*; (*C*) Španjolska *[shpanyolska]*
spanner ključ *[klyooch]*
spare part rezervni dio (*m*) *[rezervnee deeo]*
spare tyre/tire rezervna guma *[rezervna gooma]*
spark(ing) plug svjećica *[svyecheetsa]*
speak: do you speak English? govorite li engleski? *[govoreete lee engleskee]*; **I don't speak ...** ne govorim ... *[govoreem]*; **can I speak to ...?** mogu li razgovarati sa ...? *[mogoo lee razgovaratee]*; **speaking** (*on telephone*) na telefonu
special specijalan *[spetseeyalan]*; **nothing special** ništa specijalno *[neeshta spetseeyalno]*
specialist specijalist *[spetseeyaleest]*
special(i)ty specijalnost *[spetseeyalnost]*; **the special(i)ty of the house** specijalitet kuće *[spetseeyaleetet kooche]*
spectacles (*S*) naočari *[naocharee]*; (*C*) naočale *[naochale]*
speed (*noun*) brzina *[burzeena]*; **he was speeding** prebrzo je vozio *[preburzo ye vozeeo]*
speedboat gliser *[gleeser]*
speed limit ograničenje brzine *[ograneechenye burzeene]*
speedometer brzinomjer *[burzeenomyer]*
spell: how do you spell it? kako se to piše? *[kako se to peeshe]*
spend potrošiti *[potrosheetee]*; **I've spent all my money** potrošio sam sav novac *[potrosheeo sam sav novats]*
spice začin *[zacheen]*
spicy: it's very spicy veoma je začinjeno *[veoma ye zacheenyeno]*; (*very hot*) veoma je ljuto *[lyooto]*
spider pauk *[paook]*
spin-dryer centrifuga *[tsentreefooga]*
splendid (*very good*) divan *[deevan]*
splint (*for limb*) udlaga *[oodlaga]*

splinter (*in finger*) iver *[eever]*
splitting: I've got a splitting headache strašno me boli glava *[strashno me bolee glava]*
spoke (*in wheel*) žbica *[Jbeetsa]*
sponge spužva *[spooJva]*
spoon (*S*) kašika *[kasheeka]*; (*C*) žlica *[Jleetsa]*
sport sport
sport(s) jacket sportska jakna *[yakna]*
spot (*on face*) prišt *[preesht]*; **will they do it on the spot?** hoće li to uraditi smjesta? *[hoche lee to ooradeetee smyesta]*
sprain: I've sprained my ... iščašio sam ... *[eeshchasheeo]*
spray (*for hair*) lak
spring (*season*) proljeće *[prolyeche]*; (*of car, seat*) opruga *[oprooga]*
square (*in town*) trg *[turg]*; **ten square meters** deset kvadratnih metara *[deset kvadratneeн metara]*
squash (*sport*) skvoš *[skvosh]*
stain (*noun: on clothes*) mrlja *[murlya]*
stairs stepenice *[stepeneetse]*
stale (*bread*) star; (*taste*) bljutav *[blyootav]*
stall: the engine keeps stalling motor se stalno gasi *[motor se stalno gasee]*
stalls (*in theatre*) parter
stamp (*noun*) marka; **a stamp for England, please** marku za Englesku, molim *[markoo za engleskoo, moleem]*
stand: I can't stand ... (*can't tolerate*) ne mogu podnositi ... *[mogoo podnoseetee]*
standard (*adjective*) standardan
standby stendbaj *[stendbɪ]*
star zvijezda *[zvyezda]*; (*in movies*) filmska zvijezda *[feelmska]*
start (*noun*) početak *[pochetak]*; **when does the film start?** kad počinje film? *[pocheenye feelm]*; **the car won't start** kola neče da upale *[kola neche da oopale]*
starter (*of car*) anlaser; (*food*) predjelo *[predyelo]*
starving: I'm starving umirem od gladi *[oomeerem od gladee]*
state (*in country*) država *[durJava]*; **the States** (*USA*) Sjedinjene Američke Države *[syedeenyene amereechke durJave]*

station (S) stanica *[staneetsa]*; (C) kolodvor

statue kip *[keep]*

stay: we enjoyed our stay uživali smo u boravku *[ooJeevalee smo oo boravkoo]*; **where are you staying?** gdje ste odsjeli? *[gdye ste odsyelee]*; **I'm staying at ...** odsjeo sam u ... *[odsyeo sam oo]*; **I'd like to stay another week** ostao bih još tjedan *[ostao beeн yosh tyedan]*; **I'm staying in tonight** večeras ne izlazim *[vecheras ne eezlazeem]*

steak biftek

steal ukrasti *[ookrastee]*; **my bag has been stolen** ukrali su mi tašnu *[ookralee soo mee tashnoo]*

steep (hill) strm *[sturm]*

steering sistem za upravljanje *[seestem za oopravlyanye]*; **the steering is slack** razlabavio se volan *[razlabaveeo se volan]*

steering wheel volan

step (in front of house etc) stepenica *[stepeneetsa]*

stereo stereo

sterling sterling *[sterleeng]*

stew pirjano meso *[peerjano meso]*

steward (on plane) stjuard *[styooard]*

stewardess stjuardesa *[styooardesa]*

sticking plaster flaster

sticky: it's sticky ljepljivo je *[lyeplyeevo ye]*

sticky tape ljepljiva traka *[lyeplyeeva]*

still: I'm still waiting još čekam *[yosh chekam]*; **will you still be open?** hoćete li još biti otvoreni? *[hochete lee yosh beetee otvorenee]*; **it's still not right** još nije u redu *[yosh neeye oo redoo]*; **that's still better** to je još bolje *[ye yosh bolye]*; **keep still!** budite mirni! *[boodeete meernee]*

sting: a bee sting ujed pčele *[ooyed pchele]*; **I've been stung** nešto me ujelo *[neshto me ooyelo]*

stink (noun) smrad *[sumrad]*; **it stinks** smrdi *[smurdee]*

stockings čarape *[charape]*

stolen ukraden *[ookraden]*; **my wallet's been stolen** ukraden mi je novčanik *[mee ye novchaneek]*

stomach stomak; **do you have something for an upset stomach?** imate li nešto za pokvaren stomak *[eemate lee neshto za pokvaren]*

stomach-ache bol u stomaku *[bol oo stomakoo]*

stone (rock) kamen; *see page 121*

stop (bus stop) stanica *[staneetsa]*; **which is the stop for ...?** koja je stanica za ...? *[koya ye]*; **please stop here** (to taxi driver etc) molim vas, stanite ovdje *[moleem vas, staneete ovdye]*; **do you stop near ...?** stajete li blizu ...? *[styete lee bleezoo]*; **stop doing that!** prestanite s tim! *[prestaneete s teem]*

stopover prekid putovanja *[prekeed pootovanya]*

store (shop) (S) prodavnica *[prodavneetsa]*; (C) prodavaonica *[prodavaoneetsa]*

stor(e)y (of building) (S) sprat; (C) kat

storm oluja *[olooya]*

story (tale) priča *[preecha]*

stove peć (f) *[pech]*

straight (road etc) prav; **it's straight ahead** pravo naprijed *[napryed]*; **straight away** odmah; **a straight whisky** nerazblažen viski *[nerazblaJen veeskee]*

straighten: can you straighten things out? (sort things out) da li biste to mogli srediti? *[lee beeste to moglee sredeetee]*

strange (odd) čudan *[choodan]*; (unknown) nepoznat

stranger stranac *[stranats]*; **I'm a stranger here** ovdje sam stranac *[ovdye]*

strap (S) kaiš *[ka-eesh]*; (C) remen

strawberry jagoda *[yagoda]*

streak: could you put streaks in? (in hair) možete li mi staviti pramenove? *[moJete lee mee staveetee]*

stream potok

street ulica *[ooleetsa]*; **on the street** na ulici *[ooleetsee]*

street café ulična kavana *[ooleechna]*

streetcar tramvaj *[tramvı]*

streetmap plan grada

strep throat upala grla *[oopala gurla]*

strike: they're on strike štrajkuju *[shtrıkooyoo]*

string špaga *[shpaga]*; **have you got some string?** imate li špage? *[eemate lee shpage]*

striped prugast *[proogast]*

striptease striptiz *[streepteez]*
stroke: he's had a stroke udarila ga je kap *[oodareela ga ye]*
stroll: let's go for a stroll hajdemo da se prošetamo *[hidemo da se proshetamo]*
stroller (*for babies*) kolica za bebu *[koleetsa za beboo]*
strong (*person, drink*) jak *[yak]*; (*taste*) oštar *[oshtar]*
stroppy neljubazan *[nelyoobazan]*
stuck zaglavljen *[zaglavlyen]*; **the key's stuck** zaglavio se ključ *[zaglaveeo se klyooch]*
student (*male*) student *[stoodent]*; (*female*) (S) studentkinja *[stoodentkeenya]*; (C) studentica *[stoodenteetsa]*
stupid glup *[gloop]*; **that's stupid** to je glupo *[ye gloopo]*
sty(e) (*in eye*) (S) čmičak *[chmeechak]*; (C) ječmenac *[yechmenats]*
subtitles (*film*) titlovi *[teetlovee]*
suburb predgrađe *[predgradje]*
subway (*underground*) podzemna željeznica *[Jelyezneetsa]*
successful: were you successful? jeste li imali uspjeha? *[yeste lee eemalee oospyeha]*
suddenly naglo
sue: I intend to sue namjeravam tužiti *[namyeravam tooJeetee]*
suede prevrnuta koža *[prevurnoota koJa]*
sugar šećer *[shecher]*
suggest: what do you suggest? šta predlažete? *[shta predlaJete]*
suit (*clothes*) odijelo *[odyelo]*; **it doesn't suit me** (*clothes etc*) ne stoji mi dobro *[stoyee mee dobro]*; **it suits you** dobro vam stoji *[vam stoyee]*; **that suits me fine** (*arrangements*) to mi sasvim odgovara *[mee sasveem]*
suitable (*time, place*) pogodan
suitcase (S) kofer; (C) kufer *[koofer]*
sulk: he's sulking mrzovoljan je *[murzovolyan ye]*
sultry (*weather, climate*) sparan
summer ljeto *[lyeto]*; **in the summer** ljeti *[lyetee]*
sun sunce *[soontse]*; **in the sun** na suncu *[soontsoo]*; **out of the sun** van domašaja sunca *[domashIya soontsa]*; **I've had too much sun** previše mi je

sunca *[preveeshe mee ye]*
sunbathe sunčati se *[soonchatee]*
sunblock pomada za sunčanje *[soonchanye]*
sunburn: have you got something for sunburn? imate li šta za opaljenost od sunca? *[eemate lee shta za opalyenost od soontsa]*
sunburnt izgorio od sunca *[eezgoreeo od soontsa]*
Sunday nedjelja *[nedyelya]*
sunglasses naočari za sunce *[naocharee za soontse]*
sun lounger (*chair*) ležaljka *[leJalyka]*
sunny: if it's sunny ako bude sunčano *[ako boode soonchano]*; **a sunny day** sunčan dan *[soonchan]*
sunrise izlazak sunca *[eezlazak soontsa]*
sun roof otvoreni krov *[otvorenee]*
sunset zalazak sunca *[zalazak soontsa]*
sunshade suncobran *[soontsobran]*
sunshine sunčev sjaj *[soonchev syI]*
sunstroke sunčanica *[soonchaneetsa]*
suntan: to get a suntan preplanuti *[preplanootee]*
suntan lotion losion za sunčanje *[loseeon za soonchanye]*
suntanned preplanuo (od sunca) *[preplanoo-o (od soontsa)]*
suntan oil ulje za sunčanje *[oolye za soonchanye]*
sun worshipper lud za suncem *[lood za soontsem]*
super! izvanredan *[eezvanredan]*; **super!** izvanredno! *[eezvanredno]*
superb veličanstven *[veleechanstven]*
supermarket supermarket *[soopermarket]*
supper večera *[vechera]*
supplement (*extra charge*) doplata
suppose: I suppose so tako pretpostavljam *[tako pretpostavlyam]*
suppository supozitorijum *[soopozeetoreeyoom]*
sure: I'm sure siguran sam *[seegooran]*; **are you sure?** jeste li sigurni *[yeste lee seegoornee]*; **he's sure** siguran je *[ye]*; **sure!** naravno!
surfboard daska za serfing *[serfeeng]*
surfing: to go surfing ići na serfing *[eechee na serfeeng]*
surname prezime *[prezeeme]*
surprise (*noun*) iznenađenje

[eeznenadjenye]
surprising: that's not surprising to
nije neočekivano *[neeye neochekee-
vano]*
suspension (*of car*) opruge točkova
[oprooge tochkova]
swallow (*verb*) gutati *[gootatee]*
swearword psovka
sweat (*verb*) znojiti se *[znoyeetee]*;
(*noun*) znoj *[znoy]*; **covered in sweat**
obliven znojem *[obleeven znoyem]*
sweater džemper *[djemper]*
sweatshirt majica *[mıyeetsa]*
Sweden Švedska *[shvedska]*
sweet (*taste*) sladak; (*noun: dessert*)
dezert
sweets slatkiši *[slatkeeshee]*
swelling otok
sweltering: it's sweltering velika je
zapara *[veleeka ye zapara]*
swerve: I had to swerve (*when driving*) morao sam naglo skrenuti
[morao sam naglo skrenootee]
swim (*verb*) plivati *[pleevatee]*; **I'm
going for a swim** idem na kupanje
[eedem na koopanye]; **do you want
to go for a swim?** želiš li se kupati?
[Jeleesh lee se koopatee]; **I can't
swim** ne znam plivati

swimming plivanje *[pleevanye]*; **I like
swimming** volim plivati *[voleem
pleevatee]*
swimming costume kupači kostim
[koopachee kosteem]
swimming pool bazen
swimming trunks kupaće gaćice
[koopache gacheetse]
Swiss (*adjective*) (S) švajcarski
[shvıtsarski]; (C) švicarski *[shveets-
arskee]*; (*man*) (S) Švajcarac *[shvıts-
arats]*; (C) Švicarac; (*woman*) (S)
Švajcarka *[shvıtsarka]*; (C) Švicarka
[shveetsarka]
switch (*noun*) prekidač *[prekeedach]*;
could you switch it on? uključite,
molim vas! *[ooklyoocheete moleem
vas]*; **could you switch it off?**
isključite, molim vas! *[eesklyoocheete]*
Switzerland (S) Švajcarska *[shvıts-
arska]*; (C) Švicarska *[shveetsarska]*
swollen otekao
swollen glands otekle žlijezde
[Jlyezde]
sympathy suosjećajnost (*f*) *[soo-
osyechınost]*
synagogue sinagoga *[seenagoga]*
synthetic sintetičan *[seenteteechan]*

T

table (S) sto (*m*); (C) stol (*m*); **a table
for two** sto/stol za dvoje *[dvoye]*; **at
our usual table** za našim
uobičajenim stolom *[nasheem oo-
obeechıyeneem stolom]*
tablecloth stolnjak *[stolnyak]*
table tennis stoni tenis *[stonee tenees]*
table wine stono vino *[stono veeno]*
tactful (*person*) taktičan *[takteechan]*
tailback kolona vozila *[vozeela]*
tailor krojač *[kroyach]*
take uzeti *[oozetee]*; **will you take this
to room 12?** da li biste odnijeli ovo
u sobu 12? *[lee beeste odnyelee ovo
oo soboo dvana-est]*; **will you take
me to the airport?** da li biste me
odvezli na aerodrom? *[lee beeste me
odvezlee na a-erodrom]*; **do you take**

credit cards? primate li kreditne
kartice? *[preemate lee kredeetne
karteetse]*; **OK, I'll take it** u redu,
uzet ću *[oo redoo oozet choo]*; **how
long does it take?** koliko vremena
treba za to? *[koleeko]*; **it'll take 2
hours** trebat će 2 sata *[che]*; **is this
seat taken?** je li ovo mjesto zauzeto?
[ye lee ovo myesto zaoozeto]; **I can't
take too much sun** ne mogu
predugo biti na suncu *[mogoo
predoogo beetee na soontsoo]*; **to take
away** (*food*) za ponijeti *[ponyetee]*;
will you take this back, it's broken
da li biste primili ovo nazad,
slomljeno je *[preemeelee ovo nazad,
slomlyeno ye]*; **could you take it in
at the side?** (*dress, jacket*) da li biste

mogli suziti sa strane *[moglee soozeetee]*; **when does the plane take off?** kad poleće avion? *[poleche aveeon]*; **can you take a little off the top?** (*to hairdresser*) možete li skratiti malo na vrhu *[moɹete lee skrateetee malo na vurhoo]*

talcum powder talk

talk (*verb*) govoriti *[govoreetee]*

tall (*person, building*) visok *[veesok]*

tampax (*tm*) higijenski tamponi *[heegeeyenskee tamponee]*

tampons tamponi *[tamponee]*

tan preplanulost *[preplanoolost]*; **I want to get a good tan** želim dobro pocrnjeti *[ɹeleem dobro potsurnyetee]*

tank (*of car*) rezervo-ar

tap slavina *[slaveena]*

tape (*for cassette*) traka; (*sticky*) ljepljiva *[lyeplyeeva]*

tape measure krojački centimetar *[kroyachkee tsenteemetar]*

tape recorder magnetofon

taste (*noun*) ukus *[ookoos]*; **can I taste it?** mogu li probati? *[mogoo lee probatee]*; **it has a peculiar taste** ima neobičan ukus *[eema neobeechan]*; **it tastes very nice** veoma je ukusno *[veoma ye ookoosno]*; **it tastes revolting** ima odvratan ukus

taxi taksi (*m*) *[taksee]*; **will you get me a taxi?** molim vas, pozovite mi taksi *[moleem vas pozoveete mee]*

taxi-driver taksista (*m*) *[takseesta]*

taxi rank, taxi stand taksi-stanica *[taksee-staneetsa]*

tea (*drink*) čaj *[chɪ]*; **tea for two please** čaj za dvoje, molim *[dvoye moleem]*; **could I have a cup of tea?** (*S*) molim vas šolju čaja *[sholyoo chɪya]*; (*C*) molim vas šalicu čaja *[shaleetsoo]*

teabag čaj u kesici *[chɪ oo keseetsee]*

teach: could you teach me? možete li me učiti? *[moɹete lee me oocheetee]*; **could you teach me Serbocroat?** da li biste me mogli učiti srpskohrvatski *[lee beeste me moglee ... surpsko-Hurvatskee]*

teacher (*male, junior*) učitelj *[oocheetel-yuh]*; (*female, junior*) učiteljica *[oocheetelyeetsa]*; (*male, secondary*) profesor; (*female, secondary*) profesorica *[profesoreetsa]*

team (*S*) tim *[teem]*; (*C*) momčad (*n*)

[momchad]

teapot čajnik *[chɪneek]*

tea towel kuhinjska krpa *[kooheenyska kurpa]*

teenager tinejdžer *[teeneydjer]*

teetotal: he's teetotal on je trezvenjak *[ye trezvenyak]*

telegram telegram; **I want to send a telegram** želim poslati telegram *[ɹelem poslatee]*

telephone telefon; **can I make a telephone call?** mogu li telefonirati? *[mogoo lee telefoneeratee]*; **could you talk to him for me on the telephone?** da li biste s njim govorili telefonom umjesto mene? *[lee beeste s nyeem govoreelee telefonom oomyesto mene]*

telephone box/booth telefonska govornica *[telefonska govorneetsa]*

telephone directory telefonski imenik *[telefonskee eemeneek]*

telephone number telefonski broj *[telefonskee broy]*; **what's your telephone number?** koje je vaš telefonski broj? *[koye ye vash]*

telephoto lens teleobjektiv *[tele-obyekteev]*

television televizija *[televeezeeya]*; **I'd like to watch television** želio bih gledati televiziju *[ɹeleeo beeH gledatee televeezeeyoo]*; **is the match on television?** je li meč na televiziji? *[ye lee mech na televeezeeyee]*

tell: could you tell him ...? da li biste mu rekli ...? *[lee beeste moo reklee]*

temperature (*weather, fever*) temperatura *[temperatoora]*; **he has a temperature** ima temperaturu *[eema temperatooroo]*

temple (*religious*) Hram

temporary privremen *[preevremen]*

tenant (*of apartment*) stanar

tennis tenis *[tenees]*

tennis ball teniska lopta *[teneeska]*

tennis court teniski teren *[teneeskee]*; **can we use the tennis court?** možemo li se poslužiti teniskim terenom? *[moɹemo lee se poslooɹeetee teneeskeem]*

tennis racket teniski reket *[teneeskee]*

tent šator *[shator]*

term (*at school*) tromjesečje *[trom-yesechye]*

terminus (*rail*) krajnja stanica *[krɪnya staneetsa]*

terrace terasa; **on the terrace** na terasi *[terasee]*

terrible grozan

terrific izvanredan *[eezvanredan]*

testicle mudo *[moodo]*

than nego; **smaller than** manji nego *[manyee]*

thanks, thank you hvala *[Hvala]*; **thank you very much** hvala lijepo *[lyepo]*; **thank you for everything** hvala za sve; **no thanks** ne, hvala

that: that woman ta žena *[ʃena]*; **that man** taj čovjek *[tɪ chovyek]*; **that one** onaj *[onɪ]*; **I hope that ...** nadam se da ...; **that's perfect** to je savršeno *[ye savursheno]*; **that's strange** to je čudno *[choodno]*; **is that ...?** je li to ...? *[ye lee]*; **that's it** (*that's right*) tako je *[tako ye]*; **is it that expensive?** je li tako skupo? *[ye lee tako skoopo]*

the *see page 102*

theater, theatre (*S*) pozorište *[pozoreeshte]*; (*C*) kazalište *[kazaleeshte]*

their njihov *[nyeehov]*; **their house** njihova kuća *[nyeehova koocha]*; *see page 109*

theirs njihov *[nyeehov]*; *see page 112*

them njih *[nyeeн]*; **for them** za njih; **with them** sa njima *[nyeema]*; **I gave it to them** dao sam njima *[dao sam nyeema]*; **who?** — **them** ko? — oni *[onee]*; *see page 111*

then (*at that time*) tada; (*after that*) onda

there tamo; **over there** tamo; **up there** gore; **is there ...?** ima li ...? *[eema lee]*; **are there ...?** ima li ...? **there is ...** ima ...; **there are ...** ima ...; **there you are** (*giving something*) izvolite *[eezvoleete]*

thermal spring (*S*) topli izvor *[toplee eezvor]*; (*C*) toplice *[topleetse]*

thermometer termometar

thermos flask termos

thermostat (*in car*) termostat

these ovi *[ovee]*; **can I have these?** molim vas ove? *[moleem vas ove]*

they oni *[onee]*; **are they ready?** jesu li spremni? *[yesoo lee spremnee]*; **are they coming?** dolaze li? *[dolaze lee]*; *see page 111*

thick debeo; (*stupid*) priglup *[preegloop]*

thief lopov

thigh bedro

thin (*material*) tanak; (*person*) mršav *[murshav]*

thing stvar; **have you seen my things?** jeste li vidjeli moje stvari? *[yeste lee veedyelee moye stvaree]*; **first thing in the morning** rano ujutro *[rano ooyootro]*

think misliti *[meesleetee]*; **what do you think?** šta mislite? *[shta meesleete]*; **I think so** mislim da je tako *[meesleem da ye tako]*; **I don't think so** ne mislim da je tako; **I'll think about it** razmislit ću o tome *[razmeesleet choo o tome]*

third-class (*S*) treća klasa *[trecha]*; (*C*) treći razred *[trechee]*

third party insurance osiguranje protiv trečeg lica *[oseegooranye proteev trecheg leetsa]*

thirsty: I'm thirsty žedan sam *[ʃedan]*

this: this hotel ovaj hotel *[ovɪ hotel]*; **this street** ova ulica *[ova ooleetsa]*; **this one** ovaj; **this is my wife** ovo je moja žena *[ovo ye moya ʃena]*; **is this yours?** je li ovo vaše? *[ye lee ovo vashe]*

those oni *[onee]*; **not these, those** ne ovi, oni *[ovee]*

thread (*noun*) konac *[konats]*

throat grlo *[gurlo]*

throat lozenges pastile za grlo *[pasteele za gurlo]*

throttle (*on motorbike*) gas

through kroz; **does it go through Zagreb?** prolazi li kroz Zagreb? *[prolazee lee]*; **Monday through Friday** od ponedjeljka do petka; **straight through the city centre** pravo kroz centar grada *[tsentar]*

through train (*S*) direktni voz *[deerektnee]*; (*C*) direktni vlak

throw (*verb*) baciti *[batseetee]*; **don't throw it away** ne bacajte to *[batsɪte]*; **I'm going to throw up** povraćat ću *[povrachat choo]*

thumb palac *[palats]*

thumbtack (*S*) rajssnegla *[rɪsnegla]*; (*C*) čavlić *[chavlich]*

thunder grmljavina *[gurmlyaveena]*

thunderstorm pljusak s grmljavinom

[plyoosak s gurmlyaveenom]
Thursday četvrtak *[chetvurtak]*
ticket karta; (*cloakroom*) broj *[broy]*
ticket office prodavnica karata
[prodavneetsa]
tie (*noun: around neck*) kravata
tight (*clothes etc*) tijesan *[tyesan]*; **the
waist is too tight** struk je pretijesan
[strook ye pretyesan]
tights hula-hopke *[hoola-hopke]*
time vrijeme *[vryeme]*; **what's the
time?** koliko je sati? *[koleeko ye
satee]*; **at what time do you close?** u
koliko sati zatvarate? *[oo koleeko
satee zatvarate]*; **there's not much
time** nema mnogo vremena; **for the
time being** za sada; **from time to
time** s vremena na vrijeme; **right on
time** tačno na vrijeme *[tachno]*; **this
time** ovaj put *[ovı poot]*; **last time**
prošli put *[proshlee]*; **next time**
slijedeći put *[slyedechee]*; **four times**
četiri puta *[cheteeree poota]*; **have a
good time!** lijepo se provedite!
[lyepo se provedeete]; *see page 119*
timetable red vožnje *[voɪnye]*
tin (*can*) konzerva
tinfoil aluminijumska folija
[aloomeeneeyoomska foleeya]
tin-opener otvarač za konzerve
[otvarach]
tint (*verb: hair*) obojiti *[oboyeetee]*
tiny majušan *[mɪyooshan]*
tip (*to waiter etc*) napojnica
[napoyneetsa]; **does that include the
tip?** uključuje li to napojnicu?
[ooklyoochooye lee to napoyneetsoo]
tire (*for car*) guma *[gooma]*
tired umoran *[oomoran]*; **I'm tired**
umoran sam
tiring zamoran
tissues papirnate maramice
[papeernate marameetse]
to: to Yugoslavia/England u
Jugoslaviju/Englesku *[oo yoogo-
slaveeyoo/engleskoo]*; **to London** u
London; **to the airport** na aerodrom
[a-erodrom]; **here's to you!** u vaše
zdravlje! *[vashe zdravlye]*; *see page
119*
toast (*bread*) tost; (*drinking*) zdravica
[zdraveetsa]
tobacco (*S*) duvan *[doovan]*; (*C*)
duhan *[doohan]*

tobacconist, tobacco store trafika
[trafeeka]
today danas; **today week** danas tjedan
dana *[tjedan]*
toe nožni prst *[noɪnee purst]*
toffee karamela
together zajedno *[zɪyedno]*; **we're
together** mi smo zajedno *[mee]*; **can
we pay together?** možemo li platiti
zajedno? *[moɪemo lee plateetee]*
toilet toalet; **where's the toilet?** gdje
je toalet? *[gdye ye]*; **I have to go to
the toilet** moram ići u toalet *[moram
eechee oo]*; **she's in the toilet** ona je
u toaletu *[ona ye oo toaletoo]*
toilet paper toaletni papir *[toaletnee
papeer]*
toilet water kolonjska voda
[kolonyska]
toll (*for motorway*) (*S*) putarina
[pootareena]; (*C*) cestarina
[tsestareena]
tomato (*S*) paradajz *[paradız]*; (*C*)
rajčica *[rıcheetsa]*
tomato juice (*S*) sok od paradajza
[paradıza]; (*C*) sok od rajčice
[rıcheetse]
tomato ketchup kečap *[kechap]*
tomorrow sutra *[sootra]*; **tomorrow
morning** sutra ujutro *[ooyootro]*;
tomorrow afternoon sutra popodne;
tomorrow evening sutra uveče
[ooveche]; **the day after tomorrow**
prekosutra *[prekosootra]*; **see you
tomorrow** vidimo se sutra
[veedeemo]
ton tona; *see page 120*
tongue jezik *[yezeek]*
tonic (water) tonik *[toneek]*
tonight večeras *[vecheras]*; **not tonight**
ne večeras
tonsillitis angina *[angeena]*
tonsils krajnici *[krıneetsee]*
too (*excessively*) suviše *[sooveeshe]*;
(*also*) takođe *[takodje]*; **it's too
expensive** suviše je skupo *[ye
skoopo]*; **too much** previše
[preveeshe]; **me too** i ja *[ee ya]*; **I
was there too** ja sam bio takođe
[beeo]; **I'm not feeling too good** ne
osjećam se najbolje *[osyecham se
nıbolye]*
tooth zub *[zoob]*
toothache zubobolja *[zoobobolya]*

toothbrush četkica za zube *[chetkeetsa za zoobe]*
toothpaste pasta za zube *[zoobe]*
top: on top of ... navrh ... (+G) *[navurн]*; **on top of the car** navrh kola; **on the top floor** na najgornjem spratu *[nıgornyem spratoo]*; **at the top** na vrhu *[vurhoo]*; **at the top of the hill** na vrhu brda *[burda]*; **top quality** najbolji kvalitet *[nıbolyee kvaleetet]*; **bikini top** gornji dio bikinija *[gornyeę deeo beekeeneeya]*
topless toples; **topless beach** toples plaža *[plaja]*
torch baterija *[batereeya]*
total (*money*) ukupna svota *[ookoopna]*
touch (*verb*) dodirnuti *[dodeernootee]*; **let's keep in touch** ostanimo u vezi *[ostaneemo oo vezee]*
tough (*meat*) žilav *[jeelav]*; **tough luck!** kakav peh *[peн]*
tour (*noun*) putovanje *[pootovanye]*; **is there a tour of ...?** ima li izlet za ...? *[eema lee eezlet]*
tour guide turistički vodič *[tooreesteechkee vodeech]*
tourist turist *[tooreest]*
tourist information office turistički ured *[tooreesteechkee oored]*
touristy: somewhere not so touristy negdje gdje nema toliko turista *[negdye gdye nema toleeko tooreesta]*
tour operator turistička agencija *[tooreesteechka agentseeya]*
tow: can you give me a tow? možete li me šlepati? *[moјete lee me shlepatee]*
toward(s) prema; **toward(s) Belgrade** prema Beogradu *[beogradoo]*
towel (*S*) peškir *[peshkeer]*; (*C*) ručnik *[roochneek]*
town grad; **in town** u gradu *[oo gradoo]*; **which bus goes into town?** koji autobus ide u grad? *[koyee aootoboos eede]*; **we're staying just out of town** odsjeli smo u neposrednoj blizini grada *[odsyelee smo oo neposrednoy bleezeenee]*
town hall gradska vijećnica *[vyechneetsa]*
tow rope uže za vuču *[ooјe za voochoo]*
toy igračka *[eegrachka]*
track suit trenerka

traditional tradicionalan *[tradeetseeonalan]*; **a traditional Dalmatian meal** tradicionalno dalmatinsko jelo *[tradeetseeonalno dalmateensko yelo]*
traffic saobraćaj *[saobrachı]*
traffic circle kružni tok *[krooјnee]*
traffic cop saobraćajac *[saobrachıyats]*
traffic jam zastoj saobraćaja *[zastoy saobrachıya]*
traffic light(s) semafor
trailer prikolica *[preekoleetsa]*
train (*S*) voz; (*C*) vlak; **when's the next train to ...?** kad je sljedeći voz/ vlak za ...? *[ye slyedechee]*; **by train** vozom/vlakom
trainers (*shoes*) patike *[pateeke]*
train station (*S*) željeznička stanica *[јelyezneechka staneetsa]*; (*C*) željeznički kolodvor *[јelyezneechkee]*
tram tramvaj *[tramvı]*
tramp (*person*) skitnica *[skeetneetsa]*
tranquillizers umirujuća sredstva *[oomeerooyoocha]*
transatlantic prekoatlantski *[preko-atlantskee]*
transformer (*electric*) transformator
transistor tranzistor *[tranzeestor]*
transit lounge (*at airport*) tranzitna čekaonica *[tranzeetna chekaoneetsa]*
translate prevesti *[prevestee]*; **could you translate that?** da li biste mogli to prevesti? *[lee beeste moglee]*
translation prijevod *[pryevod]*
translator prevodilac *[prevodeelats]*
transmission (*of car*) transmisija *[transmeeseeya]*
travel putovati *[pootovatee]*; **we're travel(l)ing around** putujemo naokolo *[pootooyemo]*
travel agent turistički agent *[tooreesteechkee]*
travel(l)er putnik *[pootneek]*
traveller's cheque, traveler's check putnički ček *[pootneechkee chek]*
tray (*S*) poslužavnik *[poslooјavneek]*; (*C*) tacna *[tatsna]*
tree drvo *[durvo]*
tremendous izvanredan *[eezvanredan]*
trendy pomodan
tricky kompliciran *[kompleetseeran]*
trim: just a trim please (*to hairdresser*) molim vas, samo potšišivanje *[moleem vas, samo potsheesheevanye]*
trip (*journey*) putovanje *[pootovanye]*;

I'd like to go on a trip to ... volio bih da odem na putovanje *[voleeo beeн da odem na pootovanye]*; **have a good trip** sretan put *[poot]*
tripod *(for camera)* stativ *[stateev]*
tropical *(heat)* tropski *[tropskee]*
trouble nezgoda; **I'm having trouble with ...** imam nezgodu sa ... *[eemam nezgodoo]*; **sorry to trouble you** izvinite što vas uznemiravam *[eezveeneete shto vas ooznemeeravam]*
trousers *(S)* pantalone; *(C)* hlače *[нlache]*
trouser suit *(S)* kostim s pantalonama; *(C)* kostim s hlačama *[нlachama]*
trout *(S)* pastrmka *[pasturmka]*; *(C)* pastrva *[pasturva]*
truck kamion *[kameeon]*
truck driver vozač kamiona *[vozach kameeona]*
true istinit *[eesteeneet]*; **that's not true** to nije istina *[neeye eesteena]*
trunk *(of car)* prtljažnik *[purtlyaлneek]*; *(big case)* sanduk *[sandook]*
trunks *(swimming)* kupaće gaćice *[koopache gacheetse]*
truth istina *[eesteena]*; **it's the truth** istina je *[ye]*
try probati *[probatee]*; **please try** molim vas probajte *[moleem vas probιte]*; **will you try for me?** da li biste probali umjesto mene? *[lee beeste probalee oomyesto mene]*; **I've never tried it** nikad nisam probao *[neekad neesam]*; **can I have a try?** mogu li probati? *[mogoo lee]*; **may I try it on?** mogu li probati?
T-shirt majica *[mιyeetsa]*
tube *(for tyre)* unutrašnja guma *[oonootrashnya gooma]*

Tuesday utorak *[ootorak]*
tuition: I'd like tuition želio bih da uzimati satove *[лeleeo beeн oozeematee]*
tulip tulipan *[tooleepan]*
tuna fish tuna *[toona]*
tune *(noun)* melodija *[melodeeya]*
tunnel tunel *[toonel]*
Turkey Turska *[toorska]*
turn: it's my turn now sad je na mene red *[ye]*; **turn left** skrenite lijevo *[skreneete lyevo]*; **where do we turn off?** gdje skrećemo *[skrechemo]*; **can you turn the air-conditioning on?** da li biste uključili erkondišn? *[lee beeste ooklyoocheelee erkondeeshun]*; **can you turn the air-conditioning off?** da li biste isključili erkondišn? *[eesklyoocheelee]*; **he didn't turn up** nije se pojavio *[neeye se poyaveeo]*
turning *(in road)* skretanje *[skretanye]*
TV televizija *[televeezeeya]*
tweezers pinceta *[peentseta]*
twice dvaput *[dvapoot]*; **twice as much** dvaput toliko *[toleeko]*
twin beds dva kreveta
twin room dvokrevetna soba
twins blizanci *[bleezantsee]*
twist: I've twisted my ankle uganuo sam nogu *[ooganoo-o sam nogoo]*
type *(noun)* vrsta *[vursta]*; **a different type of ...** drukčija vrsta ... *(+G)* *[drookcheeya]*
typewriter *(S)* pisaća mašina *[peesacha masheena]*; *(C)* pisaći stroj *[peesachee stroy]*
typhoid tifus *[teefoos]*
typical *(dish etc)* tipičan *[teepeechan]*; **that's typical!** to je tipično! *[ye teepeechno]*
tyre guma *[gooma]*

U

ugly (*person, building*) ružan *[rooJan]*
ulcer čir *[cheer]*
Ulster Alster
umbrella kišobran *[keeshobran]*
uncle: my uncle (*mother's brother*) moj ujak *[moy ooyak]*; (*father's brother*) moj stric *[streets]*
uncomfortable (*chair etc*) neudoban *[ne-oodoban]*
unconscious nesvjestan *[nesvyestan]*
under ispod *[eespod]*
underdone (*meat*) nepečen *[nepechen]*
underground (*rail*) podzemna željeznica *[podzemna Jelyezneetsa]*
underpants gaće *[gache]*
undershirt potkošulja *[potkoshoolya]*
understand: I don't understand ne razumijem *[razoomyem]*; **I understand** razumijem; **do you understand?** razumijete li? *[razoomyete lee]*
underwear donje rublje *[donye rooblye]*
undo (*clothes*) otkopčati *[otkopchatee]*
uneatable: it's uneatable ne može se jesti *[moJe se yestee]*
unemployed nezaposlen
unfair: that's unfair to je nepravedno
unfortunately na žalost *[Jalost]*
unfriendly neprijazan *[nepreeyazan]*
unhappy nesretan
unhealthy (*person, climate etc*) nezdrav
United States Sjedinjene Države *[syedeenyene durJave]*; **in the United States** u Sjedinjenim Državama *[oo syedeenyeneem durJavama]*
university univerzitet *[ooneeverzeetet]*
unlimited mileage (*on hire car*) neograničena kilometraža *[neogran-eechena keelometraJa]*
unlock otključati *[otklyoochatee]*; **the door was unlocked** vrata su bila otključana *[soo beela otklyoochana]*

unpack otpakovati *[otpakovatee]*
unpleasant neprijatan *[nepreeyatan]*
unpronounceable: it's unpronounceable to se ne može izgovoriti *[moJe eezgovoreetee]*
untie odvezati *[odvezatee]*
until do; **until we meet again** (*said as parting words*) do ponovnog susreta! *[soosreta]*; **not until Wednesday** ne do srijede *[sryede]*; **until he returns** ne dok se ne vrati *[vratee]*
unusual neobičan *[neobeechan]*
up gore; **further up the road** dalje uz cestu *[dalye ooz tsestoo]*; **up there** tamo gore; **he's not up yet** (*not out of bed*) još nije ustao *[yosh neeye oostao]*; **what's up?** šta je? *[shta ye]*
upmarket (*restaurant, hotel, goods etc*) luksuzan *[looksoozan]*
upset stomach pokvaren stomak
upside down naopako
upstairs gore
urgent hitan *[heetan]*; **it's very urgent** veoma je hitno *[veoma ye heetno]*
urinary tract infection infekcija mokraćnih organa *[eenfektseeya moκrachneeн]*
us nas; **with us** s nama; **for us** za nas; *see page 111*
use (*verb*) upotrijebiti *[oopotryeb-eetee]*; **may I use ...?** mogu li upotrijebiti ...? *[mogoo lee]*
used: I used to swim a lot nekad sam mnogo plivao *[pleevao]*; **when I get used to the heat** kad se naviknem na vrućinu *[naveeknem na vroocheenoo]*
useful koristan *[koreestan]*
usual običan *[obeechan]*; **as usual** kao obično *[kao obeechno]*
usually obično *[obeechno]*
U-turn promjena pravca *[promyena pravtsa]*

V

vacancy: do you have any vacancies? (*hotel*) imate li slobodnih soba? *[eemate lee slobodneeн soba]*

vacation raspust *[raspoost]*; we're here on vacation ovdje smo na raspustu *[ovdye smo na raspoostoo]*

vaccination vakcinacija *[vaktseenatseeya]*

vacuum cleaner usisivač *[ooseeseevach]*

vacuum flask termos

vagina vagina *[vageena]*

valid (*ticket etc*) važeći *[vaлechee]*; how long is it valid for? koliko važi? *[koleeko vaлee]*

valley dolina *[doleena]*

valuable (*adjective*) dragocjen *[dragotsyen]*; can I leave my valuables here? mogu li ostaviti ovdje svoje dragocjenosti? *[mogoo lee ostaveetee ovdye svoye dragotsyenostee]*

value (*noun*) vrijednost *[vryednost]*

van kombi *[kombee]*

vanilla vanilija *[vaneelya]*; a vanilla ice cream sladoled od vanilije *[vaneelye]*

varicose veins proširene vene *[prosheerene]*

variety show varijete *[vareeyete]*

vary: it varies zavisi *[zaveesee]*

vase vaza

vaudeville varijete *[vareeyete]*

VD venerična bolest *[venereechna]*

veal teletina *[teleteena]*

vegetables povrće *[povurche]*

vegetarian: I'm a vegetarian (*man*) ja sam vegeterijanac *[ya sam vegetereeyanats]*; (*woman*) ja sam vegeterijanka *[vegetereeyanka]*

velvet somot

vending machine automat *[aootomat]*

ventilator ventilator *[venteelator]*

very veoma, vrlo *[vurlo]*; it's very

cheap veoma je jevtino *[ye yevtino]*; just a very little Serbocroat sasvim malo srpskohrvatski *[sasveem malo surpsko-нurvatskee]*; just a very little for me za mene veoma malo; I like it very much mnogo mi se dopada *[mnogo mee see]*

vest (*under shirt*) potkošulja *[potkoshoolya]*; (*waistcoat*) prsluk *[purslook]*

via preko; via Belgrade preko Beograda

video (*noun: film*) video (*m*) *[veedeo]*; (*recorder*) video rikorder *[reekorder]*

view pogled; what a superb view! kakav krasan pogled!

viewfinder tražilo *[traлeelo]*

villa vila *[veela]*

village selo

vine loza

vinegar (*S*) sirće *[seerche]*; (*C*) ocat *[otsat]*

vine-growing area vinogradarski kraj *[veenogradarskee krл]*

vineyard vinograd *[veenograd]*

vintage (*of wine*) berba

vintage wine kvalitetno vino *[kvaleetetno veeno]*

visa viza *[veeza]*

visibility (*for driving etc*) vidljivost *[veedlyeevost]*

visit (*verb*) posjetiti *[posyeteetee]*; I'd like to visit ... rado bih posjetio ... *[rado beeн posyeteeo]*; come and visit us dođite nam u posjetu *[dodjeete nam oo posyetoo]*

vital: it's vital that ... bitno je da ... *[beetno ye]*

vitamins vitamini *[veetameenee]*

vodka votka

voice glas

voltage voltaža *[voltaлa]*

vomit povraćati *[povrachatee]*

W

wafer (*with ice cream*) vafla

waist struk *[strook]*

waistcoat prsluk *[purslook]*

wait čekati *[chekatee]*; **wait for me**
čekajte me *[chekɪte]*; **don't wait for
me** nemojte me čekati *[nemoyte me
chekatee]*; **it was worth waiting for**
vrijedilo je čekati *[vryedeelo ye]*; **I'll
wait until my wife comes** čekat ću
da mi dođe žena *[chekat choo da
mee dodje ɪena]*; **I'm waiting for
someone** čekam nekog *[chekam
nekog]*; **I'll wait a little longer** čekat
ću još malo *[yosh malo]*; **can you do
it while I wait?** možete li uraditi
dok čekam? *[moɪete lee ooraɖeetee]*

waiter konobar; **waiter!** konobar!

waiting room čekaonica *[cheka-
oneetsa]*

waitress konobarica *[konobareetsa]*;
waitress! konobarice! *[konobareetse]*

wake: **will you wake me up at 6.30?**
hoćete li me probuditi u 6.30?
*[hochete lee me proboodeetee oo
shest ee treedeset]*

Wales Vels

walk: **let's walk there** odšetajmo tamo
[odshetɪmo]; **is it possible to walk
there?** može li se do tamo pješke?
[moɪe lee se do tamo pyeshke]; **I'll
walk back** vratit ću se pješke *[vrateet
choo]*; **is it a long walk?** je li daleko
pješke? *[ye lee]*; **it's only a short
walk** sasvim je blizu pješke *[sasveem
ye bleezoo]*; **I'm going out for a
walk** idem u šetnju *[eedem oo
shetnyoo]*; **let's take a walk around
town** prošetajmo po gradu
[proshetɪmo po gradoo]

walking: **I want to do some walking**
želim ići u planinarenju *[ɪeleem
eechee oo planeenarenyoo]*

walking boots planinarske cipele
[planeenarske tseepele]

walking stick štap *[shtap]*

walkman (*tm*) vokman

wall zid *[zeed]*

wallet novčanik *[novchaneek]*

walnut orah *[oraн]*

wander: **I like just wandering
around** volim lutati naokolo *[voleem
lootatee naokolo]*

want: **I want a ...** želim ... *[ɪeleem]*; **I
don't want any ...** ne želim ...; **I
want to go home** želim ići kući
[eechee koochee]; **I don't want to** ne
želim; **he wants to ...** želi ... *[ɪelee]*;
what do you want? šta želite? *[shta
ɪeleete]*

war rat

ward (*in hospital*) (*S*) odjeljenje
[odyelyenye]; (*C*) odjel *[odyel]*

warm topao; **it's so warm today**
danas je tako toplo; **I'm so warm**
tako mi je toplo *[mee ye]*

warning upozorenje *[oopozorenye]*

was: **it was ...** bilo je to ... *[beelo ye]*;
see page 115

wash (*verb*) oprati *[opratee]*; **I need a
wash** treba da se operem; **can you
wash the car?** možete li oprati kola?
[moɪete lee opratee]; **can you wash
these?** možete li ih oprati? *[lee eeн]*;
it'll wash off opraće se *[oprache]*

washcloth (*S*) peškirič za lice
[peshkeereech za leetse]; (*C*) krpica za
lice *[kurpeetsa]*

washer (*for bolt etc*) brtva *[burtva]*

washhand basin umivaonik *[oomee-
vaoneek]*

washing (*clothes*) prljavo rublje
[purlyavo rooblye]; **where can I hang
my washing?** gdje mogu objesiti
rublje? *[gdye mogoo obyeseetee]*; **can
you do my washing for me?** možete
li mi oprati rublje? *[moɪete lee mee
opratee]*

washing machine (*S*) mašina za
pranje rublja *[masheena za pranye
rooblya]*; (*C*) stroj za pranje rublja
[stroy]

washing powder deterdžent
[deterdjent]

washing-up: **I'll do the washing-up**

ja ću oprati suđe *[ya choo opratee soodje]*
washing-up liquid tekućina za pranje suđa *[tekoocheena za pranye soodja]*
wasp osa
wasteful: that's wasteful to je rasipno *[ye raseepno]*
wastepaper basket (*S*) korpa za otpatke; (*C*) koš za smeće *[kosh za smeche]*
watch (*wrist-*) ručni sat *[roochnee]*; **will you watch my things for me?** hoćete li mi pripaziti stvari? *[hochete lee mee preepazeetee stvaree]*; **I'll just watch** samo ću gledati *[choo gledatee]*; **watch out!** pazite! *[pazeete]*
watch strap (*S*) kaiš za sat *[kɪ-eesh]*; (*C*) remen za sat
water voda; **may I have some water?** molim vas malo vode *[moleem]*
watercolo(u)r akvarel
waterproof (*adjective*) nepromočiv *[nepromocheev]*
waterski: I'd like to learn to waterski rado bih naučio skijati na vodi *[rado beeн naoocheeo skeeyatee na vodee]*
waterskiing skijanje na vodi *[skeeyanye na vodee]*
water sports sportovi na vodi *[sportovee na vodee]*
water wings natikači za plivanje *[nateekachee za pleevanye]*
wave (*in sea*) val
way: which way is it? kojim putem? *[koyeem pootem]*; **it's this way** u ovom pravcu *[oo ovom pravtsoo]*; **it's that way** u onom pravcu *[onom]*; **could you tell me the way to ...?** da li biste mi mogli pokazati put za ...? *[lee beeste mee moglee pokazatee poot]*; **is it on the way to Split?** je li na puta za Split? *[ye lee na pootoo za speet]*; **you're blocking the way** zakrčili ste put *[zakurcheelee]*; **is it a long way to ...?** je li daleko do ...? *[ye lee]*; **would you show me the way to do it?** da li biste mi pokazali kako da to uradim? *[mee pokazalee kako da to ooradeem]*; **do it this way** uradite ovako *[ooradeete]*; **no way!** ni govora! *[nee]*
we mi *[mee]*; *see page 111*
weak (*person, drink*) slab

wealthy bogat
weather vrijeme *[vryeme]*; **what foul weather!** kakvo gadno vrijeme!; **what beautiful weather!** kakvo prekrasno vrijeme!
weather forecast prognoza vremena
wedding vjenčanje *[vyenchanye]*
wedding anniversary godišnjica vjenčanja *[godeeshnyeetsa vyenchanya]*
wedding ring burma *[boorma]*
Wednesday srijeda *[sryeda]*
week tjedan *[tyedan]*; **a week (from) today** danas tjedan dana; **a week (from) tomorrow** sutra tjedan dana *[sootra]*; **Monday week** ponedjeljak tjedan dana *[ponedyelyak]*
weekend vikend *[veekend]*; **at/on the weekend** preko vikenda *[veekenda]*
weight težina *[teɹeena]*; **I want to lose weight** želim smršati *[ɹeleem smurshatee]*
weight limit dozvoljena težina *[dozvolyena teɹeena]*
weird čudan *[choodan]*
welcome: welcome to ... dobrodošli u ... *[dobrodoshlee oo]*; **you're welcome** (*don't mention it*) nema na čemu *[nema na chemoo]*
well: I don't feel well ne osjećam se dobro *[osyecham se dobro]*; **I haven't been very well** nisam se osjećao najbolje *[neesam se osyechao nɪbolye]*; **she's not well** ne osjeća se dobro *[osyecha]*; **how are you — very well, thanks** kako ste — odlično, hvala *[odleechno нvala]*; **you speak English very well** veoma dobro govorite engleski *[govoreete engleskee]*; **me as well** ja takođe *[ya takodje]*; **well done!** čestitam! *[chesteetam]*; **well well!** (*surprise*) vidi! vidi! *[veedee]*
well-done (*meat*) dobro pečeno *[dobro pecheno]*
wellingtons gumene čizme *[goomene cheezme]*
Welsh velški *[velshkee]*
were *see page 115*
west zapad; **to the west of ...** zapadno od ...; **in the west** na zapadu *[zapadoo]*
wet mokro; **it's all wet** potpuno je vlažno *[potpoono ye vlaɹno]*; **it's**

been **wet** all **week** cijeli tjedan pada kiša *[tsyelee tyedan pada keesha]*
wet suit ronilačko odijelo *[roneelachko odyelo]*
what? šta? *[shta]*; **what's that?** šta je to? *[ye]*; **what is he saying?** šta govori? *[govoree]*; **I don't know what to do** ne znam šta da radim *[radeem]*; **what a view!** kakav pogled!
wheel točak *[tochak]*
wheelchair invalidska kolica *[eenvaleedska koleetsa]*
when? kada? ; **when we get back** kad se vratimo *[vrateemo]*; **when we got back** kad smo se vratili *[vrateelee]*
where gdje? *[gyde]*; **where is ...?** gdje je ...? *[ye]*; **I don't know where he is** ne znam gdje je; **that's where I left it** tu sam ostavio *[too sam ostaveeo]*
which: which bus? koji autobus? *[koyee aootoboos]*; **which one?** koji? ; **which is yours?** koji je vaš *[ye vash]*; **I forget which it was** zaboravio sam koji je bio ... *[zaboraveeo sam koyee ye beeo]*; **the one which ...** onaj koji ... *[onɪ]*; *see page 113*
while *(conjunction)* dok; **while I'm here** dok sam ovdje *[ovdye]*
whipped cream šlag *[shlag]*
whisky viski *[veeskee]*
whisper *(verb)* šaptati *[shaptatee]*
white bijel *[byel]*
white wine bijelo vino *[byelo veeno]*
who? ko? ; **who was that?** ko je to bio? *[ye to beeo]*; **the man who ...** čovjek koji ... *[chovyek koyee]*
whole: the whole week cijeli tjedan *[tsyelee tyedan]*; **two whole days** dva cijela dana *[tsyela]*; **the whole lot** sve
whooping cough hripavac *[ʜreepavats]*
whose: whose is this? čije je ovo? *[cheeye ye ovo]*
why? zašto? *[zashto]*; **why not?** zašto da ne?; **that's why it's not working** eto zašto ne radi *[zashto ne radee]*
wide širok *[sheerok]*
wide-angled lens širokokutni objektiv *[sheerokootnee obyekteev]*
widow udovica *[oodoveetsa]*
widower udovac *[oodovats]*
wife: my wife moja žena *[moya ʒena]*
wig perika *[pereeka]*

will: will you ask him hoćete li ga pitati *[hochete lee ga peetatee]*; *see page 116*
win *(verb)* pobijediti *[pobyedeetee]*; **who won?** ko je pobijedio? *[ye pobyedeeo]*
wind *(noun)* vjetar *[vyetar]*
window prozor; **near the window** blizu prozora *[bleezoo prozora]*; **in the window** *(of shop)* u izlogu *[oo eezlogoo]*
window seat sjedište pored prozora *[syedeeshte]*
windscreen, windshield vjetrobran *[vyetrobran]*
windscreen wipers, windshield wipers brisači *[breesachee]*
windsurf: I'd like to windsurf rado bih išao na serfing *[beeʜ eeshao na serfeeng]*
windsurfing serfing *[serfeeng]*
windy vjetrovit *[vyetroveet]*; **it's so windy** tako je vjetrovito *[tako ye vyetroveeto]*
wine vino *[veeno]*; **can we have some more wine?** molim vas još malo vina *[moleem vas yosh malo veena]*
wine glass vinska čaša *[veenska chasha]*
wine list vinska karta *[veenska]*
wine-tasting probanje vina *[probanye veena]*
wing *(of plane, bird, car)* krilo *[kreelo]*
wing mirror bočno ogledalo *[bochno]*
winter zima *[zeema]*; **in the winter** zimi *[zeemee]*
winter holiday zimski odmor *[zeemskee]*
wire žica *[ʒeetsa]*
wireless radio *(m)* *[radeeo]*
wiring električna instalacija *[elektreechna eenstalatseeya]*
wish: wishing you were here *(as written on postcards)* želio bih da ste i vi ovdje *[ʒeleeo beeʜ da ste ee vee ovdye]*; **best wishes** najbolje želje *[nɪbolye ʒelye]*
with sa; **I'm staying with ...** odsjeo sam kod ... *(+G)* *[odsyeo]*; **she is with her mother** ona je s majkom *[ona ye s mɪkom]*; **with love** s ljubavlju *[lyoobavlyoo]*; **with difficulty** s naporom; **with a pencil** olovkom

without bez

witness svjedok *[svyedok]*; **will you be a witness for me?** hoćete li biti moj svjedok? *[hochete lee beetee moy]*

witty duhovit *[doohoveet]*

wobble: it wobbles klima se *[kleema]*

woman žena *[jena]*

women žene *[jene]*

wonderful divan *[deevan]*

won't: it won't start neće da upali *[neche da oopalee]; see page 116*

wood (*material*) drvo *[durvo]*

woods (*forest*) šuma *[shooma]*

wool vuna *[voona]*

word riječ *[ryech]*; **you have my word** dajem vam riječ *[dıyem vam ryech]*

work (*verb*) raditi *[radeetee]*; (*noun*) rad; **how does it work** kako radi? *[radee]*; **it's not working** ne radi; **I work in ...** radim u *[radeem oo]*; **do you have any work for me?** imate li ikakvog posla za mene? *[eemate lee eekakvog]*; **when do you finish work?** kada završavate posao? *[zavurshavate]*

work permit radna dozvola

world svijet *[svyet]*; **all over the world** po cijelom svijetu *[tsyelom svyetoo]*

worn-out (*person*) iscrpljen *[eestsurplyen]*; (*shoes, clothes*) pohaban

worry: I'm worried about her zabrinut sam za nju *[zabreenoot sam za nyoo]*; **don't worry** ne brinite se *[breeneete]*

worse: it's worse gore je *[gore ye]*; **it's getting worse** pogoršava se *[pogorshava]*

worst najgori *[nıgoree]*

worth: it's not worth 500 dinars ne vrijedi 500 dinara *[vryedee petsto deenara]*; **it's worth more than that** vrijedi više *[veeshe]*; **is it worth a visit?** vrijedi li posjetiti? *[lee posyeteetee]*

would: would you give this to ...? da li biste ovo dali ... (+*D*) *[lee beeste ovo dalee]*; **what would you do?** šta biste vi radili? *[shta beeste vee radeelee]*

wrap: could you wrap it up? da li biste mogli umotati? *[lee beeste moglee oomotatee]*

wrapping omot

wrapping paper papir za umotavanje *[papeer za oomotavanye]*

wrench (*tool*) ključ za odvijanje *[klyooch za odveeyanye]*

wrist ručni zglob *[roochnee]*

write pisati *[peesatee]*; **could you write it down?** da li biste mogli zapisati? *[lee beeste moglee zapeesatee]*; **how do write it?** kako se piše? *[peeshe]*; **I'll write to you** pisat ću vam *[peesat choo]*; **I wrote to you last month** pisao sam vam prošlog mjeseca *[peesao ... proshlog myesetsa]*

write-off: the car is a write-off kola su potpuno uništena *[kola soo potpoono ooneeshtena]*

writer pisac *[peesats]*

writing pisanje *[peesanye]*

writing paper papir za pisanje *[papeer za peesanye]*

wrong: you're wrong niste u pravu *[neeste oo pravoo]*; **the bill's wrong** račun je pogrešan *[rachoon ye pogreshan]*; **sorry, wrong number** žao mi je, pogrešan broj *[jao mee ye ... broy]*; **I'm on the wrong bus** u pogrešnom sam autobusu *[oo pogreshnom sam aootoboosoo]*; **I went to the wrong room** otišao sam u pogrešnu sobu *[oteeshao sam oo pogreshnoo soboo]*; **that's the wrong key** to je pogrešan ključ *[ye ... klyooch]*; **there's something wrong with ...** nešto nije u redu sa ... *[neshto neeye o redoo sa]*; **what's wrong?** šta nije u redu? *[shta]*; **what's wrong with it?** u čemu je greška? *[oo chemoo ye greshka]*

X

X-ray rendgen

Y

yacht jahta *[yahta]*
yacht club jaht-klub *[yaht-kloob]*
yard: in the yard u dvorištu *[oo dvoreeshtoo]*; *see page 120*
year godina *[godeena]*
yellow žut *[JOOt]*
yellow pages poslovni telefonski imenik *[poslovnee telefonskee eemeneek]*
yes da
yesterday juče *[yooche]*; **yesterday morning** juće ujutro *[ooyootro]*; **yesterday afternoon** juče popodne *[popodne]*; **the day before yesterday** prekjuče *[prekyooche]*
yet: has it arrived yet? je li već stiglo? *[ye lee vech steeglo]*; **not yet** još nije *[yosh neeye]*
yobbo siledžija *(m)* *[seeledjeeya]*
yog(h)urt jogurt *[yogoort]*
you *(familiar, singular)* ti *[tee]*; *(polite, singular, plural)* vi *[vee]*; **this is for you** ovo je za vas; **with you** sa vama; *see page 112*
young mlad

young people omladina *[omladeena]*
your *(familiar, singular)* tvoj *[tvoy]*; *(polite, singular, plural)* vaš *[vash]*; **your camera** vaša kamera *[vasha]*; *see page 109*
yours *(familiar, singular)* tvoj *[tvoy]*; *(polite, singular, plural)* vaš *[vash]*; *see page 112*
youth hostel omladinski hotel *[omladeenskee]*; **we're youth hostel(l)ing** putujemo odsijedajući u omladinskim hotelima *[pootooyemo odsyedıyoochee oo omladeenskeem hoteleema]*
Yugoslav *(adjective)* (S) jugoslovenski *[yoogoslovenskee]*; (C) jugoslavenski *[yoogoslavenskee]*; *(man)* (S) Jugosloven *[yoogosloven]*; (C) Jugoslaven *[yoogoslaven]*; *(woman)* (S) Jugoslovenka; (C) Jugoslavenka; **the Yugoslavs** (S) Jugosloveni; (C) Jugoslaveni
Yugoslavia Jugoslavija *[yoogoslaveeya]*

Z

zero nula *[noola]*
zip, zipper patent-zatvarač *[patent-zatvarach]*; **could you put a new zip on?** da li biste mogli staviti novi patent-zatvarač? *[lee beeste moglee staveetee novee]*
zoo zoološki vrt *[zo-oloshkee vurt]*
zoom lens zum-objektiv *[zoom-obyekteev]*

Serbocroat-English

A

aerodrom airport
aerodromska zgrada air terminal
ajvar *[ivar]* relish made of aubergine/
eggplant and peppers
alarmno zvono alarm bell
alaska čorba *[alaska chorba]*
fisherman's bouillabaisse (rich fish
stew served with fried bread)
alat tools
Albanija, Albanska Albania
alkoholna pića wines and spirits
ambasada embassy
ambulanta surgery, doctor's office
Amerikanac, Amerikanka American
ananas *[ananas]* pineapple
animirani film animated film
antifriz antifreeze
aparat za gašenje požara fire
extinguisher

apartman suite
apatinski paprikaš *[apateenskee
papreekash]* Apatin bouillabaisse
(freshwater fish stew with onions,
peppers, chillies, peeled tomatoes
and wine, served with noodles)
apoteka chemist, pharmacy
Austrija Austria
autobus bus, coach
autobusna stanica bus/coach station
autobusni red vožnje bus timetable/
schedule
autoput motorway, highway
avenija avenue
avgust August
avion aircraft
avionom by airmail
avionska pošta airmail

B

bademi *[bademee]* almonds
bakalar *[bakalar]* cod
baklava *[baklava]* rich cake made of
thin layers of pastry, filled with walnuts and soaked in syrup
balkon upper circle; balcony
banja spa
banka bank
barbun *[barboon]* red mullet
baren *[baren]* boiled
bareno jaje *[bareno yiye]* boiled egg
barokni Baroque
batak *[batak]* leg (*poultry*)
bazen za djecu paddling pool
bazen za plivanje swimming pool
bečki ordrezak *[bechkee odrezak]*
Wiener Schnitzel
benzinska pumpa petrol/gas pump

Beograd Belgrade
bešamel umak *[beshamel oomak]* be-
chamel sauce
biblioteka library
bijela kafa *[byela kafa]* white coffee,
coffee with milk
bijeli kruh/hljeb *[byelee krooн/нlyeb]*
white bread
bijeli luk *[byelee look]* garlic
bijelo meso *[byelo meso]* breast (*poultry*)
bijelo vino *[byelo veeno]* white wine
bioskop cinema, movie theater
biro za nađene stvari lost property
bitango jedna! *[beetango yedna]*
bastard!
bižuterija jewel(le)ry
blagajna cashier; ticket office

boje i lakovi paints and varnishes
bojenje colo(u)r rinse
bolnica hospital
boranija *[boraneeya]* French beans
boranija sa svinjskim mesom *[boraneeya sa sveenyskeem mesom]* French beans with pork
boravišna taksa residence tax
borovnice *[borovnitse]* blackcurrants
Bosanac, Bosanka Bosnian
bosanski lonac *[bosanskee lonats]* Bosnian hot-pot/casserole
Bosna Bosnia (*region in central Yugoslavia*)
br. (broj) number
brašno *[brashno]* flour
bravetina *[braveteena]* mutton
brdo hill
brendi brandy
breskve *[breskve]* peaches
brijanje shave
brišite noge please wipe your feet
britanska vojna misija British Military Mission

brizle *[breezle]* sweetbreads
brodet *[brodet]* fish stew
brodet na dalmatinski način *[brodet na dalmateenskee nacheen]* bouillabaisse Dalmatian style (fried carp or sea bream in a sauce made of onions, tomatoes, wine, vinegar, Tabasco (*tm*) sauce and white pepper)
broj garderobe baggage slip
broj je zauzet *[broy ye zaoozet]* the line is engaged/busy
broj leta flight number
broj pasoša passport number
broj sobe room number
brzi vlak/voz fast train
bubrezi *[boobrezee]* kidneys
budalo! *[boodalo]* fool!
Bugarska Bulgaria
bulevar boulevard
burek *[boorek]* minced meat/ground beef pie
but *[boot]* leg (*of meat*)
buter *[booter]* butter
butik boutique

C

carina Customs
carinska deklaracija customs declaration
celer *[tseler]* celery
centar grada city centre/center
cesta road
cigarete cigarettes
cijediti ručno wring by hand
cijena price; charge
cikla *[tseekla]* beetroot, red beet
cikorija *[tseekoreeya]* chicory
cipal *[tseepal]* grey mullet
cjenovnik price list
couvert cover charge

crkva church
Crna Gora Montenegro (*a republic of Yugoslavia*)
crna kafa *[tsurna kafa]* black coffee
crni kruh/hljeb *[tsurnee kroоn/Hlyeb]* brown bread
crni luk *[tsurnee look]* onion
Crnogorac, Crnogorka Montenegrin
crno vino *[tsurno veeno]* red wine
crtani film cartoon
Crveni krst Red Cross
crveni luk *[tsurvenee look]* onion
cvekla *[tsvekla]* beetroot, red beet
cvjećara florist

Serbocroat alphabetical order: c č ć; d dž đ; lu lj; nu nj; s š; z ž

Č

čaj tea *[chɪ]*
čaj sa limunom *[chɪ sa leemoonom]* tea with lemon
čamci za iznajmljivanje boats to rent
čaše glasses
ček cheque, check
čekaonica waiting room
češnjak *[cheshnyak]* garlic
četvrtak Thursday
čista svila pure silk
čistiti samo kemijski dry clean only
čorba *[chorba]* (thick) soup
čorba od goveđeg repa *[chorba od govedjeg repa]* oxtail soup

čorba od kupusa *[chorba od koopoosa]* cabbage soup
čorba od mladog graška *[chorba od mladog grashka]* green pea soup
čorbast pasulj sa kobasicama *[chorbast pasool-yuh sa kobaseetsama]* bean stew with sausages
čorbast pasulj sa svinjskim nožicama *[chorbast pasool-yuh sa sveenyskeem noɪeetsama]* bean stew with pig's trotters
čuvaj se psa beware of the dog
čuvati na hladnom i suhom mjestu store in a cool, dry place

Ć

ćebad blankets
ćevabdžinica type of café serving 'ćevapčići' made on the premises
ćevapčići *[chevapcheechee]* minced/ground meat rolls
ćufte na kajmaku *[choofte na kɪmakoo]* meat balls with 'kajmak'
ćufte od džigerice *[choofte od djeegereetse]* liver balls

ćufte u sosu od rajčica *[choofte oo sosoo od rɪcheetsa]* meatballs in tomato sauce
ćulbastija *[cholbasteeya]* grilled slice of well-matured best rib of beef
ćuretina *[chooreteena]* turkey
ćurka na podvarku *[choorka na podvarkoo]* turkey with sauerkraut

D

d (dinar) dinar
da yes
dagnje *[dagnye]* mussels
da, hvala *[ʜvala]* yes thank you
Dalmacija Dalmatia (*region of western Yugoslavia along the Adriatic*)
Dalmatinac, Dalmatinka Dalmatian

danas today
datum rođenja date of birth
dezert dessert
dežurna apoteka/ljekarna emergency pharmacy/chemist
dežurstvo duty
dimljen *[deemlyen]* smoked

dimljeni bakalar *[deemlyenee bakalar]* smoked cod

dimljeni sir *[deemlyenee seer]* smoked cheese

dinar dinar, Yugoslav unit of currency

dinja *[deenya]* melon

direktni vlak/voz through train

direktor manager

divljač *[deevlyach]* game (*meat*)

dizel gorivo diesel-oil

dječja odjeća children's wear

dječja porcija children's portion

dnevno per day

dobar dan *[dobar]* good afternoon

dobar tek *[dobar]* enjoy your meal

dobrodošli u ... welcome to ...

dobro jutro *[dobro yootro]* good morning

dobro pečen *[dobro pechen]* well-done (*meat*)

dobro promućkati prije upotrebe shake well before using

dobro veče *[dobro veche]* good evening

dođavola! *[dodjavola]* damn it!

dolar dollar

dolasci arrivals

dolazak arrival

dole down

dolina valley

dolma *[dolma]* stuffed vegetables

domaće kobasice na žaru *[domache kobaseetse na ʝaroo]* grilled home-made sausages

domaći letovi domestic flights

dopisnice postcards

doručak breakfast

dotrajao kolovoz worn road surface

doviđenja *[doveedjenya]* so long

doza za djecu/odrasle dosage for children/adults

dozvoljena brzina speed limit

dozvoljena težina weight limit

dozvoljena visina maximum height

drago mi je *[drago mee ye]* pleased to meet you

drogerija drugstore

drugi kat/sprat (*UK*) second floor, (*USA*) third floor

drugi razred second class

državljanstvo nationality

držimo marke we sell stamps

držite odstojanje keep your distance

dunja *[doonya]* quince

dvokrevetna soba double room

dvosmjerni saobraćaj two-way traffic

DŽ

džamija mosque

džem *[djem]* jam

džem od bresaka *[djem od bresaka]* peach jam

džem od šipaka *[djem od sheepaka]* rose-hip jam

džigerica na žaru *[djeegereetsa na ʝaroo]* grilled liver

džin *[djeen]* gin

Đ

đuveč *[djoovech]* dish made of meat, rice and various vegetables

E

ekspres pismo express letter
električar electrician
električna roba electrical goods
električni aparati electrical ap-
pliances
Engleska England
Englez, Engleskinja English

F

faširane šnicle *[fasheerane shneetsle]* beefburger style steaks
fazan *[fazan]* pheasant
feferoni *[feferonee]* hot chillies
filijala branch
flekice *[flekeetse]* macaroni squares
formular form
fotograf photographer
fotokopiranje photocopying service
freske frescoes
frizer hairdresser
funta sterlinga pound sterling

G

g. (gospodin) Mr
galerija gallery
garancija guarantee
garaža garage
garderoba left luggage, baggage checkroom
gđa (gospođa) Mrs
gđica (gospođica) Miss
gibanica *[geebanitsa]* layered cheese pie
girice *[geereetse]* whitebait
glavna pošta main post office
glavno jelo main course
gljive *[glyeeve]* mushrooms
god. (godina) year
godina rođenja year of birth
godišnje per annum
gore up
gostiona inn
gotova jela set dishes (*items on menu immediately available*)
gotski Gothic
govedina *[govedeena]* beef
govedina sa hrenom *[govedeena sa нrenom]* cold beef with horseradish
goveđa supa *[govedja soopa]* beef

broth
goveđe pečenje *[govedje pechenye]* roast beef
goveđi bujon *[govedjee booyon]* beef bouillon
goveđi gulaš *[govedjee goolash]* beef goulash
goveđi jezik *[govedjee yezeek]* ox tongue
goveđi odrezak sa lukom *[govedjee odrezak sa lookom]* beef steak with onion
grad town, city
gradska bolnica city hospital
gradska vijećnica town hall
grah *[граɴ]* beans

gramofonske ploče records
grašak *[grashak]* peas
Grčka Greece
grejpfrut *[graypfroot]* grapefruit
grne *[gurne]* stuffed onions
groblje cemetry
grožde *[groɪdje]* grapes
grožđice *[groɪdjeetse]* raisins
grupno putovanje group travel
gubi se! *[goobee]* bugger off!
guraj push
guska goose
guščetina *[gooshcheteena]* goose
guščja jetra *[gooshcheeya yetra]* goose liver
gvoždara ironmonger, hardware store

H

hemijska čistiona dry cleaning
Hercegovac, Hercegovka Herzegovinian
Hercegovina Herzegovina *(region in west central Yugoslavia)*
historijski spomenici historic monuments
hlače trousers, pants
hladna zakuska *[ʜladna zakooska]* mixed hors d'oeuvres

hladnjaci fridges
hljeb *[ʜlyeb]* bread
hrana foodstuffs
hren *[ʜren]* horseradish
hrenovke *[ʜrenovke]* frankfurters; hot-dogs
Hrvat, Hrvatica Croat
Hrvatska Croatia *(a republic of Yugoslavia)*
hvala *[ʜvala]* thank you

I

idi do đavola! *[eedee do djavola]* go to hell!
idiote! *[eedeeote]* idiot!
igračke toys
igrani film feature film
ime first name
informacije information
integralna riža *[eentegralna reeʝa]* brown rice
Irska Ireland
isplata withdrawals
istarski brodet *[eestarskee brodet]*

bouillabaisse *(fish stew)* as made in Istria
istok east
Istra Istria *(peninsula in the Adriatic)*
Istranin, Istranka Istrian
Italija Italy
izdaje se samo na ljekarski recept available only on prescription
izdavanje prtljaga baggage claim
izlaz exit; gate
izlaz broj ... gate number
izlaz na peron to the platforms/tracks

Serbocroat alphabetical order: c č ć; d dž đ; lu lj; nu nj; s š; z ž

izlaz na prednja/srednja/zadnja vrata exit at front/centre/center/rear only
izlaz u slučaju opasnosti emergency exit
izlaz u slučaju požara fire exit

izlaz za teretna vozila heavy goods exit
izlet u ... trip to ...
izložbena dvorana exhibition hall
izložbeni paviljon exhibition hall
izvinite *[eezveeneete]* sorry

J

jabuke *[yabooke]* apples
jabuke u šlafroku *[yabooke oo shlafrokoo]* sliced apples in batter
Jadran Adriatic
Jadransko more Adriatic sea
jagnjeća čorba *[yagnyecha chorba]* lamb soup
jagnjeća kapama *[yagnyecha kapama]* braised lamb with spinach
jagnjeća koljenica *[yagnyecha kolyeneetsa]* shank of lamb
jagnjeća plećka *[yagnyecha plechka]* shoulder of lamb
jagnjeće pečenje *[yagnyeche pechenye]* roast lamb
jagnjeći but *[yagnyechee boot]* leg of lamb
jagnjeći perkelt *[yagnyechee perkelt]* lamb stew
jagnjetina *[yagnyeteena]* lamb
jagode *[yagode]* strawberries
jaja na kajmaku *[yıya na kımakoo]* eggs fried on 'kajmak', a type of creamy, fatty cheese
jaja sa šunkom *[yıya sa shoonkom]* ham and eggs
jaje na oko *[yıye na oko]* fried egg sunny side up
janjetina *[yanyeteena]* lamb
jarebica *[yarebeetsa]* partridge
jasle creche
jastog *[yastog]* lobster

JAT (Jugoslovenski aerotransport) Yugoslav airlines
jedan smjer one-way street
jednokrevetna soba single room
jednosmjerna ulica one-way street
jednosmjerni saobraćaj one-way traffic
jegulja *[yegoolya]* eel
jela po porudžbini dishes à la carte
jela sa roštilja grilled dishes
jelovnik menu
jesetra *[yesetra]* sturgeon
jetrena pašteta *[yetrena pashteta]* liver pâté
jezero lake
JNA (Jugoslovenska narodna armija) Yugoslav People's Army
jogurt *[yogoort]* yoghurt
JRM (Jugoslavenska ratna mornarica) Yugoslav Navy
JRT (Jugoslovenska radiotelevizija) Yugoslav Radio-Television
jug south
Jugosloven, Jugoslovenka Yugoslav
juha *[jooha]* soup
juhe soups
jul July
jun June
jutros this morning
JŽ (Jugoslovenske željeznice) Yugoslav Railways/Railroads

K

kabare cabaret
kabina za probanje fitting room
kačamak *[kachamak]* polenta (*a type of porridge eaten with meat*)
kačkavalj *[kachkaval-yuh]* hard full-fat cheese, cacciocavallo
kadaif *[kada-eef]* very thin noodles in syrup with walnuts, raisins and honey
kafa coffee
kafana, kafić café
kajgana *[kıgana]* scrambled eggs
kajmak *[kımak]* 'kajmak', a rich creamy cheese
kajsije *[kıseeye]* apricots
kajsijevača *[kıseeyevacha]* apricot brandy
kakao cocoa
kalja *[kalya]* cabbage with onion and meat (mutton or pork)
kamenice *[kameneetse]* oysters
kameno doba Stone Age
kamp oprema camping equipment
kapi ... ... drops
karfiol *[karfeeol]* cauliflower
karta ticket
karte za sve smjerove tickets for all destinations
kasa cash desk
kasarna barracks
kasato *[kasato]* cassata
kaštradina *[kashtradeena]* smoked mutton cooked with cabbage, potatoes and beans
kat floor
katedrala cathedral
kavana café
kazališna predstava theatrical performance
kečiga *[kecheega]* sterlet (*type of fish*)
keks biscuit, cookie
kej quay
kelj *[kel-yuh]* savoy cabbage
kemijska čistiona dry cleaner
kesten *[kesten]* chestnut

kesten pire *[kesten peere]* chestnut purée
kiflice sa makom *[keefleetse sa makom]* sweet filled croissants with poppy seeds
kiflice sa orasima *[keefleetse sa oraseema]* sweet filled croissants with walnuts
kikiriki *[keekeereekee]* peanuts
kino cinema, movie theater
kisela pavlaka *[keesela pavlaka]* sour cream
kisela voda *[keesela voda]* mineral water
kisele paprike *[keesele papreeke]* pickled peppers
kiselo mlijeko sour milk
kiselo vrhnje *[keeselo vurhnye]* sour cream
klekovača *[klekovacha]* plum brandy with juniper
klisura gorge
klizav put slippery road
klozet toilet, rest room
knedla *[knedla]* dumpling
knedle od sira sa kiselim mlijekom *[knedle od seera sa keeseleem mlyekom]* cheese dumplings with sour milk
knjižara bookshop, bookstore
kobasica *[kobaseetsa]* sausage
kockarnica casino
kočnica u slučaju opasnosti emergency brake
kolači cakes
kola hitne pomoći ambulance
kola za iznajmljivanje cars for hire/ to rent
kola za ručavanje dining car
kola za spavanje sleeping car
kolosjek platform, track
kolovoz August
komovica *[komoveetsa]* grape brandy
kompot *[kompot]* stewed fruit, compote

Serbocroat alphabetical order: c č ć; d dž đ; lu lj; nu nj; s š; z ž

kompot od ... *[kompot ...]* stewed ...
koncert concert
koncertna dvorana concert hall
konfekcija ready-to-wear clothes
konjak *[konyak]* cognac
konsome *[konsome]* consommé
konzervirana hrana canned food
konzulat consulate
Kosovo Kosovo *(autonomous region in south central Yugoslavia)*
košulje shirts
kotlet *[kotlet]* chop
kozmetika cosmetics
kožni proizvodi leather goods
kraj autoputa end of motorway/ highway
kraj zabrane end of parking restrictions
kranjska kobasica *[kranyska kobaseetsa]* Kranj sausage *(from Slovenian province of Kranj-Carniola)*
krastavac *[krastavats]* cucumber
kravate ties, neckties
kreditna kartica credit card
kreditno pismo letter of credit
krema za brijanje shaving cream
krempita *[krempeeta]* custard slice
krem supa od povrča *[soopa od povurcha]* cream of vegetable soup
krilo *[kreelo]* wing *(poultry)*
kristal cut glass
krivina bend
krofne *[krofne]* doughnuts
krojač tailor
krompir *[krompeer]* potatoes

krompir paprikaš *[krompeer papreekash]* potato stew
krompir pire *[krompeer peere]* mashed potatoes
krompiruša *[krompeeroosha]* potato pie
kruh *[krooh]* bread
kruške *[krooshke]* pears
kruškovača *[krooshkovacha]* pear brandy
kružni tok roundabout, rotary
krvav *[kurvav]* rare
krvavica *[kurvaveetsa]* black pudding, blood sausage
krznar furrier
krzno furs
kucajte prije ulaska knock before entering
kućne potrepštine household products
kuhan *[koohan]* boiled
kuhinja kitchen
kuhinjski namještaj kitchen furniture
kukuruzno brašno *[kookooroozno brashno]* cornflour
kupaći kostimi swimwear
kupine *[koopeene]* blackberries
kupovni kurs bank buys
kupus *[koopoos]* cabbage
kurs exchange rate
kušet couchette
kutija za prvu pomoć first aid box
kuvan *[koovan]* boiled
kuver cover charge

L

lampe lamps
leća *[lecha]* lentils; lenses
lepinja *[lepeenya]* type of pitta bread
leskovačka mučkalica *[leskovachka moochkaleetsa]* pork escalope with onions and hot peppers
leskovački ćevapi *[leskovachkee chevapee]* very hot minced/ground meat rolls
lički kupus sa suhim mesom *[leechkee koopoos sa sooheem mesom]* Lika cabbage with smoked meat (layers of sauerkraut and smoked pork or ribs of mutton)
lignje *[leegnye]* squid
liker *[leeker]* liqueur
limun *[leemoon]* lemon
limunada *[leemoonada]* lemonade
lipanj June
list *[leest]* sole

lista čekanja standby
lokal ... extension ...
lokal local train
losos *[losos]* salmon
lozovača *[lozovacha]* grape brandy
loža box (*theatre*)
lubenica *[loobeneetsa]* watermelon
luk onion

luka port
ljekarna chemist, pharmacy
ljekar opće prakse general practitioner
lješnjaci *[lyesh-nyatsee]* hazelnuts
ljetni red letenja summer flight schedule

M

Mađarska Hungary
mahune *[mahoone]* French beans
maj May
majoneza *[mıyoneza]* mayonnaise
Makedonac, Makedonka Macedonian
Makedonija Macedonia (*a republic of south Yugoslavia*)
makovnjača *[makovynacha]* poppy seed roll
maksimalna visina maximum headroom
maline *[maleene]* raspberries
manastir monastery; convent
marame scarves
maramice handkerchiefs
marelice *[mareleetse]* apricots
marinirana skuša *[mareeneerana skoosha]* marinated mackerel
marke stamps
marmelada *[marmelada]* jam
mart March
maslac *[maslats]* butter
masline *[masleene]* olives
maslinovo ulje *[masleenovo oolye]* olive oil
mast ointment; fat, lard
mašine za pranje posuđa dishwashers
mašine za pranje rublja washing machines
med honey
medenjaci *[medenyatsee]* honey biscuits
međugradski razgovor long distance call, trunk call
međunarodni letovi international flights

međunarodni put international motorway/highway
međunarodni razgover international call
meko bareno jaje *[meko bareno yıye]* soft-boiled egg
melun *[meloon]* melon
meni set menu
mesara butcher
meso meat
miješana salata *[myeshana salata]* mixed salad
miješano meso na žaru *[myeshano meso na ʒaroo]* selection of grilled meats
miješano povrće *[myeshano povurche]* mixed vegetables
mileram *[meeleram]* sour cream
mineralna voda *[meeneralna voda]* mineral water
mjenjačnica exchange bureau, bureau de change
mjesečno per month
mjesto rođenja place of birth
mladi krompir sa jagnjećim mesom *[mladee krompeer sa yagnyecheem mesom]* new potatoes with roast lamb
mladi sir *[mladee seer]* fresh white cheese
mliječni proizvodi dairy products
mlijeko *[mlyeko]* milk
mlinci *[mleentsee]* flat savo(u)ry pastry made from flour, eggs and water
mljevena govedina *[mlyevena govedeena]* minced/ground beef
mljeveno meso *[mlyeveno meso]*

minced/ground meat
moka torta *[moka torta]* coffee gâteau
molim *[moleem]* please; pardon; you're welcome; it's all right
molim vas čekajte! *[moleem vas cheekıte]* please wait
molim vas pričekajte *[moleem vas preechekıte]* please wait
more sea
morski rakovi *[morskee rakovee]* sea crabs

mrkva *[murkva]* carrots
mozak *[mozak]* brains
musaka od plavih patlidžana *[moosaka od plaveeн patleedjana]* aubergine/eggplant moussaka
muška odijela men's suits
muška odjeća menswear
muški gents, men's room
mušule *[mooshoole]* mussels
muzej museum

N

na buteru *[booteru]* in butter
nacionalni park national park
nadjeven *[nadyeven]* stuffed
nadjeveni golubovi *[nadyevenee goloobovee]* stuffed pigeons
nadjeveno pile *[nadyeveno peele]* stuffed chicken
nafta diesel-oil
na gradele barbecued
na kajmaku *[kımakoo]* in 'kajmak'
nakit jewel(le)ry
namještaj furniture
naplata toll
naplata cestarine road toll
na pr. (na primjer) for example
na prodaju for sale
narandža *[narandja]* orange
naravni odrezak *[naravnee odrezak]* plain veal escalope
naravno *[naravno]* of course
na ražnju *[raınyoo]* spit-roast
narodna nošnja folk costume
narodno kazalište/pozorište national theatre/theater
na roštilju *[na roshteelyoo]* barbecued; grilled
na sat per hour
natur šnicla *[natoor shneetsla]* plain escalope of veal
na ulju *[oolyoo]* cooked in oil
na žaru *[ıaroo]* grilled
ne bacajte otpatke no litter
ne centrifugirati do not spin-dry
ne dirajte (robu) do not touch

(goods)
nedjelja Sunday
nedjeljno per week
ne gazi travu keep off the grass
ne glačati do not iron
ne hvala *[нvala]* no thank you
nema na čemu *[nema na chemoo]* don't mention it, you're welcome
ne naginji se kroz prozor do not lean out of the window
ne otvaraj vrata dok se vlak ne zaustavi do not open the door until the train has stopped
ne propušta vodu waterproof
ne sadrži ... does not contain
nesreća accident
neto težina net weight
ne uzimati na prazan stomak not to be taken on an empty stomach
ne uzimati više od propisane doze do not exceed the stated dose
ne uznemiravajte do not disturb
nezaposlenim pristup zabranjen no admittance except for staff
nezaslađeno unsweetened
ne znam I don't know
nije za prodaju not for sale
niste u pravu *[neeste oo pravoo]* you are wrong
ništa za carinjenje nothing to declare
noćni klub night club
novčana uputnica money order
novčanica od ... dinara ... dinar

note
nudle *[noodle]* dumplings

nužnik toilet, rest room

O

obavještenja enquiries
oboreno svjetlo dipped headlights
obuća footwear
obućar cobbler
ocat *[otsat]* vinegar
od of, from, since
od ... do ... from ... to ...
odjeća za bebe babywear
odjeća za mlade young fashions
odjeljenje ... ... department
odjeljenje hitne pomoći casualty
odjeljenje za strance aliens' department
odlasci departures
odlično *[odleechno]* excellent
odmah se vraćam back in a minute
odmor intermission
odron kamenja rockslide/danger of falling rocks
oglasna ploča notice board, bulletin board
ograničenje brzine speed limits apply
ohridska pastrmka *[oнreedska pasturmka]* lake Ohrid trout
omladinski hostel youth hostel
omlet sa graškom *[omlet sa grashkom]* omelet(te) with peas
omlet sa pečurkama *[omlet sa pechoorkama]* mushroom omelet(te)
opasna krivina dangerous bend
opasnost danger
opasnost od požara fire risk

oprostite *[oprosteete]* excuse me
optičar optician
orahnjača *[oraнnyacha]* walnut roll
oranžada *[oranJada]* orange juice
orasi *[orasee]* walnuts
orasnica *[orasneetsa]* walnut cake
osim nedjeljom Sundays excepted
osim za ... except for ...
osim za utovar i istovar except for loading and unloading
osim za vozila ... except for vehicles of ...
oslić *[osleech]* hake
oslobođen od carine duty-free
osnovna škola primary school
osobno dizalo lift, elevator
ostanite na liniji *[ostaneete na leeneeyee]* hold the line
ostrvo island
osvježavajuća pića soft drinks
otkazan cancelled
otok island
otprema putnika check-in
otvoreno open
otvoriti u slučaju opasnosti open in case of emergency
ovčetina *[ovcheteena]* mutton
ovčji sir *[ovcheeyee seer]* ewe cheese
ovdje otvoriti open here
ovseni kruh/hljeb *[ovsenee krooн/нlyeb]* oat bread
ožujak March

P

p. (para) para (100th part of dinar)
palačinke *[palacheenke]* pancakes
palenta *[palenta]* polenta (*a type of porridge eaten with meat or milk*)
pamuk cotton
pansion boarding house
papazjanija *[papazyaneeya]* beef hot-pot/casserole
papirnica stationery
paprika *[papreeka]* pepper
paprike punjene sirom *[papreeke poonyene seerom]* peppers stuffed with cheese
paradajz *[paradız]* tomatoes
parfemi perfumes
pariški odrezak *[pareeshkee odrezak]* veal or pork escalope in batter
parking za hotelske goste parking for hotel guests only
parter stalls
partizani Partisans
pasoš passport
pasoška kontrola passport control
pasta za zube toothpaste
pastrmka *[pasturmka]* trout
pastrnjak *[pasturnyak]* parsnip
pasulj *[pasool-yuh]* beans
pasulj bez mesa *[pasool-yuh bez mesa]* bean stew without meat
paškanat *[pashkanat]* parsnip
paški sir *[pashkee seer]* hard, dry cheese from Adriatic island of Pag
pašticada *[pashteetsada]* rich Dalmatian stewed beef with prunes
patka *[patka]* duck
pauza interval
pavlaka *[pavlaka]* cream
pazi na vlak/voz beware of the train
pecivo *[petseevo]* roll, bun
pečen *[pechen]* roast
pečene brizle *[pechene breezle]* baked sweetbreads
pečeno jaje *[pecheno yıye]* fried egg
pečurke *[pechoorke]* mushrooms
pečurke na kajmaku *[pechoorke na kımakoo]* mushrooms fried in 'kajmak'
pekara bakery
pekmez *[pekmez]* jam
pelene nappies, diapers
periona laundry
peron platform, track
peršun *[pershoon]* parsley
petak Friday
picerija pizzeria
pidžame pyjamas, pajamas
pijaca market
piktije *[peekteeye]* brawn
pileća čorba *[peelecha chorba]* chicken soup
pileći paprikaš *[peelechee papreekash]* chicken stew
pile na roštilju *[peele na roshteelyoo]* barbecued chicken
piletina *[peeleteena]* chicken
pile u paradajzu *[peele oo paradızoo]* chicken in tomato sauce
pilule pills, tablets
pilule za spavanje sleeping pills
pindžur *[peendjoor]* relish made of peppers, tomatoes and aubergines/eggplants
pire *[peere]* purée
pire od spanaća sa prženicama *[peere od spanacha sa purjeneetsama]* creamed spinach with French toast
pirinač *[peereenach]* rice
pirjan *[peeryan]* braised
pita *[peeta]* pie
pita sa jabukama *[peeta sa yabookama]* apple pie
pita sa orasima *[peeta sa oraseema]* walnut pie
pivnica beer house
pivo *[peevo]* beer
pjenušavo vino *[pyenooshavo veeno]* sparkling wine
pješaci pređite na drugu stranu pedestrians please cross to the other side (of the street)

pješačka zona pedestrian precinct
pješački prelaz pedestrian crossing
plan grada street map, town plan
planina mountain
plava zona restricted parking area
plavi patlidžan *[plavee patleedjan]* aubergine, eggplant
plaža beach
ples dance
Plitvička jezera Plitvice lakes
pljeskavica *[plyeskaveetsa]* large hamburger
početak autoputa start of motorway/ highway
početak predstave performance starts
početna cijena minimum charge
podignite slušalicu lift receiver
podijum za ples dance floor
podmazivanje lubrication
podrum cellar
podvarak *[podvarak]* roast meat on sauerkraut
podzemni prolaz underpass
pogača *[pogacha]* type of flat, round bread
pogačice sa čvarcima *[pogacheetse sa chvartseema]* flat buns with crackling
pohovan *[pohovan]* prepared in batter or breadcrumbs and fried
pojas za spasavanje life-belt
pokretne stepenice escalator
polazak departure
poluautomatski razgovori calls through the operator
polubijeli kruh/hljeb *[poloobyeli krooн/Hlyeb]* semi-white bread
polupansion half board, European plan
pomfrit *[pomfreet]* French fries, chips
ponedjeljak Monday
po osobi per person
popust discount
porcelan porcelain
porcija ... portion of ...
poriluk *[poreelook]* leek
poriluk sa svinjskim mesom *[poreelook sa sveenyskeem mesom]* leeks with pork
portir porter
poslastičarnica confectionery; cake shop

poslije jela after meals
posljednja predstava last showing
poslovni vlak/voz business train, luxury train
posteljina bed linen
postolar cobbler
post restant poste restante, general delivery
posuđe kitchen utensils
poširana jaja *[posheerana yya]* poached eggs
pošta post office
poštanski pretinac PO Box
poštansko sanduče letter box
poštarina za ... postage rates for ...
potaž *[potaı]* thick broth
potpis signature
povrće *[povurche]* vegetables
povući u slučaju opasnosti pull in case of emergency
poziv na račun broja koji se zove collect call, reverse charge call
pozorišna predstava theatrical performance
pozornica stage
pranje i vodena shampoo and set
pranje kola car wash
prasa *[prasa]* leek
prasetina *[praseteena]* sucking pig
prati posebno wash separately
prati ručno wash by hand
pravoslavna crkva Orthodox church
prebranac *[prebranats]* baked beans with onions
predaja paketa parcels
predaja preporučenih pisama registered letters
predaja telegrama telegrams
predbroj STD code, area code
predjela *[predyela]* starters, appetizers
premijum two-star petrol, regular gas
prepelica *[prepeleetsa]* quail
presjesti u ... change at ...
pretplatne karte season tickets
prezime surname
pribor za jelo cutlery
prijatno *[preeyatno]* enjoy your meal
prijava registration form
prije jela before meals
prilog side dish
prizemlje (*UK*) ground floor, (*USA*) first floor

Serbocroat alphabetical order: c č ć; d dž đ; lu lj; nu nj; s š; z ž

prodaja karata tickets
prodaja maraka sale of stamps
prodajni kurs bank sells
prodavnica shop, store
prodavnica duhana tobacconist, tobacco store
prodavnica namještaja furniture shop/store
prodavnica novina newsagent, news vendor
prodavnica obuće shoeshop, shoestore
prodavnica ploča record shop/store
prodavnica prehrambene robe grocer
prodavnica sportske opreme sports shop/store
proja *[proya]* corn bread
prokletstvo! *[prokletstvo]* damn!
prokule *[prokoole]* Brussels sprouts
prolaz passage, lane
promjena ulja oil change
prosinac December
proso *[proso]* millet
prsluk za spasavanje life-jacket
prstaci *[purstatsee]* kind of mussel
pršut *[purshoot]* smoked ham
prva pomoć first aid
prva predstava first showing
prvi kat/sprat *(UK)* first floor, *(USA)* second floor
prvi razred first class

pržen *[purʃen]* fried
pržen hljeb/kruh *[purʃen Hlyeb/krooH]* croutons
prženi krompirići *[purʃenee krompeereechee]* fried new potatoes
prženo jaje *[purʃeno yɪye]* fried egg
pšenični kruh/hljeb *[psheneechnee krooH/Hlyeb]* wheat bread
pšenično brašno *[psheneechno brashno]* wheat flour
PTT (Pošta, telegraf, telefon) Post Office
puding *[poodeeng]* custard-like pudding
puni pansion full board, American plan
punjen *[poonyen]* stuffed
punjena jaja *[poonyena yɪya]* stuffed eggs
punjeno u ... bottled in ...
puno hvala *[poono Hvala]* thank you very much
pura *[poora]* polenta (*a type of porridge eaten with meat or milk*)
puran *[pooran]* turkey
puslice *[poosleetse]* meringues
put road; time
putna agencija travel agency
putne potrepštine travel goods
putnički ček traveller's cheque, traveler's check

R

račić *[racheech]* prawn
račun receipt, bill
računari calculators
radarska kontrola radar speed checks
radni dani working days
radnja shop, store
radnja preseljena u ... business transferred to ...
radno vrijeme office hours; opening times
radovi na putu roadwork(s)
rahatlokum *[rahatlokoom]* Turkish delight
rajčica *[rɪcheetsa]* tomato
rak crab
rakija *[rakeeya]* brandy
rampa level crossing, grade crossing
rasprodaja sale
rasprodato sold out
rastopiti u vodi dissolve in water
rastvor solution
ratluk *[ratlook]* Turkish delight
razgledanje sightseeing
razglednice picture postcards
ražan kruh/hljeb *[raʃan krooH/Hlyeb]*

rye bread
ražnjići *[raɪ-nyeechee]* kebabs
rebra *[rebra]* ribs
recepcija reception
red row; queue, line
red letenja flight timetable/schedule
red vošnje timetable, schedule
reklama advertisement
reklamacije complaints
ren horseradish
renesansa Renaissance
restoran restaurant
restovan *[restovan]* fried with onions
rezanci *[rezantsee]* tagliatelle
rezanci za supu *[rezantsee za soopoo]*
  soup noodles
rezervacija reservation
rezervacija karata advance booking
rezervirano reserved
rezervni dijelovi spare parts
riba na gradele *[reeba na gradele]*
  barbecued fish
ribane tikvice *[reebane teekveetse]*
  grated courgettes/zucchinis
ribarnica fishmonger
ribizle *[reebeezle]* currants
riblja čorba *[reeblya chorba]* fish soup
riblji restoran fish/restaurant
ribolov fishing
ričet *[reechet]* thick barley broth
rijeka river

rimokatolička crkva Roman Catholic
  church
ringlice *[reengleetse]* anchovy fillets
riva promenade
rizi-bizi *[reezee beezee]* rice with peas
riža *[reeʒa]* rice
robna kuća department store
rok trajanja ... sell by ...
rok upotrebe ... expiry date ...
rolat od oraha *[rolat od oraha]* walnut roll
rolat sa šunkom *[rolat sa shoonkom]*
  ham roll
romanski romanesque
roštilj barbecue
rotkvica *[rotkveetsa]* radish
rovinjski rizoto *[roveenyskee rizoto]*
  Rovinian risotto (rice with a seafood
  sauce cooked with onions, tomatoes,
  olives, capers, garlic and wine
rozbratna sa lukom *[rozbratna sa
  lookom]* sirloin steak with onions
ručak lunch
ručni prtljag hand baggage
rujan September
Rumunija, Rumunjska Romania
ruska salata *[rooska salata]* Russian
  salad
ružica *[rooɪeetsa]* rosé wine
ručnici towels

S

s, sa with
SAD (Sjedinjene Američke Države)
  USA
sahat-kula clock tower
salata *[salata]* salad
salata od kiselih krastavaca *[salata
  od keeseleeн krastavatsa]* pickled
  gherkin salad
salata od kiselog kupusa *[salata od
  keeselog koopoosa]* pickled cabbage
  salad
salata od slatkog kupusa *[salata od
  slatkog koopoosa]* cabbage salad
sala za ručavanje dining room

samoposluga supermarket
samostan monastery; convent
samousluga supermarket
samo za autobuse buses only
samo za članove members only
samo za oralnu upotrebu to be tak-
  en orally only
samo za vanjsku upotrebu for
  external use only
samo za vozila GSP public transport
  vehicles only
sapun soap
sapun za brijanje shaving soap
sardele *[sardele]* sardines

---

sardine *[sardeene]* sardines
sarma od kiselog kupusa *[sarma od keeselog koopoosa]* stuffed pickled cabbage leaves
sarma od slatkog kupusa *[sarma od slatkog koopoosa]* stuffed cabbage leaves
sarma od vinovog lišća *[sarma od veenovog leeshcha]* stuffed vine leaves
sastav composition
sataraš *[satarash]* stew made of onions, tomatoes, peppers and eggs
satovi watches and clocks
savijača *[saveeyacha]* strudel, apple *etc* turnover
sekelji gulaš *[sekelyee goolash]* pork and sauerkraut goulash
selo village
senf mustard
serkl dress circle
servirati hladno serve cold
servisna stanica service station
service nije uključen service not included
sezonski popust seasonal reductions
SFRJ (Socijalistička Federativna Republika Jugoslavija) Socialist Federal Republic of Yugoslavia
siječanj January
sinagoga synagog(ue)
sipa *[seepa]* cuttlefish
sir *[seer]* cheese
sirće *[seerche]* vinegar
sirnica *[seerneetsa]* cheese pie
sirup za kašalj cough syrup
Sjedinjene Američke Države United States of America
sjedište seat
sjever north
skuša *[skoosha]* mackerel
slačica *[slacheetsa]* mustard
sladoled *[sladoled]* ice cream
sladoled od banane *[sladoled od banane]* banana ice cream
slanina *[slaneena]* bacon
slani štapići *[slanee shtapeechee]* savo(u)ry sticks
Slapovi Krke Krka waterfalls
slastičarna confectionery; cake shop
slatkiši desserts
slatko *[slatko]* fruit in thick syrup, fruit preserve
slatko od ... *[slatko]* ... in syrup, ... preserve
slatko vino sweet wine
slijedeća predstava next performance
slobodan for hire, to rent; vacant
slobodno *[slobodno]* come in
Slovenac, Slovenka Slovene
Slovenija Slovenia (*a republic of northwest Yugoslavia*)
smanjite brzinu reduce speed
smokve *[smokve]* figs
smrznuta hrana frozen foods
smuđ *[smoodj]* perch
snek-bar snack bar
sniženje cijena reduced prices
so *[so]* salt
soba room
soba sa kupaonicom/kupatilom room with bathroom
soba sa tušem room with shower
sobe za izdavanje rooms to let/rent
sočivo *[socheevo]* lentils
soja *[soya]* soya-beans
sok juice
sok od marelice *[mareleetse]* apricot juice
sol salt
som catfish
somun *[somoon]* type of pitta bread
spanać *[spanach]* spinach
spavaonica dormitory
specijalista za ... ... specialist, consultant for ...
specijalista za uho, grlo i nos ear, throat and nose specialist
SPI (Služba pomoći i informacija) breakdown services
spomenik pod zaštitom države listed monument
sportska oprema sports goods
sportski tereni sports grounds
sprat floor
spustite slušalicu replace the receiver
sranje! *[sranye]* shit!
Srbija Serbia
Srbin, Srpkinja Serb
sremska kobasica *[sremska kobaseetsa]* smoked sausage from Srem province in north-west Serbia

srijeda Wednesday
srneći medaljoni *[surnechee meda-lyonee]* medaillons of venison
srnetina *[surneteena]* venison
srnetina sa sokom od limuna *[surneteena sa sokom od leemoona]* venison with lemon juice
srpanj July
srpska salata *[surpska salata]* Serbian salad (tomatoes, cucumbers, onions and peppers with salt and oil)
stadion stadium
stajalište taksija taxi rank/stand
staklo glassware
stalna adresa permanent address
stanica stop
stanica milicije police station
stanica na zahtjev request stop
stanica prve pomoći first aid post
stan za izdavanje apartment to let/rent
staza za skijanje ski run
stećak type of old Bosnian tombstone
stolar joiner, carpenter
stolnjaci tablecloths
stono vino table wine
strana valuta foreign currency
struška jegulja *[strooshka yegoolya]* Struga eel (*cooked in wine*)
studeni November

stvari koje podležu carini dutiable articles
subota Saturday
suho vino dry wine
sulc *[soolts]* jelly
suncokretno ulje *[soontsokretno oolye]* sunflower oil
supa *[soopa]* soup
supa od griza *[soopa od greeza]* wheat groats soup
supa od pirinča *[soopa od peereencha]* rice soup
supe soups
super four-star petrol, premium gas
sušenje fenom blow dry
suteren basement
sutljaš *[sootlyash]* rice pudding
suženje puta road narrows
svaka tableta sadrži ... each tablet contains ...
svibanj May
svinjetina *[sveenyeteena]* pork
svinjska krmenadla *[sveenyska kurmenadla]* pork chop
svinjska vješalica *[sveenyska vyeshaleetsa]* grilled pork fillet
svinjski ražnjići *[sveenyskee raj-nyeechee]* pork kebabs
svi pravci all directions
svježe obojeno wet paint

šampita *[shampeeta]* thin layer of pastry topped with soft meringue
šampon shampoo
šaran *[sharan]* carp
šaran pečen sa pavlakom *[sharan pechen sa pavlakom]* carp baked in sour cream
šargarepa *[shargarepa]* carrots
šatobrijan za dvije osobe *[shatobreeyan za dveeye osobe]* chateaubriand steak for two
šećer *[shecher]* sugar
šeširi hats
šišanje haircut, trim
škampe *[shkampe]* scampi

škampe na buzaru *[shkampe na boozaroo]* scampi buzara style (fried in oil with onion, garlic and parsley and cooked in wine)
škola school
školska odjeća school wear
Škotska Scotland
šljive *[shlyeeve]* plums
šljivovica *[shleevoveetsa]* slivovitz, plum brandy
šnenokle *[shnenokle]* floating island (*dessert*)
šopska salata *[shopska salata]* mixed salad with cheese
špagete *[shpagete]* spaghetti

Serbocroat alphabetical order: c č ć; d dž đ; lu lj; nu nj; s š; z ž

špargla *[shpargla]* asparagus
špar(o)ga *[shpar(o)ga]* asparagus
špinat *[shpeenat]* spinach
štanglice od badema *[shtangleetse od badema]* almond sticks
štanglice od bjelanaca *[shtangleetse od byelanatsa]* meringue sticks
štrudla od jabuka *[shtroodla od yabooka]* apple strudel

štruklji *[shtruklyee]* buckwheat roll
štuka *[shtooka]* pike
štuka sa slaninom *[shtooka sa slaneenom]* pike with bacon
šuma forest
šumske jagode *[shoomske yagode]* wild strawberries
šunka *[shoonka]* ham

T

tablete tablets, pills
taksi taxi
taksimetar taximeter
taksi stanica taxi rank/stand
tapetar upholsterer
tapete wallpaper
tarana *[tarana]* dough pellets
tarator *[tarator]* cucumber with soured milk
tartar-sos *[tartar sos]* tartar sauce
tartufi *[tartoofee]* truffles
taške *[tashke]* ravioli
tekući račun current account, checking account
teleća čorba *[telecha chorba]* veal soup
teleća džigerica *[telecha djeegeritsa]* calf's liver
teleća rozbratna *[telecha rozbratna]* veal entrecôte
teleća vješalica *[telecha vyeshaleetsa]* grilled fillet of veal
teleće grudi *[teleche groodee]* breast of veal
teleće pečenje *[teleche pechenye]* roast veal
teleći medaljon *[telechee medalyon]* fillet of veal
teleći odrezak *[telechee odrezak]* escalope of veal
teleći paprikaš *[telechee papreekash]* veal stew
telefonski imenik telephone directory
teletina *[teleteena]* veal
televizori television sets

teniski tereni tennis courts
tepisi carpets
teretna vozila heavy vehicles
teretni vlak/voz goods train, freight train
težina weight
tikvica *[teekveetsa]* courgettes, zucchinis
tikvopita *[teekvopeeta]* pumpkin pie
tiskanica printed matter
titlovan with subtitles
tkanine textiles, fabrics
toalet toilet, rest room
toaletni pribor toiletries
to je sve? *[ye]* is that everything?
torta *[torta]* gâteau
trajekt ferry
trajna perm
tranzitni putnici transit passengers
trapist *[trapeest]* trappist cheese (*similar to Port Salut*)
travanj April
travarica *[travareetsa]* brandy made with aromatic herbs
travnički sir *[travneechkee seer]* Travnik cheese (*white sheep's cheese*)
treći kat/sprat (*US*) third floor, (*USA*) fourth floor
trenutak *[trenootak]* just a moment
trešnje *[treshnye]* cherries
trg square
trgovina shop, store
trkalište race course
trpezarija dining room
tučeno vrhnje *[toocheno vurнnye]* whipped cream

tufahije *[toofaheeye]* baked apples with sugar and walnuts
tuna *[toona]* tuna
tuna na gradele *[toona na gradele]* barbecued tuna
tunj *[toon-yuh]* tuna
turistički ured tourist office

turistički vodič tourist guide
turska kafa *[toorska kafa]* Turkish coffee
turšija *[toorsheeya]* pickled foods
tvrdo bareno jaje *[tvurdo bareno yıye]* hard-boiled egg

U

u in
ubacite novac insert coin
uđite bez kucanja enter without knocking
ugor *[oogor]* conger eel
uključen servis service included
u kvaru out of order
ul. (ulica) street
ulaz entrance
ulaz na druga vrata use other door
ulaznica admission ticket
ulica street
ulje *[oolye]* oil
umak *[oomak]* sauce
umirujuće sredstvo tranquillizer
umjetnička galerija art gallery
upalite svjetlo switch on your lights
uplata deposits
u pola cijene half price
upotreba prema priloženom uputstvu to be used according to the enclosed instructions
u pravu ste *[oo pravoo]* you are right

uputstva za pranje washing instructions
uputstvo za upotrebu instructions for use
ured office
urmašice *[oormasheetse]* finger-shaped cakes in syrup
u slučaju opasnosti in an emergency
utorak Tuesday
u umaku *[oo oomakoo]* with sauce
uzbuna alarm
uzimati poslije jela to be taken after meals
uzimati prema priloženom uputstvu to be taken according to the enclosed instructions
uzimati prije jela to be taken before meals
uzimati ... puta na dan to be taken ... times per day
uzimati svakih ... sati to be taken every ... hours
uzmite korpu please take a basket

V

vagon restoran restaurant car
valjušci *[valyooshtsee]* dumplings
valuta currency
vanilice *[vaneelitse]* small crescent-shaped vanilla cakes (*as dessert*)
vansezonske cijene low season rates
vatrogasna stanica fire station
važi do ... expiry date ...

večera dinner
večeras this evening
veličina size
veliko hvala *[veleeko нvala]* thank you very much
veliko sniženje big reductions
veljača February
Vels Wales

Serbocroat alphabetical order: c č ć; d dž đ; lu lj; nu nj; s š; z ž

veš underwear
veterinar veterinary surgeon
vez embroidery
veza connection
vežite pojaseve please fasten your seatbelts
vinjak *[veenyak]* wine brandy
vino *[veeno]* wine
vinska karta wine list
viski whisky
višnje *[veeshnye]* morello cherries
viza visa
vlak train
voće *[voche]* fruit
voće i povrće greengrocer
voćna salata *[vochna salata]* fruit salad
voćni kolač *[vochnee kolach]* fruit cake
voćni sok *[vochnee]* fruit juice
voda nije za piće not drinking water
voda za piće drinking water

vodič guide
vodoinstalater plumber
Vojvodina Vojvodina (*autonomous region in north-east Yugoslavia*)
voltaža voltage
votka vodka
voz train
vozi desno drive on the right
vozi lagano drive slowly
vozi pažljivo drive with care
vraćam se za jedan sat back in an hour
vrhnje *[vurHnye]* cream
vrijeme dolaska arrival time
vrijeme polaska departure time
vrijeme posjete visiting hours
vrlo dobro *[vurlo dobro]* very well
vuci pull
vulkanizer tyres/tires repaired
vuna wool
vunica wool

Z

zabavište kindergarten
zabavni park amusement park
zaboga! *[zaboga]* for God's sake!
zabranjena upotreba sirene do not sound your horn
zabranjeno autostopiranje no hitch-hiking
zabranjeno bacanje smeća no dumping
zabranjeno fotografiranje no photographs
zabranjeno hraniti životinje do not feed the animals
zabranjeno je razgovarati sa vozačem do not speak to the driver
zabranjeno kupanje no bathing
zabranjeno lijepljenje plakata stick no bills
zabranjeno loviti ribu no fishing
zabranjeno ložiti vatru it is forbidden to light fires
zabranjeno parkiranje no parking
zabranjeno pljuvanje no spitting

zabranjeno preticanje no overtaking/passing
zabranjeno pušenje no smoking
zabranjeno skretanje lijevo no left turn
zabranjen pristup no admittance
zabranjen prolaz keep out
zabranjen ulaz no entry
zadruga cooperative society
zahod toilet, rest room
za izdavanje for hire, to rent
za iznajmljivanje for hire, to rent
zakašnjenje delay
zakuska *[zakooska]* mixed starter (*smoked ham, salami, cheese etc*)
zaliv bay
zamrzivači freezers
zanimanje occupation
zaobilazni put detour, diversion
zapad west
zaštitni znak trade mark
zatvaraj vrata please close the door
zatvoreni bazen indoor swimming

pool
zatvoreno closed
zatvoreno za publiku closed to the public
zatvoreno za vrijeme ručka closed at lunchtime
zatvoreno zbog žalosti closed due to bereavement
zatvoren put road closed
zauzet engaged, occupied
zavjese curtains
zbogom goodbye
zdravo hello

zdravstveno uvjerenje health certificate
zec *[zets]* rabbit
zečevina *[zecheveena]* hare
zelena salata *[zelena salata]* lettuce
zeljanica *[zelyanitsa]* spinach pie
zemička *[zemeechka]* roll, bun
zemlja country
zimski red letenja winter flight schedule
zubar dentist
zubatac *[zoobatats]* dentex (*type of fish*)

Ž

željeznička stanica railway station, train station
željeznički kolodvor railway station, train station
ženska odjeća ladies' wear
ženske čarape tights and stockings

ženski ladies, ladies' room
žestoka pića spirits
žito *[jeeto]* wheat with sugar and ground walnuts
žurnal newsreel

Serbocroat alphabetical order: c č ć; d dž đ; lu lj; nu nj; s š; z ž

Reference Grammar

ARTICLES

There are no articles in Serbocroat, no words for 'a' or 'the'. So, for example:

motocikl

can mean either 'a motorbike' or 'the motorbike' depending on the context. For example:

želim iznajmiti motocikl
I want to hire a motorbike

motocikl je bio na krivoj strani ulice
the motorbike was on the wrong side of the road

NOUNS

GENDER
Nouns can be masculine, feminine or neuter.

Most masculine nouns end in a consonant:

pasoš	passport
hotel	hotel

but some masculine nouns end in **-o**:

auto	car
radio	radio

Feminine nouns usually end in **-a**:

sestra	sister
plaža	beach

but some feminine nouns (mostly abstract) end in a consonant:

ljubav	love
noć	night

Neuter nouns end in **-o** or **-e**:

selo	village
dijete	child

In the English-Serbocroat part of this book we have marked all feminine nouns ending in a consonant with (*f*) and all masculine nouns ending in **-o** with (*m*).

PLURALS
To form the plurals of nouns, follow the rules given below:

Masculine nouns
Masculine nouns ending in a consonant: add -i

   hotel/hoteli   hotel/hotels

Masculine nouns of one syllable ending in a 'hard' consonant: add -ovi

   grad/gradovi   town/towns

Masculine nouns of one syllable ending in a 'soft' consonant (**j, lj, nj, c, ć, č, š, dž, đ, ž**):   add -evi

   muž/muževi   husband/husbands

Masculine nouns ending in -**k** change the final consonant into -**c** before adding the plural ending -**i**:

   potok/potoci   stream/streams
   otok/otoci   island/islands

Feminine nouns
Feminine nouns ending in -**a**:   change -a
                                                                      to -e

   žena/žene   woman/woman

Feminine nouns ending in a consonant: add -i

   noć/noći   night/nights

Neuter nouns
Neuter nouns: change -o
                                                 or -e into -a

   vino/vina   wine/wines
   jaje/jaja   egg/eggs

Many neuter nouns insert -**en** or -**et** between the stem and the plural ending:

   ime/imena   name/names
   dugme/dugmeta button/buttons

Some nouns exist only in a plural form (and take a plural verb and plural adjective endings) although they are singular in meaning, for example:

   vrata   door
   novine   newspaper
   kola   car

If you want to say 'cars' or 'newspapers' etc the Serbocroat word remains unchanged:

   ova kola   these cars
   engleske novine English newspapers

Some nouns have an irregular plural:

   čovjek/ljudi   man/men
   otac/očevi   father/fathers
   brat/braća   brother/brothers

Declensions 104

THE DECLENSION OF NOUNS

Serbocroat is an 'inflected' language. This means that nouns and adjectives change their endings according to their function in the sentence. There are seven cases:

nominative, vocative, accusative, genitive, dative, instrumental and locative.

The NOMINATIVE is used for the subject of a sentence, for example:

moj muž nije ovdje
my husband isn't here

The VOCATIVE is used for addressing animate creatures (people and animals), for example:

zdravo Ivane
hello Ivan

The ACCUSATIVE is used for the direct object of a sentence, for example:

ne znam *njegovo ime*
I don't know *his name*

It is also used after some prepositions when they convey the idea of motion or direction (**kroz** through; **pod** under; **pred** in front of; **u** in; **niz** down, **na** on), for example:

idem kroz grad
I'm going through town

idem na krov
I'm going up onto the roof

The GENITIVE denotes possession ('of'), for example:

Petrova knjiga
Peter's book

It is also used after some prepositions (**od** from; **iza** behind; **bez** without; **blizu** near; **do** until etc), for example:

iza hotela
behind the hotel

The genitive is also used after **evo** (here is), **eno** (there is), and **koliko** (how many), after adverbs of quantity (**nekoliko** some; **mnogo** much; **malo** a little) and nouns of measure (**litar** litre; **komad** piece; **kilogram** kilogram), for example:

eno Petra
there's Peter

tri komada papira
three pieces of paper

tri kilograma šećera
three kilos of sugar

The DATIVE is used to denote direction (but not motion) towards someone or something. It is used for the indirect object with verbs of giving, sending etc, often preceded in English by the preposition 'to', for example:

dao sam ključ *direktoru*
I gave the key *to the manager*

The INSTRUMENTAL is used to denote the means by which an action is carried out, for example:

on je pokazao *prstom*
he pointed *with his finger*

It is also used for the idea of being together with, or in the company of, other persons or objects, for example:

bio sam *s Nadom* u kinu
I went to the cinema *with Nada*

It is also in several expressions of time, for example:

nedjeljom
on Sundays

mjesecima
for months

godinama
for years

The LOCATIVE is used after prepositions denoting location, for example:

u Splitu	in Split
na plaži	on the beach
pri luci	near the harbour

Here are declension tables for Serbocroat nouns:

Masculine nouns

	hotel hotel		**prijatelj** friend	
	sing.	pl.	sing.	pl.
N	hotel	hoteli	prijatelj	prijatelji
V	hotele	hoteli	prijatelju	prijatelji
A	hotel	hotele	prijatelja	prijatelje
G	hotela	hotela	prijatelja	prijatelja
D	hotelu	hotelima	prijatelju	prijateljima
I	hotelom	hotelima	prijateljem	prijateljima
L	hotelu	hotelima	prijatelju	prijateljima

	grad town, city		**muž** husband	
	sing.	pl.	sing.	pl.
N	grad	gradovi	muž	muževi
V	grade	gradovi	muže	muževi
A	grad	gradove	muža	muževe
G	grada	gradova	muža	muževa
D	gradu	gradovima	mužu	muževima
I	gradom	gradovima	mužem	muževima
L	gradu	gradovima	mužu	muževima

The accusative *singular* ending of masculine nouns differs depending on whether they are animate (indicating persons and animals) or inanimate. If the noun is inanimate the accusative is the same as the nominative (**hotel**, **grad**); if the noun is animate it is the same as the genitive (**prijatelja**, **muža**).

Masculine nouns which end in **-k** change the **-k** into **-c** before adding **-i** or **-ima**. For example:

singular: **putnik**

pl.: N **putnici**   D **putnicima**
V **putnici**   I **putnicima**
A **putnike**   L **putnicima**
G **putnika**

Masculine nouns which end in **-k** and **-g** change the final consonant into **-č** and **-ž** respectively in front of **-e** in the vocative singular case, for example:

putnik   **putniče**   traveller
drug   **druže**   friend, comrade

Feminine nouns

	žena woman, wife		**noć** night	
	sing.	pl.	sing.	pl.
N	žena	žene	noć	noći
V	ženo	žene	noći	noći
A	ženu	žene	noć	noći
G	žene	žena	noći	noći
D	ženi	ženama	noći	noćima
I	ženom	ženama	noći	noćima
L	ženi	ženama	noći	noćima

Feminine nouns ending in **-ka**, **-ga**, and **-ha** change these into **-ci**, **-zi** and **-si** respectively in the dative and locative singular, for example:

majka   **majci**   mother
knjiga   **knjizi**   book
snaha   **snasi**   daughter-in-law

Neuter nouns

	selo village, countryside		**more** sea	
	sing.	pl.	sing.	pl.
N	selo	sela	more	mora
A	selo	sela	more	mora
G	sela	sela	mora	mora
D	selu	selima	moru	morima
I	selom	selima	morem	morima
L	selu	selima	moru	morima

	ime name		**dugme** button	
	sing.	pl.	sing.	pl.
N	ime	imena	dugme	dugmeta
A	ime	imena	dugme	dugmeta
G	imena	imena	dugmeta	dugmeta
D	imenu	imenima	dugmetu	dugmetima
I	imenom	imenima	dugmetom	dugmetima
L	imenu	imenima	dugmetu	dugmetima

The noun **dijete** (child) has the irregular plural form **djeca**. **Djeca** is declined as a feminine singular noun, but it takes a plural verb.

ADJECTIVES

Adjectives agree with the nouns they refer to in gender, number, and case. In Serbocroat there are two forms of most adjectives – indefinite and definite. In the English-Serbocroat section of this book we have given the masculine indefinite form of the adjective. In general practice the indefinite form is used when the adjectives are used after the noun, for example:

moj novi kaput je *crven*   my new coat is *red*

The definite form is used when the adjective comes before the noun, for example:

moj *crveni* kaput je nov   my *red* coat is new

To form the feminine and neuter forms of an adjective add **-a** to the masculine indefinite form for feminine and **-o** for neuter. The indefinite declension is:

	m	f	n
(red)	**crven**	**crvena**	**crveno**
(new)	**nov**	**nova**	**novo**
(old)	**star**	**stara**	**staro**

The plurals of the adjectives are formed by the addition of the endings **-i** for masculine, **-e** for feminine and **-a** for neuter to the masculine indefinite form:

m	f	n
crveni	**crvene**	**crvena**
novi	**nove**	**nova**
stari	**stare**	**stara**

The declension of definite adjectives

mladi young

	singular			plural		
	m	f	n	m	f	n
N	**mladi**	**mlada**	**mlado**	**mladi**	**mlade**	**mlada**
V	**mladi**	**mlada**	**mlado**	**mladi**	**mlade**	**mlada**
A	**mladi, mladog**	**mladu**	**mlado**	**mlade**	**mlade**	**mlada**
G	**mladog**	**mlade**	**mladog**	**mladih**	**mladih**	**mladih**
D	**mladom**	**mladoj**	**mladom**	**mladim**	**mladim**	**mladim**
I	**mladim**	**mladom**	**mladim**	**mladim**	**mladim**	**mladim**
L	**mladom**	**mladoj**	**mladom**	**mladim**	**mladim**	**mladim**

Examples:

došao sam sa svojom mladom sestrom
I came with my young sister

to je za moju mladu sestru
that's for my young sister

COMPARATIVES (BIGGER, BETTER etc)

Most comparatives are formed by the addition of the endings **-iji** (m), **-ija** (f) and **-ije** (n) to the indefinite adjective. In the plural the feminine ending is changed to **-ije**, the neuter ending to **-ija**, and the masculine remains the same:

		singular			plural	
	m	f	n	m	f	n
(red)	**crven – crveniji**	**crvenija**	**crvenije**	**crveniji**	**crvenije**	**crvenija**
(new)	**nov – noviji**	**novija**	**novije**	**noviji**	**novije**	**novija**
(old)	**star – stariji**	**starija**	**starije**	**stariji**	**starije**	**starija**

These words take the normal adjective case endings (see page 107).

ona je starija
she's older

ona je sa starijom sestrom
she's with her older sister

To express 'than' use **od**:

ona je starija od mene
she's older than me

Other adjectives have the ending **-ji**, although it is not always 'visible' because of regular consonant changes:

d + j	gives	**đ**	**tvrd**	**tvrđi**	(hard-harder)
g + j	gives	**ž**	**drag**	**draži**	(dear-dearer)
h + j	gives	**š**	**tih**	**tiši**	(quiet-quieter)
k + j	gives	**č**	**jak**	**jači**	(strong-stronger)
t + j	gives	**ć**	**ljut**	**ljući**	(hot, angry-hotter, angrier)

Most of the adjectives ending in **-ak, -ek, -ok** drop this ending in the comparative:

blizak (fem. **bliska**)	**bliži** (close-closer)
dalek	**dalji** (far-further)
dubok	**dublji** (deep-deeper)
kratak	**kraći** (short-shorter)
plitak	**plići** (shallow-shallower)
sladak	**slađi** (sweet-sweeter)
širok	**širi** (broad-broader)
težak	**teži** (hard, heavy-harder, heavier)
uzak	**uži** (narrow-narrower)

Some common adjectives have irregular comparative forms:

dobar	**bolji, bolja, bolje** (good-better)
loš	**gori, gora, gore** (bad-worse)
velik	**veći, veća, veće** (big-bigger)
malen	**manji, manja, manje** (small-smaller)

SUPERLATIVES (BIGGEST, BEST etc)

The superlatives are formed by adding the prefix **naj-** to the comparative:

bliži	**najbliži**	(closer-closest)
sladak	**najslađi**	(sweeter-sweetest)
bolji	**najbolji**	(better-best)
veći	**najveći**	(bigger-biggest)

najskuplji hotel u gradu
the most expensive hotel in town

POSSESSIVE ADJECTIVES (MY, YOUR etc)
They are:

moj	my
tvoj	your (*singular familiar*)
njegov	his, its
njen	her, its
naš	our
vaš	your (*singular polite, plural familiar and polite*)
njihov	their

The declension of **moj**

		singular			plural	
	masc.	fem.	neuter	masc.	fem.	neuter
N	moj	moja	moje	moji	moje	moja
A	moj, moga	moju	moje	moje	moje	moja
G	mog(a)	moje	mog(a)	mojih	mojih	mojih
D	mom(e)	mojoj	mom(e)	mojim	mojim	mojim
I	mojim	mojom	mojim	mojim	mojim	mojim
L	mom(e)	mojoj	mom(e)	mojim	mojim	mojim

Tvoj and **svoj** are declined in the same way.

The declension of **njegov**

		singular			plural	
	masc.	fem.	neuter	masc.	fem.	neuter
N	njegov	njegova	njegovo	njegovi	njegove	njegova
A	njegov, njegovog	njegovu	njegovo	njegove	njegove	njegova
G	njegovog	njegove	njegovog	njegovih	njegovih	njegovih
D	njegovom	njegovoj	njegovom	njegovim	njegovim	njegovim
I	njegovim	njegovom	njegovim	njegovim	njegovim	njegovim
L	njegovom	njegovoj	njegovom	njegovim	njegovim	njegovim

Njen and **njihov** are declined in the same way.

The declension of **naš**

| | singular | | | plural | | |
	masc.	fem.	neuter	masc.	fem.	neuter
N	naš	naša	naše	naši	naše	naša
A	naš, našeg	našu	naše	naše	naše	naša
G	našeg	naše	našeg	naših	naših	naših
D	našem	našoj	našem	našim	našim	našim
I	našim	našom	našim	našim	našim	našim
L	našem	našoj	našem	našim	našim	našim

Vaš is declined in the same way.

> **moj bicikl**
> my bicycle

> **moja prijateljica**
> my friend (*female*)

> **u našem autu, u našim kolima**
> in our car

There are two forms for the accusative masculine singular in all these declensions. The one identical with the genitive is used if the noun is animate:

> **vidim naš hotel**   I can see our hotel
> **vidim našeg prijatelja tamo**   I can see our friend over there

There is in Serbocroat a reflexive possessive adjective **svoj** (one's own). It is used when the possessed object or person belongs to the subject of the sentence:

> **uzet ću tvoj auto**
> I'll take your car

> **uzet ću svoj auto**
> I'll take my (own) car

> **uzet će svoj auto**
> he'll take his (own) car

DEMONSTRATIVE ADJECTIVES (THIS, THAT etc)
See section on Demonstrative Pronouns (page 113) as the forms are the same.

PRONOUNS

PERSONAL PRONOUNS

sing.:	**ja**	I
	ti	you (*singular familiar*)
	on	he
	ona	she
	ono	it

pl.:	**mi**	we
	vi	you (*singular polite, plural polite and familiar*)
	oni	they (m)
	one	they (f)
	ona	they (n)

The declension of personal pronouns

singular

N	**ja**	**ti**	**on**	**ona**	**ono**
A	**mene, me**	**tebe, te**	**njega, ga**	**nju, je, ju**	**njega, ga**
G	**mene, me**	**tebe, te**	**njega, ga**	**nje, je**	**njega, ga**
D	**meni, mi**	**tebi, ti**	**njemu, mu**	**njoj, joj**	**njemu, mu**
I	**mnom,**	**tobom**	**njim,**	**njom,**	**njim**
	mnome		**njime**	**njome**	**njime**
L	**meni**	**tebi**	**njemu**	**njoj**	**njemu**

plural

N	**mi**	**vi**	**oni, one, ona**
A	**nas**	**vas**	**njih, ih**
G	**nas**	**vas**	**njih, ih**
D	**nama, nam**	**vama, vam**	**njima, im**
I	**nama**	**vama**	**njima**
L	**nama**	**vama**	**njima**

As you can see, in some cases personal pronouns have two forms. The long, stressed forms are used for emphasis and after prepositions; the short forms are not stressed, and cannot start a sentence. The accusative of **ona** has two short forms: **je** and **ju**. **Je** is the form which is generally used; **ju** is used only when the preceding word ends in **-je**, or the following word begins with **je-**.

to je za mene	**daj to meni**	**dao sam ih njoj**
that's for me	give it to me	I gave them to her

Serbocroat often omits the personal pronoun when it is the subject of a sentence, for example:

gdje je?	**ne mogu**	**ne želim**
where is he/she/it?	I can't	I don't want to

But the pronoun is used for emphasis:

on ne radi, a ja radim
he's not working but I am

YOU
There are two ways of saying 'you' in Serbocroat. They are:

ti (sing.)   used for addressing a child, a relative, a friend; it is also used between young people.

vi (pl.)   used more formally to address a person the speaker does not know well. It is also the plural form of **ti**. The verbs used are always in the plural.

ti si moj prijatelj
you are my friend

da li ste vi direktor?
are you the manager?

vi ste moji prijatelji
you are my friends

REFLEXIVE PRONOUNS (MYSELF, YOURSELF etc)
There is only one reflexive pronoun in Serbocroat: **se** (or **sebe**), and it corresponds to all English reflexive pronouns. It is used instead of a personal pronoun when the verb refers to the subject of the sentence:

on se stalno gleda
he's always looking at himself

ja sam se zatvorio u kući
I locked myself in the house

Serbocroat uses many more verbs reflexively than English. Some are truly reflexive, i.e. **se** refers to the subject:

perem se svaki dan
I wash (myself) every day

Others are reflexive in form only:

bojim se vode   I am afraid of the water
sjećam se mora   I remember the sea
šetali smo se po gradu   we walked around the city

The declension of the reflexive pronoun

There is no nominative or vocative case. The same forms are used for both the singular and the plural:

A   **sebe, se**
G   **sebe, se**
D   **sebi, si**
I   **sobom**
L   **sebi**

   govorio sam sam sa sobom
   I was just talking to myself

POSSESSIVE PRONOUNS (MINE, YOURS etc)
Possessive pronouns have the same form as possessive adjectives (see page 109).

Like the possessive adjectives, possessive pronouns agree in gender, number and case with the noun they replace:

ovi koferi su vaši?
are these suitcases yours?

nije vaša tašna – moja je
that's not your handbag – it's mine

DEMONSTRATIVE PRONOUNS

These are: **ovaj, ova, ovo** (this); **onaj, ona, ono** (that over there); **taj, ta, to** (that).
They are all declined in the same way.

	singular			plural		
	masc.	fem.	neuter	masc.	fem.	neuter
N	ovaj	ova	ovo	ovi	ove	ova
A	ovaj, ovog	ovu	ovo	ove	ove	ova
G	ovog(a)	ove	ovog(a)	ovih	ovih	ovih
D	ovom(e)	ovoj	ovom(e)	ovim(a)	ovim(a)	ovim(a)
I	ovim(e)	ovom	ovim(e)	ovim(a)	ovim(a)	ovim(a)
L	ovom(e)	ovoj	ovom(e)	ovim(a)	ovim(a)	ovim(a)

neću ovaj auto, hoću onaj
I don't want this car, I want that one

pošto su ove cipele?
how much are these shoes?

INTERROGATIVE PRONOUNS

The interrogative pronouns are **ko** (who), **što** or **šta** (what), **koji** (which), and **čiji**
(whose).

*The declension of **ko** and **što** (**šta**)*

N	ko	što (šta)
A	koga	što (šta)
G	koga	čega
D	kome	čemu
I	kim(e)	čim(e)
L	kome	čemu

kome si dao?
who did you give it to?

Neko (somebody) and **niko** (nobody) are declined like **ko**. **Ništa** (nothing) is
declined like **šta**; **nešto** is also declined like **šta**, except that in the accusative it has
the same form as the nominative, **nešto**.

*The declension of **koji***

	singular			plural		
	masc.	fem.	neuter	masc.	fem.	neuter
N	koji	koja	koje	koji	koje	koja
A	koji/kojeg	koju	koje	koje	koje	koja
G	kojeg	koje	kojeg	kojih	kojih	kojih
D	kojem	kojoj	kojem	kojim	kojim	kojim
I	kojim	kojom	kojim	kojim	kojim	kojim
L	kojem	kojoj	kojem	kojim	kojim	kojim

u kojoj sobi?
in which room?

Čiji is declined in the same way.

VERBS

PRESENT TENSE
There is only one form of the present tense in Serbocroat and it has three main sets of endings. It is important to know the 1st person singular, present tense of every verb in order to determine the endings (see the list on page 118).

	imati (to have)	**govoriti** (to speak)	**putovati** (to travel)
(ja)	imam	govorim	putujem
(ti)	imaš	govoriš	putuješ
(on, ona, ono)	ima	govori	putuje
(mi)	imamo	govorimo	putujemo
(vi)	imate	govorite	putujete
(oni, one, ona)	imaju	govore	putuju

Personal pronouns are rarely used in Serbocroat as subjects, except for emphasis (see also page 111):

govorim engleski
I speak English

The verbs are made NEGATIVE by placing **ne** immediately before the verb:

ne govorim, ne goviriš, ne govori etc; **ne pišem, ne pišes, ne piše** etc:

ne govorim srpskohrvatski
I don't speak Serbocroat

But the verb **imati** (to have) has its own negative form: **nemam, nemaš, nema, nemamo, nemate, nemaju**:

nemam novaca
I don't have any money

*The verb 'to be' (**biti**)*

	(long form)	(short form)	(negative)
(ja)	jesam	sam	nisam
(ti)	jesi	si	nisi
(on, ona, ono)	jeste	je	nije
(mi)	jesmo	smo	nismo
(vi)	jeste	ste	niste
(oni, one, ona)	jesu	su	nisu

The long forms are used for emphasis, at the beginning of a sentence or when answering a question with a simple 'yes, I am' etc:

jesi li Englez? are you English?
jesam yes, I am
jesu li Englezi? are they English?
jesu yes, they are

Some other important verbs are irregular:

	htjeti* (to want, wish)			moći (to be able to)	ići (to go)
	(long form)	(short)	(negative)		
(ja)	hoću	ću	neću	mogu	idem
(ti)	hoćeš	ćeš	nećeš	možeš	ideš
(on, ona, ono)	hoće	će	neće	može	ide
(mi)	hoćemo	ćemo	nećemo	možemo	idemo
(vi)	hoćete	ćete	nećete	možete	idete
(oni, one, ona)	hoće	će	neće	mogu	idu

*This verb is used as an auxiliary for the future tense (see page 116).

THE PAST TENSE

There is only one past tense in common use in Serbocroat. It is composed of the short form of the present tense of the verb **biti** (**sam, si, je, smo, ste, su**) and the past participle of the verb concerned. In all verbs ending in **-ti** (**imati, govoriti, putovati**), the participle is formed by replacing **-ti** with the following endings:

	sing.	pl.	sing.	pl.	sing.	pl.
masc.	ima-o	ima-li	govori-o	govori-li	putova-o	putova-li
fem.	ima-la	ima-le	govori-la	gogovi-le	putova-la	putova-le
neut.	ima-lo	ima-la	govori-lo	govori-la	putova-lo	putova-la

The past participle used agrees in number and gender with the subject of the sentence:

> **putovao** I travelled (said by man)

> **putovala** I travelled (said by woman)

If the infinitive of a verb does not end in **-ti**, but, for example, in **-sti** or **-ći** it is best to learn the past participle as you come across it (see the list on page 118).

The verb 'to be'

ja sam bio/bila (I was)	**mi smo bili/bile** (we were)
ti si bio/bila (you were)	**vi ste bili/bile** (you were)
on je bio (he was)	**oni su bili** (they were)
ona je bila (she was)	**one su bile** (they were)
ono je bilo (it was)	**ona su bila** (they were)

Word order

Normally the personal pronoun is omitted and the word order reversed when the past tense expression comes at the beginning of a sentence:

bio sam žedan (said by man)
I was thirsty

bila sam žedna (said by woman)
I was thirsty

imao je puno novaca
he had a lot of money

stigle su rano
they arrived early (*feminine form*)

The negative form of the past tense

The negative form of the past tense is composed of the negative form of the verb to be (**nisam, nisi, nije, nismo, niste, nisu**) and the past participle of the verb concerned:

nisam otputovao	I didn't leave
nije došao	he didn't arrive
nisu jele	they didn't eat (*feminine form*)

THE FUTURE TENSE

The future tense is formed from the short form of the present tense of the verb **htjeti** (see page 115) and the infinitive of the verb concerned. For the negative form use the negative form of the verb **htjeti** and the infinitive. For example:

biti (to be)

ja ću biti (I will be)	**neću biti** (I will not be)
ti ćeš biti (you will be)	**nećeš biti** (you will not be)
on/ ona/ ono će biti (he, she, it will be)	**neće biti** (he, she, it will not be)
mi ćemo biti (we will be)	**nećemo biti** (we will not be)
vi ćete biti (you will be)	**nećete biti** (you will not be)
oni/one/ona će biti (they will be)	**neće biti** (they will not be)

When the personal pronoun is omitted, the word order is different. In the Serbian (Eastern) variant of the language, the verbs ending in **-ti** drop the infinitive ending and the auxiliary verb is added to the stem; the two words are written together:

biću, bićeš, biće, bićemo, bićete, biće (I will be etc)
radiću, radićeš, radiće, radićemo, radićete, radiće (I will work etc)

In the Croatian (Western) variant, the final **-i** of the infinitive is omitted and the auxiliary verb is added, but it is written separately:

bit ću, bit ćeš, bit će, bit ćemo, bit ćete, bit će
radit ću, radit ćeš, radit će, radit ćemo, radit ćete, radit će

Verbs ending in **-ći** do not drop their ending, and the auxiliary is always written as a separate word:

doći ću, doći ćeš, doći će, doći ćemo, doći ćete, doći će (I will come etc)
moći ću, moći ćeš, moći će, moći ćemo, moći ćete, moći će (I will be able etc)

THE IMPERATIVE (COMMANDS, SUGGESTIONS)

There are three forms, the second person singular and the first and second persons plural. They are formed by adding the endings **-i, -imo, -ite** or **-j, -jmo, -jte** to the verb stem (see page 118).

First set:

govoriti	to speak	–	**govori, govorimo, govorite**
kupiti	to buy	–	**kupi, kupimo, kupite**
pisati	to write	–	**piši, pišimo, pišite**
jesti	to eat	–	**jedi, jedimo, jedite**

The second set of endings is used with verbs which have the vowel **a** in the ending of the present tense, and with verbs in which the present tense stem ends in **-j**:

pitati	to ask	–	**pitaj, pitajmo, pitajte**
slušati	to listen	–	**slušaj, slušajmo, slušajte**
piti	to drink	–	**pij, pijmo, pijte**
čitati	to read	–	**čitaj, čitajmo, čitajte**

kupi kruha
buy some bread

idemo jesti
let's go and eat

govorite engleski
speak English

The negative imperative is formed by placing **ne** in front of the imperative:

ne govorite tako brzo
don't speak so fast

QUESTIONS

To ask questions use the following patterns: **da li** + the appropriate tense of the verb.

da li imate ...?	do you have ...?
da li pliva?	does he/she swim?

Here is a list of common verbs, giving the parts that you will need to know in order to form the tenses given on the preceding pages.

Infinitive		1st pers. sing. present	past participle
biti	to be	jesam	bio
činiti	to do	činim	činio
čitati	to read	čitam	čitao
dati	to give	dajem	dao
dobiti	to get (obtain)	dobim	dobio
doći	to come	dođem	došao
donijeti	to bring	donosim	donio
držati	to hold	držim	držao
gledati	to look at, watch	gledam	gledao
govoriti	to speak	govorim	govorio
gurati	to push	guram	gurao
hodati	to walk	hodam	hodao
htjeti	to want	hoću	htio
imati	to have	imam	imao
ići	to go	idem	išao
izgubiti	to lose	izgubim	izgubio
jesti	to eat	jedem	jeo
kupiti	to buy	kupim	kupio
misliti	to think	mislim	mislio
moći	to be able	mogu	mogao
ostati	to stay	ostajem	ostao
otvoriti	to open	otvorim	otvorio
pitati	to ask	pitam	pitao
piti	to drink	pijem	pijo
početi	to begin	počnem	počeo
pomaknuti	to move (something)	pomaknem	pomaknuo
pomoći	to help	pomognem	pomogao
poslati	to send	pošaljem	poslao
praviti	to make	pravim	pravio
putovati	to travel	putujem	putovao
raditi	to work	radim	radio
razumjeti	to understand	razumijem	razumio
reći	to say	reknem	rekao
smijati se	to laugh	smijem se	smijao sam se
spavati	to sleep	spavam	spavao
staviti	to put	stavim	stavio
trčati	to run (person)	trčim	trčao
uzeti	to take	uzmem	uzeo
vidjeti	to see	vidim	vidio
voljeti	to like, love	volim	volio
voziti	to drive	vozim	vozio
vući	to pull	vućem	vukao
zatvoriti	to close	zatvorim	zatvorio
znati	to know	znam	znao
željeti	to want	želim	želio

da li ste imali ...?	did you have ...?
da li se kupao/kupala?	did he/she go swimming?
da li ćete se vratiti dogodine?	will you be coming back next year?

TELLING THE TIME

what time is it?	koliko je sati? *[koleeko ye satee]*
it is ...	sada je ... *[sada ye]*
one o'clock	jedan sat *[yedan sat]*
seven o'clock	sedam sati *[sedam satee]*
one a.m.	jedan ujutro *[yedan ooyootro]*
seven a.m.	sedam ujutro *[sedam ooyootro]*
one p.m.	jedan poslije podne *[yedan poslye podne]*
seven p.m.	sedam uveče *[sedam ooveche]*
midday	podne
midnight	ponoć *[ponoch]*
five past eight	osam i pet *[ee]*
five to eight	pet do osam
half past ten	pola jedanaest* *[pola yedana-est] or* deset i pol
quarter past eleven	jedanaest i četvrt *[chetvurt]*
quarter to eleven	četvrt do jedanaest

*note that this way of saying 'half past ten' means literally 'half eleven', the Serbocroat equivalent of 'half past' being 'half to' (as in German).

CONVERSION TABLES

1. LENGTH

centimetres, centimeters
1 cm = 0.39 inches

metres, meters
1 m = 100 cm = 1000 mm
1 m = 39.37 inches = 1.09 yards

kilometres, kilometers
1 km = 1000 m
1 km = 0.62 miles = 5/8 mile

km	1	2	3	4	5	10	20	30	40	50	100
miles	0.6	1.2	1.9	2.5	3.1	6.2	12.4	18.6	24.9	31.1	62.1

inches
1 inch = 2.54 cm

feet
1 foot = 30.48 cm

yards
1 yard = 0.91 m

miles
1 mile = 1.61 km = 8/5 km

miles	1	2	3	4	5	10	20	30	40	50	100
km	1.6	3.2	4.8	6.4	8.0	16.1	32.2	48.3	64.4	80.5	161

2. WEIGHT

gram(me)s
1 g = 0.035 oz

g	100	250	500
oz	3.5	8.75	17.5 = 1.1 lb

kilos
1 kg = 1000 g
1 kg = 2.20 lb = 11/5 lb

kg	0.5	1	1.5	2	3	4	5	6	7	8	9	10
lb	1.1	2.2	3.3	4.4	6.6	8.8	11.0	13.2	15.4	17.6	19.8	22

kg	20	30	40	50	60	70	80	90	100
lb	44	66	88	110	132	154	176	198	220

tons
1 UK ton = 1018 kg
1 US ton = 909 kg

tonnes
1 tonne = 1000 kg
1 tonne = 0.98 UK tons = 1.10 US tons

ounces
1 oz = 28.35 g

pounds
1 pound = 0.45 kg = 5/11 kg

lb	1	1.5	2	3	4	5	6	7	8	9	10	20
kg	0.5	0.7	0.9	1.4	1.8	2.3	2.7	3.2	3.6	4.1	4.5	9.1

stones
1 stone = 6.35 kg

stones	1	2	3	7	8	9	10	11	12	13	14	15
kg	6.3	12.7	19	44	51	57	63	70	76	83	89	95

hundredweights
1 UK hundredweight = 50.8 kg
1 US hundredweight = 45.36 kg

3. CAPACITY

litres, liters
1 l = 1.76 UK pints = 2.13 US pints
$\frac{1}{2}$ l = 500 cl
$\frac{1}{4}$ l = 250 cl

pints
1 UK pint = 0.57 l
1 US pint = 0.47 l

quarts
1 UK quart = 1.14 l
1 US quart = 0.95 l

gallons
1 UK gallon = 4.55 l
1 US gallon = 3.79 l

4. TEMPERATURE

centigrade/Celsius
$C = (F - 32) \times 5/9$

C	−5	0	5	10	15	18	20	25	30	37	38
F	23	32	41	50	59	64	68	77	86	98.4	100.4

Fahrenheit
$F = (C \times 9/5) + 32$

F	23	32	40	50	60	65	70	80	85	98.4	101
C	−5	0	4	10	16	20	21	27	30	37	38.3

NUMBERS

0	nula *[noola]*	1st	(*m*) prvi *[purvee]*
1	(*m*) jedan *[yedan]*		(*f*) prva *[purva]*
	(*f*) jedna *[yedna]*		(*n*) prvo *[purvo]*
	(*n*) jedno *[yedno]*	2nd	drugi *[droogee]*
2	(*m, n*) dva	3rd	treći *[trechee]*
	(*f*) dvije *[dveeye]*	4th	četvrti *[chetvurtee]*
3	tri *[tree]*	5th	peti *[petee]*
4	četiri *[cheteeree]*	6th	šesti *[shestee]*
5	pet	7th	sedmi *[sedmee]*
6	šest *[shest]*	8th	osmi *[osmee]*
7	sedam *[sedam]*	9th	deveti *[devetee]*
8	osam *[osam]*	10th	deseti *[desetee]*
9	devet *[devet]*		
10	deset *[deset]*		
11	jedanaest *[yedana-est*		
12	dvanaest *[dvana-est]*		
13	trinaest *[treena-est*		
14	četrnaest *[cheturna-est]*		
15	petnaest *[petna-est]*		
16	šesnaest *[shesna-est]*		
17	sedamnaest *[sedamna-est]*		
18	osamnaest *[osamna-est]*		
19	devetnaest *[devetna-est]*		
20	dvadeset *[dvadeset]*		
21	dvadeset jedan *[dvadeset yedan]*		
22	dvadeset dva *[dvadeset]*		
30	trideset *[treedeset]*		
31	trideset jedan *[treedeset yedan]*		
40	četrdeset *[chetur-deset]*		
50	pedeset *[pedeset]*		
60	šezdeset *[shezdeset]*		
70	sedamdeset *[sedamdeset]*		
80	osamdeset *[osamdeset]*		
90	devedeset *[devedeset]*		
100	sto		
110	sto deset *[deset]*		
200	dvjesto *[dvyesto]*		
300	tristo *[treesto]*		
400	četiristo *[cheteereesto]*		
500	petsto *[petsto]*		
600	šesto *[shesto]*		
1000	(*S*) hiljada *[heelyada]*		
	(*C*) tisuća *[tisoocha]*		
2000	dvije hiljade/tisuće *[dveeye heelyade/teesooche]*		
1,000,000	(*Serbian*) milion *[meelee-on]*		
	(*Croatian*) milijun *[mili-oon]*		